Miss

Try, if you can, to imagine the loss of a child.

Try to imagine losing your memory.

Try to imagine how a teenager feels, coping with life.

Traumatic events weave their way through this story of loss and pain, love and rejection.

Stories often have happy endings.

But life can be cruel.

Chapter 1

Elizabeth Lyonaisse endures life, not enjoys it. The last two years have been traumatic. The story of her daughter and son-in-law emigrating after their child went missing are believed by many…but both she and her husband Carl know the truth. She had wanted to sell up and move, but he had refused.

*

Elizabeth tucked the folds of her silk nightdress beneath her as she sits at the dressing table. She took a box from one of the drawers. It had once held a pair of child's dancing shoes. Now it holds only memories. A multi-coloured yo-yo. A simple picture scrawled with crayons, two large stick-figures, holding hands, a smaller on between them. A hairbrush with her granddaughter's hair entwined in its bristles. Hair that comes close to matching her own, or would have done before it turned grey. Holding the brush close to her face she inhaled. Her bosom heaved, fleshing out wrinkled skin.

She held her breath, eyes closed, remembering.

Elizabeth often thought back to one particular night when her granddaughter, Mary, came to stay for the weekend. They held hands and gazed up at the dark sky. Mary asked who turned the stars off in the daytime. Elizabeth tried to explain they were still there, but the sun made it too bright to see them. Mary insisted someone must collect them each morning and return at night to toss them back up into the sky. Elizabeth recalled how she smiled at Mary's childlike logic.

Weeks later they, they enjoyed another lovely visit. Her daughter, Susan, dressed Mary in a plain blue dress, pinched in around the waist with a matching sash. Mary's hair was tied back with silk ribbons. Mary's father said she looked exactly like her favourite bedtime storybook character, Alice in Wonderland.

Whenever Mary visited her grandparents, she made the spare room her own, often giving tea parties to her teddy bears. Maybe the sunshine streaming through the window beckoned her out that day. Maybe she was bored with her game. No one ever knew. But for some reason she abandoned the other bears, taking only Mrs Fluffy, her favourite, into the grounds.

And just like Alice in Wonderland, she too disappeared.

But, unlike Alice, there was no happy ending.

The search for her continued late into the night. People from the village, organised by the local policeman, joined hands and walked the grounds. Torch beams probed dark places, out-buildings were searched and searched again, but Mary had vanished.

Mary's parents were devastated.

Carl Lyonaisse submerged his own feelings to comfort his wife as she cried herself to sleep.

The investigation resumed the following morning. Police from neighbouring forces threw themselves into the task. Newspapers ran the story for weeks. Financial consideration eventually forced Carl and Elizabeth's daughter and son-in-law to return home. They returned at every opportunity to resume their search.

The heartbreak brought on by the loss of Mary should have been tempered over time for Carl and Elizabeth. But it hadn't. Mary's parents had seen to that.

Chapter 2

Making a welcome appearance after all the rain; the sun climbed above woodland bordering one edge of the country estate. Its glow slowly crossed the meadow, turning the ornamental pond into liquid gold. Creeping across manicured lawns and splendid flower beds it sent long shadows towards a large house dominating the rural landscape. Warm rays caressed the brickwork and lanced against shuttered windows.

As it cleared the rooftop of the grand house, the sun warmed rabbits grazing in a meadow. Continuing its relentless advance, the golden light reached another, irregular shaped, pond. A raindrop, resting on a bulrush at the water's edge, took hold of a beam of sunlight and transformed it into a fairy palette of colours.

Twelve years previously, during the autumn of 1944, a V1 flying bomb *en route* to London had tired of its flight of destruction. The terror weapon dropped into the grounds of Oakwood House, coming to an abrupt halt fifty miles short of its intended target. It had been a narrow escape for the house and its occupants. Even so, the majority of the windows on one side of the structure had needed replacing. Over the years the bomb crater had gradually filled with water, providing sanctuary for a colony of frogs. Reeds and bulrushes now surround it. Dragonflies dance an aerial ballet, water boatmen scull over the surface.

The grandeur of this Georgian building still reflects the wealth created by sugar plantations. Money, from the exploitation of dark-skinned men thousands of miles from the centre of the British Empire, has been cleansed of guilt by the passage of time. Away from the main house stand two other dwellings, also built in the Georgian style. Both survived the uninvited wartime visitor. One provides accommodation for the housekeeper and gardener. The other, originally intended for more servants, remains empty as a result of the post-war economy. These smaller properties are the result of the frugal use of the family fortune by Carl Lyonaisse after inheriting the estate in 1926 at the age of thirty.

*

Elizabeth put down a tray and took a gold chain from around her neck. Using the key that hung from it, she opened one of the many doors in the corridor, picked up the tray and entered. Crossing the carpet, she approached a brightly painted table surrounded by equally coloured chairs. The gathered guests paid her no attention. Smiling at them she began her ritual. Removing last week's biscuits from a central plate she replaced them with fresh ones. Taking glasses of orange-juice from in front of the sightless diners she emptied them into a bowl and refilled their drinks from a jug. Her task complete she touched fingers to her lips, bent down and transferred the kiss to the back of the only empty chair. Teddy bears, sitting bolt upright in child-size seats, continued to ignore her.

She locked the door behind her as she left.

*

Elizabeth took the tray back to the kitchen before returning to her bedroom. Drawing the curtains aside she gazed through the window at Douglas Miller as he slowly pushed a wheelbarrow between raised flower beds, heading for the kitchen garden.

There was a crunch as Douglas Miller let down the heavy barrow onto the gravel path. He winced as he straightened his back. As he wiped his forehead with a handkerchief he looked up and saw Elizabeth at her bedroom window. Raising a hand, he acknowledged he had seen her. Grasping the handles of the wheelbarrow he continued pushing its load of manure towards the kitchen garden. He stopped again and drew a deep breath before moving on. The clouds of iridescent green and blue flies, settling on his decomposing load to pay homage, added colour to the dull brown fertiliser.

Miller was proud of the vegetables he grew. The vicar's wife always made a point of corralling him at the annual garden fete in order to try and wheedle his secret from him. Each year he would touch the side of his nose and tell her it was all in the preparation of the soil. *"Goodness has to go in if goodness is to come out,"* he always said.

A robin flew down and perched on the handle of the garden fork sticking up from the freshly turned soil. Miller smiled. The bird often came to visit, grateful for a chance to explore the soil his digging disturbed. As he forked manure into the prepared ground, he unearthed a small bone. Plucking it from the garden he tossed it into a bucket containing weeds, stones and shards of glass gleaned from his cultivation.

Flowers woke from their slumbers as the sun bathed the grounds of the house. Bees welcomed the blooms to a new day, dancing amongst them, diving into coloured trumpets, vying for their precious nectar. Sweet scents filled the air, competing with the gardener's pipe tobacco. His pipe finished; Douglas tapped it against one knee. Blowing through it he stuffed his addictive crutch back in the top pocket of a tweed jacket. Picking up the barrow he trundled it back to his storage shed.

Now in his sixtieth year, Miller is slightly older than Elizabeth Lyonaisse but the years have not been kind to either of them. He shares with her the mental scars of losing someone, his son, Brian. The young man was reported missing, believed dead, during one of the battles for Monte Cassino. The shared experiences of grief, hers for a daughter and granddaughter and his for a son, resulted in her reluctance to allow Carl to replace the ailing gardener.

*

Carl Lyonaisse stirred in his bed. Reaching for gold-framed glasses on the bedside table, he sat up and listened before swinging his legs out of the bed and seeking slippers with his toes. Crossing the room, he took his dressing gown from the back of the door and slipped it on.

There had been a time when he would have been awake, washed, and riding his favourite horse at this hour. But his love of Stilton cheese and an over-indulgence in glasses of fortified wine had taken its toll. His doctor told him the cheese and port, added to heightened blood pressure, had initiated his gout. He was able to cope with foregoing gastronomic pleasures, but constantly struggled with the loss that brought about his hypertension. Shuffling along the corridor he knocked on the door of his wife's bedroom. Reassured by her response he returned to his bed.

Chapter 3

The police constable whistled as he rode his bicycle through the grounds. Reaching the property occupied by the Millers he dismounted and propped his bike against the fence. Removing cycle clips securing the bottom of his trousers, he approached the front door.

Inside the house, Rex, the family collie, jumped out of his basket, tail wagging, wet tongue hanging out.

Douglas's wife, Patricia, stood at the sink rubbing the collar of a shirt with a large block of Fairy green soap. When she heard the knock, she wiped reddened hands on her pinafore and left the washing to soak in the grey water.

She knew George, the local policeman, and had done so for many years. Brushing aside his objections, she led the way back to the kitchen.

A kettle gently steamed on the cast iron cooking range. Spooning tea leaves from a tea caddy into a brown glazed teapot she added boiling water. Satisfied the tea had brewed sufficiently she poured it through a strainer and passed a cup to George. Now social etiquette had been fulfilled, she asked the reason for his visit.

His answer caused her to leap to her feet. The cup dropped from her fingers, hitting the edge of the table, spilling the hot beverage onto the flagstone floor. Seconds later her crumpled body lay in the steaming puddle.

*

Douglas found Patricia being helped to her feet. He rushed to help George get his wife onto a chair. Going to the sink he ran the cold tap for a while, held a tea towel under it, then brought the cloth to the table. Gently he laid it on her forehead. Her eyes opened. Her lips moved, but there was no sound.

Douglas gripped George's arm. 'What happened?'

Now it was his turn to receive a shock. A shock greater than the one he received while removing the frayed lead from a radio inadvertently left plugged into the mains. That had thrown him across the room. The message George brought had the same effect. 'I'm sorry Mr Miller, your phone didn't answer so I came to tell you myself. They *think* they've found your son. He's alive. They would like you to go to the hospital where he works to see if you can confirm his identity.'

'He can't be.' Douglas swallowed. 'Brian was killed at Monte Cassino.' He clenched his fists. 'Is this some sort of joke? If it is, I don't find it funny.'

George held his hands up, palms facing Douglas, as if to prevent an attack. 'I didn't mean to upset you like this. We received a telephone call from the Matron. She said a new cleaner claimed to recognise Brian.' He paused. 'I think she may be correct as she lived in the next village most of her life. Probably saw him at a dance in the Village Hall sometime.'

Patricia removed the damp cloth from her forehead. 'Could it be true?' she asked, grasping her husband's sleeve. 'Can it really be Brian? I must go and see for myself.'

'It's hard to believe. Please don't build up your hopes. I'll run over to the Big House right now and tell them where we're going. I'm sure they'll understand.'

Carl Lyonaisse was equally amazed at the news. He instructed his chauffeur to take the Millers to the hospital.

Chapter 4

The Victorian workhouse now accommodated a hospital for mentally disturbed servicemen. Its ugly façade had been softened over the years by variegated ivy clinging to the walls. Hollyhocks and sunflowers sought to distract the eye from windows protected by grim wrought-iron bars.

A silver-grey Daimler swept through the puddles in the drive and parked. The chauffeur stepped out and opened a door for his passengers. Douglas and Patricia thanked him before hurrying into the building.

They spoke to a young woman operating the telephone switchboard behind the front desk. She smiled, turned away and pushed a plug into one of the many small holes. 'Hello? Hello? Is that…? Oh, good. I've got Mr and Mrs Miller here to see one of the patients… Thank you.' Swivelling back round on her chair she said, 'Matron will be with you shortly. Please take a seat.'

Minutes later a rotund woman swept into the entrance hall. 'Mr and Mrs Miller? It's nice to meet you.'

Douglas grasped his wife's hand and gave a gentle squeeze. She managed a slight nod in return.

The Matron led the way down the corridor. 'I do hope our cleaner is right,' she called over her shoulder. 'Come along, we'll soon see.'

Following Matron into one of the side wards, Patricia stopped abruptly.

Peeling paint lingered on depressing pale green walls. The tenacious smell of Dettol, persisting around rows of

identical metal frame beds, assailed her nose. Men stared up
at enamelled light shades guarding fly encrusted bulbs.
Others lay in foetal positions.

Patricia's mouth dropped open and remained that way as
she watched a man wearing striped pyjamas march the full
length of the ward, arms swinging and head held high.
Reaching the far end he stopped and stamped his feet, but
worn carpet slippers lack the authority of army boots. He
turned, saluted and marched back.

She shielded her eyes and turned away as another patient
casually relieved himself over a cast-iron radiator. A nurse
rushed towards him, grasping a galvanised bucket. She
slipped on the wet linoleum. The resulting noise sent a man
dressed in trousers, shirt and pullover diving to the floor.
Scrambling under the nearest bed he yelled, 'Take cover!'

Matron looked at the Millers. 'I am afraid he's the man we
think may be your son. I'm so sorry.'

Douglas pointed at the man standing in front of the
radiator. 'But that's not Brian.'

Matron stared at the patient and the spreading pool of
urine. 'Not *him*. The gentleman hiding under his bed.'

Filled with trepidation the Millers followed Matron along
the ward to where the man had gone to ground. Pulling aside
the sheet and blankets, Matron crouched down and said
softly, 'It's okay. You can come out now. There's someone
here to see you.'

Douglas knelt beside her and held out a hand. 'Come on
out, son. We're here now. You'll be safe with us.'

Patricia held a handkerchief embroidered with forget-me-
not flowers to her mouth.

The man grudgingly allowed Douglas and the Matron to
coax him from beneath the bed, his eyes darting from side to
side, a nervous twitch distorting one side of his face.

Matron helped him to his feet. 'Don't worry, nothing's going to hurt you.' Turning to the Millers she spoke quietly. 'I understand you haven't seen him for many years. What do you think?'

'Do you imagine we wouldn't know our own son?' Douglas glared at Matron.

Patricia dropped her handkerchief and pushed past. Throwing her arms around him she nestled her face against the man's chest. He stood awkwardly, staring straight ahead.

'I think we should all go to my office, don't you?' Matron blinked.

'But how did Brian end up in here?' Douglas rammed tobacco into the bowl of his pipe and stared at his son. 'Why didn't he come home to us?'

'Who knows? Apart from what happened in the ward…and this isn't the first time he's reacted like this…he's fine.' Matron smiled. 'I gave him the chance to help out in the ward shortly after he was admitted as a patient. It was about two years ago wasn't it, Billy?' She smiled. 'Sorry, that's the name on the army papers he had on him when he was admitted.'

'Yes, it is. My name is Billy.' Brian sat with both hands in his lap. 'Are you really my parents? I don't remember…you do remind me of someone…' He turned away and stared straight ahead. 'Sorry.'

Patricia stifled a sob. Douglas took a freshly-laundered handkerchief from the top pocket of his tweed jacket and passed it to her. She dabbed her eyes. 'Oh, Brian, darling, it *is* us. Tell him, Douglas.'

Douglas placed his unlit pipe on Matron's desk. He reached out and put a hand on Brian's shoulder. 'Don't get upset, son. We'll soon have you right. I'll get your mother to cook you a bacon roly-poly pudding, your favourite. You must remember, surely.'

Brian's face remained blank. 'No. Sorry.'

'Never mind, it'll be all right, you'll see. Do you know how you ended up in here? We knew you were in Italy, fighting, but –'

'Please…don't talk about it. I have nightmares. Things I've seen…and done.' His facial twitch worked overtime as memories flooded back. Memories so horrific they could not be erased. Faces haunted him by day and night. Young faces, full of fear.

Matron stood up. 'Perhaps we should leave it there for the present. I'm sure he'll tell you his story when he's good and ready.'

'Can't we take him home?' Patricia's voice had an edge of pleading.

'No, I'm afraid not. You will need to speak to doctor first. I'll arrange a meeting for tomorrow if it's agreeable to you.' Matron turned her gaze towards Brian. 'And of course, it's your decision. You can always come back to us if it doesn't work out.'

Douglas got to his feet and held out a hand. 'Thank you. You've been very kind. But I'm certain it will. We've a lot of catching up to do after all these years.' He helped his wife to her feet. Her face had drained of colour, face powder and rouge defeated. She put a hand onto Matron's desk in an effort to stop her body shaking.

Matron stood. 'Billy, *oops,* sorry, force of habit. Brian, would you like to get your belongings together? Your parents and I have a few details to sort out.' Brian turned and left the office.

'Are you *sure* he's your son?' Matron looked straight at Douglas.

'Yes, of course.'

Matron placed a hand on his arm. 'Good. I'm so glad it's turning out right for you.'

'During the war we had a letter from his Commanding Officer telling us he was missing in action,' Douglas said, with a catch in his voice. 'Today we had a visit from the police telling us he's alive and well. Can you imagine how we feel?'

'No. I can't. It's just such a pity he doesn't recognise you. But please don't worry, I'm sure his memory will improve.' Pulling open a drawer in her desk, she rummaged through the contents. 'Hmm. Your mention of his Commanding Officer reminded me. You should have these.' She passed Douglas an army pay-book along with some correspondence. 'I know they aren't his, but they *were* in his possession when he was admitted. When I applied for a National Insurance number for your son, I was told William Stanton, the man on these documents, had been killed on active service.'

Douglas accepted them without a word.

Matron smiled. 'I will contact you tomorrow as soon as I can organise everything. My staff and I have grown very fond of your son.'

*

Patricia Miller took the call from the hospital early next morning. Matron was as good as her word and had arranged a meeting with the doctor.

Mr Lyonaisse instructed his chauffeur to take the Millers back to collect Brian, assuming all was well.

Patricia had risen earlier than usual and cooking smells cloaked the kitchen with the enticing smell of a bread pudding. After dusting it with sugar she cut it into oblong portions and wrapped two pieces in grease-proof paper.

Placing the remainder in a biscuit-tin she consigned it to the larder.

As they left the house Douglas Miller suddenly remembered something. Going back inside he picked up a framed photograph of Brian and the bunch of flowers Mr Lyonaisse had given him permission to pick.

Carrying an air-rifle slung over his shoulder with a shotgun nestled in the crook of one arm, MacIintyre, the estate's gamekeeper, opened the gates to allow the Daimler to leave. A brace of rabbits hanging from his leather belt showed he too had been an early riser.

*

Matron met them at the hospital door and ushered them along the corridor to meet the doctor.

Smoke hung in the air of his office. Two packets of cigarettes lay alongside a brass ashtray filled with the detritus from heavy smoking. A stethoscope hung around the neck of a skeleton suspended from a hook. Exploded views of body parts were taped to the wall. Shelves, sagging between inadequate brackets, were stacked with medical books and bound copies of journals. In pride of place on the wall behind his desk a glass-fronted oak frame protected a diploma and its red wax seal from the nicotine onslaught.

'Good morning, Doctor. This is Mr and Mrs Miller.' Turning to the nervous couple, Matron said, 'I will leave you alone to discuss Brian's future. Good luck.'

The Millers sat and waited as their son's notes were perused by the man with a cigarette stuck in the corner of his mouth. Now and then he swiped at ash as it dropped onto a page.

'Hmm…yes, now I remember…good…good.' He cleared his throat. 'Nothing to be concerned about.' He tapped the papers with a nicotine-stained finger. 'Apart from amnesia, and the nightmares he suffers from, I'd say your son is physically fit.'

'Is his loss of memory going to be permanent?' Patricia leaned forward. 'Will he ever know who we are?'

'Hard to say. I see a lot of this with these poor devils. During the first war he'd be diagnosed as having shell shock. In my opinion this man's problem has been brought on by a similar traumatic experience. He may recover, but on the other hand…'

'We'd like to take him home with us. Can we?' Patricia clasped her hands in front of her, praying.

'Well, there are no medical grounds for him to remain with us. It's only because he had nowhere else to go he was allowed to stay. We can't cure him, only time may do that.' He lit a cigarette. 'I can assure you he's never shown any tendency to violence in the two years he's been with us. If you decide to take him home, I will give my consent. But I do urge you to seriously consider all you are taking on.'

Douglas looked at Patricia. 'We have decided. We're certain it's the right thing to do. Brian will be better off with us.'

The doctor raised both hands, a token of surrender. Smoke leaked from his nostrils as he scribbled notes at the bottom of a page. 'As you wish. But I suggest you and your wife give it a trial period before making a final decision. He will need a lot of care and attention. And he must keep on with his medication. Also, I insist you make an appointment to see me in three months' time so I can give him his regular check-up. He's certainly an interesting case.' Stubbing out his cigarette he passed Douglas the medical records. 'Here, take these to Matron and she'll arrange a discharge. I wish you luck, but it won't be easy I'm afraid.'

'Thank you, Doctor.' Douglas got to his feet and held out a hand. 'Thank you very much.'

Inside Matron's office the Millers waited for their son. Douglas held out the framed photo of a young man in army uniform. 'Brian was a captain when this was taken,' he said proudly to her. 'What I still can't understand is why he had those papers when he was admitted here. They belonged to a private in his regiment. It's a complete mystery to me.'

Matron took the picture. 'I agree.' She held the frame closer. 'He doesn't seem to have changed much.'

'No, but I brought it along in case we should need to prove his identity.' Douglas reached out and held Patricia's hand.

'And I've made him a bread pudding, in case he had to stay. But now he can have it with a nice cup of tea at home.' Patricia held out the freshly-cut flowers and an envelope. 'I brought these for the cleaner to say thank you, and I've written her a letter. We had hoped to see her, it's a shame it's her day off.' She glanced at Douglas. 'Do you think it would be all right to ask the chauffeur to stop at the Post Office on the way back? I really should send Margaret a telegram as she hasn't got a telephone.'

'I don't see why not. It's a good idea and we have to pass there on the way back.'

Chapter 5

John Reardon bent down. Picking up a newspaper and a scattering of letters from the doormat, he frowned. Amongst the handful of bills and final demands a typewritten envelope, marked Private & Confidential, caught his attention. 'Who on earth sent me this?' He gave a deep sigh. 'Not the bloody Inland Revenue lot again, surely.' Tucking the letters beneath his arm he pulled the belt of his dressing gown tighter and walked back towards the kitchen. His slippers slapped against lino. The bright geometrical pattern of the floor-covering had all but gone, only the edges remained bright and relatively unmarked. The tramp of feet over the years had worn a path down the hall.

The rasping of burnt toast being scraped greeted him as he entered. His wife, Margaret, was leaning towards the kitchen window. The cold-water tap was running. Black specks clung stubbornly to the sides of the white porcelain sink in an effort to avoid joining others spiralling down the plughole.

'Not again,' he groaned. 'Is it beyond you to get my breakfast without ruining it?'

'Huh!' She turned and dropped the slices onto a plate. 'You know the answer. Do it yourself.' Tipping the egg poacher at an angle she let it drain. Prising two eggs out she slopped them on top of the toast. 'There you are. Think yourself lucky I find time to cook you anything. Some of us have got a full-time job. Since they cut your hours, you seem to spend more time down the pub than you do at the factory.'

'It's not my fault you have to work every Saturday. Anyway, mopping up piddle isn't work. Not real work. You should try standing at a lathe all day under those bloody hot lights. You might even get to sweat off a few of those pounds you keep on about.'

'Oh, would I? And if I did, would it give *me* the excuse to live down the pub?' She lit a cigarette. 'What's in the post? Anything interesting for a change?'

'No, just bills. And a letter for me.' He sat down opposite his wife and held up the daily dose of misery masquerading as a newspaper.

Margaret gazed at the silent barrier between them. Years of bickering in a loveless marriage had taken their toll. She leaned forward to read an article about the influence American music was having on British youth.

One of John's hands appeared, groped for and found his Festival of Britain mug. The sound of tea being slurped added to Margaret's disgust for her husband's table manners.

A knock on the front door startled her. 'Who's that?' she knocked the ash from her cigarette into a saucer. 'Can't be the milkman, I've paid him.'

'Is this a guessing game or are you going to answer it?'

'Why don't you go?'

'I can't. I'm reading.'

Margaret expelled smoke in his direction. 'Oh, you carry on, your majesty. I'll go as it's the servant's day off.'

Warily she opened the front door. A uniformed boy stood on the red stone step, holding out a telegram. 'Here you are, Missus.' He thrust it into her open hand. Knowing a tip would not be forthcoming from any house in this street he turned and walked away.

Margaret read the short telegram. She put a hand to her forehead and read the message again. BRIAN ALIVE. PHONE ME. MUM.

Oh – my – God! What does she mean?

It fell from her shaking hand. Bending down she picked up this bolt from the blue. With one hand pressed against the wall, she made her way back to the kitchen.

Unable to speak she held out the telegram. She shook it to attract his attention.

John didn't look up. Wiping margarine and jam from a knife, he used it to slice open the important-looking letter.

'Bastards.' He slumped in his chair, tilted his head back and shouted at the ceiling. 'Just like that. You…bastards.'

Margaret stepped forward and dropped the message onto the table. 'Quick, give me some money. I've got to phone mum. They've found Brian!'

'Do what? Your brother? Don't be so bloody daft. They can't have. He's been dead twelve years.'

'I don't need another argument. Give me some money. I've got to phone her.'

'Why? The last time you spoke to her she virtually disowned you. All over a few pounds to tide –'

'Just give it to me. *Please!*'

John thrust a hand deep into a trouser pocket and slapped a handful of coins onto the table. 'There, that's all I've got. Take it. But it's coming out of your housekeeping.'

She picked up the assorted pennies and silver and rushed to the door. 'I hope the phone box is working. Bloody yobs. If they've vandalised it again, I'll swing for them.' Opening the front door, she called out, 'What was in your letter? More bad news I suppose? No, don't bother, tell me when I get back. I must fly.'

*

Rain lashed against the red telephone box as Margaret fed coins into the slot. She pressed the button marked "A."

'Yes, it's me, Mum… Well you said he was ill last time we spoke…Anyway that's not why… Yes, it's marvellous.

Why didn't you let me know sooner? I still can't believe it. Brian and I were…but…is he? How bad? Oh, I see. I'll speak to John but I don't think there's much chance.' She nestled the phone under her cheek and fed more coins in. 'Yes, I'm still here. But that's the last of my money. Quick, tell me more about Brian.' Minutes later the line cut off.

*

Hanging her up coat, heavy now it was soaked, Margaret took off her headscarf and shook it.

'Oh, you're back, are you? I thought you'd have gone off to work.' John held out his mug. 'Get me another cuppa while you're near the pot.'

Margaret held the tea strainer with one hand and poured with the other. 'There you are. Looks a bit stewed to me.'

'Better than the gnat's piss you usually manage. Now, come on, what did the old dragon have to say? What was all the rubbish about your dead brother?'

'It's *not* rubbish. Brian *is* alive. He's back with Mum and Dad. I'll tell you more once you've told me what's in your letter. I can see it's made you more bolshie than ever.'

John tossed it onto the breakfast table. 'See for yourself. It means we won't be catching up with the rent now. Which means we'll lose this house. And my motorbike. Every bloody thing. *Your* wages won't keep us afloat and where am I supposed to find another job around here?'

'What on earth are you on about?' She rescued a sheet of paper resting on the dish of homemade jam. Carefully holding it by the edges she shook her head. 'A week's notice... Closing down... New owners unable to… What new owners?'

'Don't ask me. I didn't know the firm had changed hands. According to the letter, it happened months ago.'

Margaret's forehead wrinkled as she read on. 'I can't believe it. You all risked your lives through the bombing raids to keep the place going, and now they don't want *any* of you?'

John drummed his fingers on the table. 'That's what it says. They made a bloody fortune out of us with their military contracts. Now they're chucking us on the scrap heap. I'll be stuck at home with our layabout son.'

'And none of you knew the firm had been sold?'

'No. But I'm not surprised. Things were never the same after they employed all those darkies after the war. I don't blame them down the bus depot for striking. It's what we should have done.'

'Well, that's put the cat amongst the pigeons and no mistake. I think it's time I told you what Mother had to say.' She lit a cigarette and tried to compose her thoughts. *You're not going to like it, but things can't go on like this. Hiding behind the curtains, peering out to see who's calling for money. Walking to the shops, half expecting the landlord to jump out at me. No, this is too good to turn down. Pride's all well and good, but money makes the world go round.* Resting her cigarette against a saucer, she told him all her mother had said.

'Do what?' he spluttered. 'Move in? She must be joking. What about when you told her I'd been put on short time? She didn't want to know. Now the boot's on the other foot –'

'I suppose she thought I'd be the answer as I'm a home help. She said Brian's not at all well and dad's not so good either. She wants me to go down and give her a hand as soon as possible.'

'Huh. Typical. She just snaps her fingers and expects you to come running. What am I supposed to do? And what about Alan, that useless son of ours?' He managed a rare smile. 'Can't we just sneak off and leave him here? Make him stand on his own two feet for a change?'

'No, we *can't*. Mother says the pair of you can help look after the gardens. Make a nice change for you to work in the fresh air.'

The glass light fitting hanging from the kitchen ceiling shook. John leapt to his feet and rushed through to the hallway. At the bottom of the stairs he yelled, 'Turn that bloody row off!' Drumming his fingers against the wall he waited. Bill Haley and his Comets could still be heard, but quieter now. '*Off* I said! Do you want me to come up there?' The music died down.

Back in the kitchen he glared at his wife. 'How many times does he need telling? I'll say one thing, it'll make a change for *him* to work anywhere for more than two weeks at a time. But gardening? I don't know a thing about it. It's always been your job.'

'Not anymore, it's not. Think about it. Mum's offering us a place to stay and work for all of us. The cavalry's arrived in the nick of time if you ask me.'

'But why bloody gardening? Don't old man Lyonaisse need someone to drive that big Daimler of his? I've always fancied driving a car.'

'No, he's got a chauffeur. Now, do you want to hear how they found my brother?'

'I suppose so. Get on with it.'

'Mum said she got a telephone call telling her a new cleaner at the hospital –'

'What hospital?'

'I don't know. She didn't say. Anyway, she and Dad had to go and see if they could confirm what a cleaner had said. It seems she lived in a nearby village as a child and recognised him.'

'Who? Your brother?'

'No. Old King Cole. Aren't you listening to me?'

'Go on. I'm all ears.'

'I can't argue with that. Anyway, it *is* him. But the shame of it is he doesn't recognise Mum or Dad. Evidently, he's been working in the hospital for a couple of years. But it turns out the papers he had when he was admitted belonged to a soldier killed at Monte Cassino. Wherever that is.'

'Italy.'

'Is it? Oh yes, I remember now. Well, the matron at the hospital only found out about the papers when she offered to let him stay on.'

'I take it he's causing problems. I mean, if he doesn't know your parents–'

'Yes, but it's not his fault. Anyway, we've got a decision to make. Mum's told me she's arranged with Mr Lyonaisse to let us move into one of the houses in the grounds. I can help her, and you two can work for Mr Lyonaisse.' She glanced around the room and sighed. 'I know we won't be earning a fortune but at least we'll have somewhere to live. Besides, what choice do we have?'

'Not much I suppose. But I'm not happy about it.' He stretched his arms above his head and yawned. 'It's okay for you. You and your brother grew up down there in the country. Me? I prefer London.'

'That suits me fine. I'll go on my own. You can stay and look after yourself, and Alan of course.'

John groaned. 'You must be joking. I'd throttle him within a week. No, you win. I'll come with you.'

'I thought you might.' *More's the pity. I thought it was too good to be true for you to let me get away.*

Chapter 6

Huge cranes dominated the skyline behind the line of
terraced houses, their skeletal shapes joining reflections in
pools of water in front of the buildings. Red, white, and blue
cotton bunting hung limply across the road at one end. This
single defiant strand was a reminder of the street party held
for the Queen's Coronation three years previously. Two
small girls twirled a rope while their friends skipped over it.
Several streets away the church bell rang out to summon
worshippers for Sunday morning service.

A woman standing on her doorstep scrutinised her son
while chatting to Margaret Reardon. 'So, the first you knew
was when you got a telegram?' She frowned as she tugged
the boy's green jumper down.

'Yes. Telling me my brother wasn't killed in the war like
we all thought. Gave me one hell of a shock I can tell you.'

The woman flicked the end of a cigarette into the gutter. It
spluttered before beginning its journey in the rainwater
towards a drain. 'I bet.' She lit another, turned her head and
blew smoke away from Margaret. 'So that's it then.' The
cigarette in the corner of her mouth bobbed up and down as
she spoke. 'You're getting away from here. Lucky so and
so, I wish I was.'

'Yes, we're moving down to the country. *And* we've all
got jobs to go to.' Margaret adjusted her headscarf. 'Me old
man don't want to go, nor does Alan. But what with the
factory closing down there's not much choice is there.'

'No, suppose not, but I'm going to miss you. Where am I
going to scrounge a cup of sugar when you're gone?' She
laughed. 'Thank God my husband works in the docks, is
what I say. At least his job's safe. Well, most of the time
anyway.' Spitting on a handkerchief she attacked the jam

around her son's mouth. 'Stand still. Your dad and me paid good money for that cub uniform.' She set his cap straight and adjusted his scarf. 'You better look after it, my lad, or you'll be for it. Money doesn't grow on trees you know, more's the pity.'

Margaret smiled. 'Boys are just natural dirt magnets. Alan was just the same. I wish he'd stayed in the scouts, might have kept him away from those Teddy Boys he hangs about with now.'

The boy wriggled free from her grasp, picked up a rucksack and ran off down the street towards the scout hut where an ex-army lorry had just pulled up.

Harry, known by his cubs and scouts as Kim, was organising a human chain to move food and camping equipment from the pavement into the lorry provided by a friend of his father.

A few yards away another lorry from the same source was also being loaded, but by young girls in brown uniforms. This was to be a combined cub scout and brownie camp. The brownies were under the control of Daphne, or Brown Owl as she insisted on being addressed as. She stood in the midst of apparent chaos calmly ticking off the items as they were loaded.

With all the camping equipment and food supplies accounted for, a dozen Cubs and eight Brownies clambered up into their respective vehicles. Some rushed to secure places to sit, others waited for the tailgate to be raised and fixed into place. The lower sections of stable-type doors were swung inwards and secured. Cubs and brownies peered out at lines of parents waiting to see them off. Their annual journey to the countryside was about to begin.

Spinning his motorbike keys around one finger, Harry approached Daphne. 'All set? I'll see if I can beat you down there this time.'

'If I could have got another helper to travel with my girls, I would have been tempted to ride with you, even if it does look like we're in for more rain.' She smiled nervously and waved a hand towards the nearest lorry. 'I do hope nobody's sick this time.'

'I know what you mean. You did go through it last year, didn't you. I'm lucky some of my scouts agreed to come this year to lend a hand. They'll keep an eye on the young ones during the journey.' He jumped on the kick-start. The engine roared into life. 'Well, I'll see you down at Oakwood House, have fun.'

'I hope so,' she said, not totally convinced. 'You mind how you go on these wet roads.'

*

Harry used both feet to balance the bike on the road, waiting for the man with a handheld stop-go sign to allow him through the road works. The glorious smell of hot tar filled the air as a steamroller chugged up and down. Children skipped and hopped alongside this noisy, powerful machine. Men with shovels threw gravel onto the sticky new road surface in front of the colossus, feeding its voracious appetite. On the platform of the machine the driver tossed coal into fire, pausing only to wipe a grimy hand across an equally dirty forehead. The huge roller moved relentlessly back and forth, belching smoke and steam. Cobblestones that had sparked beneath horseshoes disappeared under a covering of pitch and stones.

Three hours later, Harry rode through the tall gates, through the formal gardens and into the meadow. Pushing the bike's foot-rest down, he dismounted. 'Done it, they're not here yet. Oops! Speak of the Devil, here they come. Time we got the marquee up and some tea brewing.'

*

Wooden tent pegs, painstakingly produced by the Cubs during dark winter nights, marked out two oblongs ten yards apart. Eager spades cut into damp grass. Turves were laid out neatly between the exposed ground and the trees bordering this side of the grounds. The wet top-soil gave little resistance to this onslaught as the volunteer scouts helped the cubs vie with each other. They piled the earth along one side of what was fast becoming a trench. Worms wriggled out of hiding, squirming in the soggy earth, until the next spade delivered its load.

Work slowed as young arms became tired. Sweating faces replaced eager smiles. Harry called a halt. Screw-topped bottles of R. White's lemonade and the few remaining sandwiches that had managed to evade the cubs during the journey were passed around.

Harry attached ropes between the posts when the digging resumed. Under the fretful eye of Daphne, he added extra guy ropes. He finished attaching canvas to provide privacy to anyone visiting these *al fresco* toilets and stood back to admire his work.

Daphne smiled. 'Let's hope it stays put this year. I can still see that poor vicar's face. How embarrassing.'

When the second trench was deep enough to meet with Harry's approval, the spades were laid against piles of spoil speckled with chalk. Scouts and cubs wandered back to their tents. Harry checked all the knots and bindings holding the wood framework over the open pits before following the boys.

Woodsmoke greeted the returning work party. A few cubs, excused from digging, had joined forces with the brownies to cook a rather late lunch.

Eggs swam in hot fat while baked beans bubbled in what could easily pass as a witches' cauldron. Curly rashers of bacon sizzled on a smoke-blackened tin tray. Thick-cut bread, impaled on sticks, was held out hopefully towards the fire. Some of the youngsters managed to achieve something resembling toast. Others watched fallen slices consumed by the flames.

After lunch Harry and Daphne organised their charges into teams. Once the usual bickering and name calling subsided, leaders were each given a flag and instructed to hide them in the woods. Harry emphasised the flags must be able to be seen this time, not buried as had been tried before. Other than that, anything was permissible.

The teams watched the flag-bearers disappear into the trees.

Harry looked at his watch, put a whistle to his mouth and blew. Boys and girls streamed through the meadow, sending clouds of indignant butterflies into the air. Daphne and Harry sauntered after them.

Deep amongst the trees, branches cracked underfoot as cubs and brownies rushed to be the first to find the opposing team's flag. Screams of delight soon announced a winner.

'We beat the boys! Brown Owl, we beat the boys!' Excited girls gathered round Daphne, their freckle-faced leader proudly holding out the trophy. 'Yes, and I climbed the tree.' She licked the palm of her hand and rubbed it over grazed knees.

Daphne smiled. 'Well done, girls. Now, let's get back to camp. I'll inspect your beds before we make the cocoa, then I think an early night is in order. It's been a long day.'

A cub briefly touched his eyes before quickly making a show of brushing imaginary dirt from his cheeks. Harry patted the boy's head. 'Never mind, lads, better luck next time. Before we go back to camp, I've got a job for you. I want you all to help me gather wood. Make sure it's dry. I don't want any more Red Indian smoke signals.' Cubs from last year's camp laughed.

Clutching slices of bread and dripping and mugs of cocoa the cubs sat around the campfire. Harry sat balanced on an upturned log, totally entrancing his audience with stories of ghosts. '…and the dog and his master were never seen again.' Crackling logs gave pale faces a false healthy glow. Harry stood and kicked a smouldering branch back onto the fire. 'That's enough for tonight, boys, time to turn in. Tomorrow…' He paused. 'Tomorrow we're going to build a rope bridge.'

The boys walked off towards their tents, some talking of ghosts, others of the chances of building the bridge. A few looked back over their shoulders into the darkness.

Two of the boys stayed by the fire, poking the logs with small branches, mesmerised by the sparks pirouetting up into the blackness.

Harry drained his mug. 'Come on you two, time for bed.'

One of the cubs dug his friend in the ribs, leant into him and whispered. 'Tell him, tell Kim what we found.'

Harry smiled. 'Yes, tell me. What did you find? Money? If it was, you can put it into the Troop Funds.'

'Go on!'

'No. You do it.'

The boys looked at each other.

'For the *last* time, just tell me. Then we can all get to bed.' Harry stood with his hands on hips.

'A hole. We found a great big hole.'

'Is that it? A hole? There are rabbit and badger holes all over the place. What's special about your one?'

'It hasn't got a bottom. It must go right down to the centre of the earth.'

Harry laughed. 'You've got too much imagination. Tell me where this hole is, then clean your teeth and get to sleep. It's getting late. I don't want your parents complaining I kept you up past your bedtime when we get back home.'

'It's under a tree. We were looking for the flag and I needed a wee. I went round the back of this tree and saw the hole. Most of it's covered by roots.'

'That's right. When I heard him yell, I ran over. We dropped stones down it, but there wasn't any sound of them hitting the bottom. I lit some of my matches and dropped them in, but they went out before we could see anything.'

'It must be bloody…sorry, Kim, it must be deep. It goes down for miles and miles.'

'Hmmm. Okay. In the morning we'll go and see if there's anything to this story of yours. Now, for the last time, *bed*.'

'Yes, Kim.'

*

Following a hurried breakfast, the two cubs led Harry through the woods. After much discussion the boys finally agreed where to turn off the established footpath. Following an animal trail through waist-high ferns they entered a copse of silver birch trees surrounding a magnificent oak.

'This is it!' The boys ran to the tree and pointed down. 'See, we told you.'

Harry caught up with them and knelt down. Lowering his face to the ground he peered into the hole.

'Hmm, looks interesting,' he said. 'But we're going to need a rope. One of you better run back to camp.'

'You could have brought the long one,' Harry sighed when the runner returned. 'I knew I should have gone myself.'

Tying the rope around the tree he leaned back to test the knot. Satisfied he sat on the edge of the hole, took hold with both hands and lowered himself into the void.

Minutes later the boys heard his voice from below. 'I've run out of rope and I'm still not down… It's very dark… Did either of you think to bring a torch?'

'No. Did you?'

Harry muttered something about the Scouts motto before climbing back up the rope. Sweating, he hauled himself from the hole.

'I can't let you go down there. We need a longer rope. And torches. And there has to be more of us. I've got the strength to climb back up but you wouldn't manage it without someone pulling on the rope.'

One of the cubs clutched the side of the tree and peered into the darkness. 'How far down *does* it go?' he asked.

'I don't know. That rope's about twenty feet long after allowing for the bit around the tree and I didn't get to the bottom.'

'Wow. Did someone dig it?'

'Yes, it's man-made all right. They're called Dene Holes. People say they were used to store grain, but no one's sure.'

A flash of lightning lit up the woods followed by the rumble of thunder reverberating in the distance.

'Where did that come from?' Harry looked puzzled. 'Not more bl…' He glanced at the cubs. 'Not more rain, surely. It wasn't forecast. I listened to the wireless before we left yesterday.' He grimaced as raindrops pattered on the leaves above their heads. 'Blast! I think we'd better get back before this lot really starts. We can come back later. And this time remember our motto. *Be prepared.* Bring a torch and our other rope.'

Harry and the cubs paused at the edge of the wood and stared upwards. Sullen rain-clouds chased cotton wool from the blue sky. Day turned to night. Lightning forked. The ground shook as thunder roared. Hailstones lashed down as the temperature plummeted. Grass, daisies and buttercups were crushed beneath the onslaught. Bumble bees deserted clover. Rabbits disappeared into burrows.

'We'll have to run for it,' Harry said, apologetically. 'Sorry, boys, I know we're going to get soaked but it's too dangerous to shelter under trees with all this lightning.'

Tents exhibited the different skill levels used to erect them. Some stood firm, balls of ice ricocheting from taut canvas. Others sagged and became receptacles for nature's angry onslaught. Wet faces peering through door flaps reflected flashes tearing the sky apart. Charcoal, floating in the fire pit, was assaulted by frozen missiles. Hailstones blanketed the ground as the intensity of the storm increased. From the relative comfort afforded by the marquee, Harry and Daphne surveyed the scene of misery.

'Never seen weather like it,' Harry grumbled. 'I remember being cold and wet on an "Outward Bound" course a couple of years back, but it was nothing compared to this. How can *this* be August? I've never known such a wet month. The whole summer's been a washout. It's more like autumn or winter if you ask me.'

Daphne nodded her agreement. 'It's such a shame. My girls have been looking forward to this so much.'

He put a hand on her shoulder. 'If it keeps up much longer, we'll be in danger of losing some of the tents. See the hailstones piling up on the ground? There must be inches of them.' As he spoke one of the ex-army shelters lost its last battle, the weight of ice bringing it down, its occupants scrambling out and running towards the marquee. 'That's right, lads,' Harry shouted above the noise of the storm. 'Over here!'

The boys stood shivering, hair plastered to their heads, uniforms sodden. Harry's forehead wrinkled. 'Shoes would have been a good idea.'

'But, Kim, we always take them off when we go in the tent like you told us to.' The boy's teeth chattered. Daphne fetched tablecloths and wrapped them around the cubs.

'There are no blankets in here I'm afraid,' she said. 'These will have to do. You shouldn't stay in those wet clothes really, but there doesn't seem much we can do about it right now.'

The canvas roof of the marquee bulged downward. Daphne looked at Harry. 'What are we going to do?' she asked.

'Abandon ship. As soon as this lot lets up, I'll go up to the house and use the phone. Let's hope the roads aren't flooded and dad's friend can arrange for the lorries to come down and collect us.' He pointed to the camp. 'Look, another tent's fallen down!'

*

Next day Mr Lyonaisse watched through an upstairs window as a pair of identical vehicles cut paths across the meadow, headlights turning raindrops into jewels. Mrs Lyonaisse approached and linked her arm through his. 'Such a pity,' she said. 'I do love having them camp here.'

'I know, I'll miss them too. But tell me, who's going to deal with those field latrines? It's too much for me to do.'

'Don't distress yourself. The gardener will take care of it, that's why we pay him.'

Leaving behind churned up grass, mud and puddles the drivers drove through the imposing gates. Inside the vehicles, cubs splashed about in water seeping from stacked canvas. Using their feet, they encouraged it to leave under the tailgate.

Following them on his motorbike Harry raised a hand and waved. Daphne wiped wet hair from her forehead and returned the gesture from the back of the lorry carrying her brownies. She bent down and spoke to her charges. They began to sing. 'Oh let the sunshine in, face it with a grin…'

Chapter 7

Rain-clouds masked the night sky, adding to the early morning gloom. Light spilled from the frontage of the newsagents, in stark contrast to darkened shops on either side. Outside the shop a young boy struggled to mount his bicycle. A heavy bag challenged his sense of balance as he wobbled down the road.

After what had happened last year, Tommy Green's birthday party was becoming a cause for anxiety for Mrs Green, the newsagent's wife. When she woke this morning, she silently prayed this year would be different. Some prayers are answered. Others are not.

Rubbing her eyes, she descended the stairs to the shop. Halfway down the poorly lit hallway, something touched her head. Instinctively she put up a hand to ward it off.

Mr Green rushed from behind the counter when he heard his wife scream. He found her sitting on the bottom stair, tearing at her hair.

'What's the matter? Did you fall?' Taking out his handkerchief he dabbed at her tears.

'No! It was a spider! A huge spider!' She turned and pointed. 'It brushed against my face! Is it in my hair? My heart's going to burst. The last time I felt this scared was when the flying bomb came down on the estate.'

Mr Green bent down and ran his fingers over her hairnet. 'There's nothing there, dear. Perhaps you imagined it.'

'I did *not*. It was a black spider as big as this!' She spread the fingers of one hand and held them up.

'If it was that size, it must have come in on a banana boat.' He helped her up. 'Come on. Let's put the kettle on and have a nice cup of tea. I could do with a cuppa after marking up all the papers for the paper round.'

She frowned. 'Is it that late? I must have overslept. Sorry, dear.'

'Yes, the paperboy has already gone. I expect you were tired after all your work yesterday. I hope Tommy appreciates it.' He lit a cigarette. 'What time is the party?'

'I made it a bit earlier this year. The magician I booked could only manage to come at four, so I said three o'clock on the invitations. That way I can get the food cleared away before he starts his show. Lucky it's half-term, so school's not a problem.'

Hearing his parents clattering about in the kitchen below, Tommy untied the length of black cotton from the bannisters and pulled the rubber spider back up. Tiptoeing to his bedroom he grinned as he hid the source of his mother's terror in a box full of comics. 'That was great. Pity I'm going to have to get rid of you, Boris, but if mum finds you, I'll be for it, so you'll have to go. I'll take you to school when we go back and swap you for something.'

*

Mrs Green checked the jellies and blancmanges sitting alongside plates piled high with home-made sausage rolls and chocolate cup-cakes on the cold-slab in her pantry. She gently prodded the icing on Tommy's birthday cake. Satisfied, she pushed ten blue candles into plastic holders and pushed them into place. 'There. That looks nice, even if I do say so myself.' She looked up at the clock. 'Another hour and they'll be here. I can't believe it's his birthday again, where *did* another year go?'

*

Six boys helped Tommy eat in minutes, everything his mother had taken hours to prepare. The mothers of Sydney, Gordon, Rowland, and the brothers, Bill and Bert would have been mortified if they could have seen their offspring. Gone was the well-scrubbed look they had when presented to Mrs Green, loving care replaced by cream and custard covered faces. Neatly ironed ties had been ripped off and stuffed into pockets leaving shirt collars askew.

*

Mrs Green stared at the man standing at the shop counter. He was carrying a fold-up table and a suitcase.

'No, thank you,' she said. 'I don't want anything. I bought brushes off the last man who called. Goodbye.'

'Just a moment, madam,' he replied. 'You're mistaken, I'm not selling anything. I'm Mysto, the magician you hired for your son's birthday.'

Mrs Green put a hand to her mouth. 'Oh, I'm so sorry. I wasn't expecting you just yet. Come through to the front room, I'll fetch you a cup of tea and something to eat.'

'Thank you. I wasn't sure how long it would take on the bus so I allowed plenty of time.' He smiled. 'Would you mind paying me now? Then I won't have to disturb you in the shop when I leave.'

'Good idea. I'll just open the till and settle up with you.'

*

The neatly laid table was now strewn with paper plates, some with evidence fish paste sandwiches were not as popular as chocolate spread or peanut butter. Empty crisp packets were blown into, screwed shut then slammed against the table adding to the noise.

'Good party, this,' Bert said. 'Let's have a jelly fight like we did at Syd's house.'

Rowland, whose waistline kept him back a little further from the table, protested. 'No! Don't waste it. I've only had two helpings.' Rowland rubbed his protruding stomach. 'Pass one of them here. I've still got plenty of room yet.'

'Want some more, do you?' Sydney asked. 'Here you are then, catch!'

The sight of Rowland in the act of half-catching, half-juggling the flying jelly sent the boys into fits of laughter. Sucking his fingers, he glared around the table. 'That's not funny,' he mumbled. 'Some of us are hungry. This is the first time I've eaten since lunchtime.'

A sausage roll bounced off his forehead, narrowly missing his National Health, fake tortoiseshell, glasses. Rowland ignored the assault and crammed the damaged pastry into his mouth. 'These are really nice. Anymore?'

Five pairs of hands grabbed sausage rolls and pelted Rowland. 'Not so fast! Ouch, that hurt. Don't!' He tried to duck beneath the table.

The door opened. 'Stop that,' Mrs Green shouted above the din. 'What do you think this is? The chimpanzees' tea party?'

'I tried to stop them, Mrs Green,' Bert said.

'Liar.' Bill punched his brother's shoulder. 'You started it.'

'Did not.'

'Did.'

'Pack it in, boys, hurry up and finish eating. Mysto is in the other room but if you don't settle down, I'll tell him you don't want to see the magic show.'

'Ohhh, please don't, Mum. We're sorry.' Tommy brushed the remains of the sausage rolls into a heap. 'We'll clear up for you.'

Rowland reached out to rescue the flaky-pastry missiles. 'These are scrummy,' he mumbled.

'Hasn't your mother told you it's rude to speak with your mouth full?'

'Is it?' Pieces of sausage roll flew in all directions.

'Urghh! He got me,' Sydney cried. 'Let's teach him a lesson.'

Mrs Green stepped in to separate the bundle of flailing arms and legs on her kitchen floor. 'Right, that's it. No magician for you.'

'But, Mum, it's not fair. Just because Rowland gets starved at home and we were trying to help him get enough to eat.' Tommy put on the "butter wouldn't melt in my mouth" look he had practised in front of the mirror in his mother's bedroom. 'Give us another chance...please.'

Mrs Green sighed. 'As it's your birthday I'll see –'

'Thanks, Mum.'

'Go on then. I give up. But you all behave yourselves in my front room.'

*

Mysto threw a square of green baize over his small folding table. Bending over a battered suitcase he selected the tricks he had chosen for today. Playing cards, metal tubes, pack of modelling balloons, a wooden box, and finally a magician's wand. He glared at his young audience. *Bloody kids,* he thought. *What have things come to when I have to resort to doing blinking kids' parties?* 'Hello children,' he said. 'My name is Mysto and I'm a magician.'

'What, like the one in the boring film my mum took me to see?' Tommy called out. 'Fantasy or something it was called.'

Mysto drew himself up and took a deep breath. 'No. To start with he was a sorcerer, and the film was called Fantasia.'

'That's right, mister,' Tommy held up his thumb. 'I thought it was something foreign.'

Mysto sighed. *I knew this was a mistake.* 'For my *first* trick I need a volunteer.' He stared around the room. Six faces stared back at him. 'Come along, there must be someone who wants to help me?'

'I will,' Rowland spluttered. 'Just give me a chance to finish this piece of cake.' He wiped both hands down his trousers as he pushed through his friends. 'What do you want me to do?'

Mysto fanned a pack of playing cards and held them out, face down, towards Rowland. 'Take a card, any card,' he said through clenched teeth. 'Look at it, show it to your friends, but don't let me see.'

Rowland chose one and held it up.

'Now, put it back in the pack.'

Rowland dutifully replaced his chosen card.

Mysto shuffled the pack. Laying the cards on the table he tapped them with the wand. Picking them up again he attempted to fan them out. The cards resisted him. Irritably, he tried to pull a card from the pack. Two came out. He held them both up as if it was what he had intended to do. 'Is one of these your card?'

The boys erupted into laughter. 'Yes, mister,' Tommy yelled. 'The one with strawberry jam and bits of cake.'

Mysto forced a smile. *Bloody kids. I ought to hang one of them as an example to the others.* 'Well done,' he said, waving Rowland away. 'You can join your friends now.' He tossed the cards back into the suitcase. *I'll have to clean those before I can use them again.* 'Okay, now for my next trick…I'm going to use this.' He held up a metal tube. 'As you can see it's perfectly empty. Using the wand, he rattled it against the inside then covered it with a square of silk. With a dramatic flourish, he made a magic pass over it. Removing the handkerchief, he pulled a string of miniature flags, interspersed with oblong pieces of coloured material, from the tube. The resulting pile built up on the table in front of him. As the last flag emerged, he bowed and waited for applause.

'You haven't got a German flag, or Japanese.' Tommy pointed. 'My uncle has, he brought them back from the war.'

'Did he? How interesting.' Mysto mimed a yawn.

'You bored too, mister? I know I am. Mum said you were a magician. You haven't even got a top hat, how are you going to produce any rabbits?' Tommy was becoming excited. 'When I grow up, I'm going to be a famous magician. A real one. I'll make lions disappear. And big –'

Mysto held up his hands. 'Let me show you how to make a lion.' He picked up the balloons and blew them up. When he had inflated three, he twisted them together and held up a shape with a head and four stubby legs. 'There you are, a lion, the king of the jungle.'

'A lion?' Tommy's incredulous voice made itself heard over the laughter of his friends. 'That's not a lion. Anyone with two eyes can see it's not. Looks more like my aunt's Scottie dog.'

Mysto tossed his creation into the case. 'It sounds as though your relatives have got just about everything.' He tapped the table with his wand. 'I know,' he said. 'As it's your birthday, Tommy, you can help me with a daring new trick, if you're brave enough. Or maybe we should get one of your friends to volunteer, shall we?'

'I can do it,' Tommy said. 'I bet I can do anything, especially daring things.'

'Good.' Mysto cleared all the objects off his table then folded it away. 'As this trick is *so* special I'll make it my last one. I've got lots of others, but this is better than all of them. Bring me your chair.'

Tommy moved his seat to where Mysto stood patiently waiting. 'Thank you. Now, I need three tumblers full of water. Can someone fetch them for me?'

Bill and Bert jumped up and made their way to the kitchen.

On their return they handed the half-pint glasses to Mysto. 'We didn't spill much, most of it's still there,' Bert said, proudly.

'Okay, Tommy, let's get started shall we. But to make this really special I'd like everyone apart from me and Tommy to leave the room and count to four hundred before coming back in. Can you do that?'

Chairs were hurriedly pushed back as the friends rushed out.

Mysto turned back to Tommy. 'Now, let's see how daring you are, shall we?'

Outside, Tommy's friends were all counting out loud as Mysto stepped out from the room carrying his folding table and suitcase. 'Make sure it's four hundred,' he said. 'Or the trick will be spoilt. Bye, boys. Enjoy the rest of the party.'

He waved to Mrs Green as he walked back through the shop. 'Goodbye, Mrs Green.'

'Off already?' she raised her eyebrows. 'That was quick. Still, it sounds as though the boys enjoyed it. Thank, you.'

'Three hundred and ninety-nine, four hundred!' Sydney pushed open the front room door and laughed. His friends pushed past and joined in.

Tommy was sitting on the chair with a glass of water balanced on his head and another two on the backs of his outstretched hands. Beads of sweat and trembling arms revealed the concentration needed to keep the glasses in place.

'Don't just stand there laughing your stupid heads off. Come and help me. If I spill water all over mum's carpet, I'll *really* be for it.'

Bert and Bill stepped forward and took the glasses off Tommy's hands. Tommy reached up and carefully removed the other glass. 'You just wait. I'm going to get him for this.'

Chapter 8

The driver and his mate carried items of furniture and tea-chests into the empty house with unusual efficiency. Their task had been made easier by Mrs Reardon's judicious use of coloured chalk to mark the boxes with the name of the rooms they were destined for. Beds were jostled up the narrow stairs. Existing furniture was pushed aside to make room for the new arrivals being deposited in the designated rooms. The house became a cross between a jumble sale and an inexpensive version of Aladdin's Cave. Nothing much of value, that was true. But what there was, had been hard earned.

Douglas Miller divided his attention between watching the men emptying the Pickford's van and the high gates. Nervously pacing up and down he removed his wristwatch, shook it, then used thumb and finger to wind it. He strapped it back on his wrist and tapped the glass. 'They should have been here by now,' he muttered.

In the adjoining house his wife, Patricia, busied herself making tea for everyone.

An hour later, the removal van drove off in a cloud of dust but had to stop at the gate to give way to a taxi.

'They're here.' Taking a briar pipe from his pocket Douglas packed it with tobacco. Tamping it down he struck a match, sucked on the stem and inhaled. His eyes watered from the coughing attack. 'That's better,' he said, taking in another mouthful of smoke.

Mrs Miller joined him as the taxi drew up.

Clutching a brown paper parcel, containing items she considered too precious to be in the hands of removal men, Mrs Reardon stepped out. She was followed by Alan holding a box of vinyl records.

Mr Reardon begrudgingly paid the fare as mother and daughter embraced.

'Mum! How nice to see you both after all this time. But where's Brian?'

'Hello, Margaret, dear. He's in the house. Been like a frog on a hot rock all morning. Come and see for yourself.'

'Has he changed very much? You worried me when we spoke on the phone. And your letter didn't say much either.'

'All I can say is it's a miracle he's home again. We just have to be patient.'

Margaret stared into her mother's eyes, seeking re-assurance. Turning towards her husband she said, 'You and Alan start sorting out your things. I'm going with Mum. I'll be back in a minute.'

*

Margaret threw her arms around her brother. 'Brian! I can't believe it. After all these years.'

He stood still, rubbing his hands together, unsure how to react.

'Don't you remember me?' Releasing him from her bear-hug she took a step back. The smile deserted her face. 'Brian? What's the matter?'

Gripping her mother's wrist, she stared at her long-lost brother. 'Why doesn't he recognise me? What's wrong?'

Mrs Miller took a deep breath. 'We're not sure. The hospital said it would take time. He's happy here with us, but…'

Margaret sank into a chair. Her natural colour drained from her cheeks, leaving face powder and lipstick struggling to present a look of normality.

*

Alan frowned as he stared around his room. A small leaded window allowed a small amount of light to penetrate the gloom. The bed, with its rose-patterned quilt, looked lost between veneered bedside cabinets. Spare blankets smothered a Lloyd Loom chair. Stacks of *Picture Post* and *Life* magazines harboured layers of dust, sprinkled with dead moths and flies.

'What am I supposed to do with this load of junk? Where am I supposed to put my record player?' He stepped around abandoned suitcases and turned the small key in a wardrobe door. 'Shit!' Pursing his lips he blew out his breath and slammed the door shut. 'Bloody mothballs. They *stink*. This'll have to go. I want my own one, not this bleedin' old thing.'

His mother entered the room and put a hand on his shoulder. 'Never mind, dear. I'll soon have it sorted out, you'll see. It was nice of your grandma to find us a house of our own, wasn't it.'

'Nice? Stuck out in the country miles from anywhere? No coffee bars, no youth club, no nothing? What's nice about it?' He kicked the door frame. 'I didn't want to come here in the first place. I hate it!'

Alan's father poked his head out of the doorway opposite. 'Good. Does that mean we'll be seeing the back of you? I could manage your train fare with a bit of a squeeze.'

'*John.*' Margaret turned to face her husband. 'Leave him alone. He's only a child.'

'Child? He's seventeen for Christ's sake.'

'Take no notice, dear. He's just having one of his airs-and-graces. None of us chose to do this. But your Nan needs a bit of help. It won't be forever.'

'I know, Mum. But it's horrible.' He waved a hand. 'Look at it. I've got a rotten little room in a rotten little house. Like I said, I hate it.'

She turned at the sound of boots on lino. John's face warned her not to get involved.

'You useless piece of shit. Hate it do you? Well, I've got news for you, boy. If you don't like it here then you can sod off. I've grafted to keep you and your mother fed and keep a decent roof over our heads. I've –'

'Failed.' Alan sneered. 'Call that place we had, decent? I don't. It was a dump.'

John raised his arm. 'Why you smarmy little git.'

Margaret forced herself between them. 'Mind your language. You're not at work now.' She glared at her husband. 'And don't you hit him again.'

Alan pulled his shoulders back and thrust out his chest. 'He wouldn't dare. I'm not having it anymore.'

Margaret gently pushed her son aside. 'Go downstairs. Help me with all those boxes. I can't do it all on my own.'

'No…well, all right. I will in a minute, just don't keep on at me all the time.' He crossed the room and moved a table. Dust danced in the air, free to choose a different place to rest. 'God knows how I'm going to make room in here for all my stuff.'

Margaret shrugged her shoulders and descended the stairs.

'Put the kettle on while you're down there. I'm gagging for a drink,' John yelled after her.

'It's already on the range! I'm just waiting for it to boil.' Margaret peered through the window. A heron stood sentinel at the edge of the pond. 'I think Mum's right,' she murmured. 'She always says, "A watched pot never boils." This one's still going to be ages yet.' Standing at the front door she called up the stairs. 'You two, I'm going over the house to see Brian. I've put the whistle on the kettle. Help yourselves when it's ready. I won't be long.' Before either John or Alan could reply, the door closed behind her.

*

'Hello, Mum, I've come to see Brian.' Margaret stood on the doorstep, gazing over her mother's shoulder into the room.

'He's upstairs in his room. It's all been a bit too much for him I'm afraid.' She fiddled with her hairnet. 'Your dad's gone up to the Big House with a list of things he needs for the grounds, so come in while it's quiet. We can catch up on each other's news and I'll make some tea.'

Margaret put a cushion behind her back and settled into an armchair. Waiting for the promised cup of tea, she stared around the room to see if anything had altered since her childhood.

Her grandparent's sepia photos loomed over the piano, dominating one end of the room. On the sideboard the Ekco radio took pride of place between a pair of ugly Victorian vases. The mantlepiece above the open fire provided a home for the eight-day chiming clock she fondly remembered, still ticking inexorably towards the end of time. A coal scuttle with its companion set of shovel, brush and poker stood in the hearth. The hand-tinted picture of King George VI had been replaced by a colour print, a portrait of a radiant young Queen. But apart from that, nothing had changed.

Balancing a cup of tea on her lap, Margaret smiled. 'Before we start, I really must tell you what happened in the village as we drove through. I shouldn't have laughed but I just couldn't help it.'

Her mother dunked a biscuit. 'Go on then, tell me.'

'A woman and a policeman were trying to free a boy's head from railings in front of the pub. He was tugging at him while she rubbed lard or something into the boy's hair. You should have heard the racket he was making. I know it wasn't funny but –'

'I *bet* it was Tommy Green. Just the sort of thing he would do. He's always getting into scrapes, trespassing and scrumping apples. If there's mischief about you can bet your last shilling Tommy's at the heart of it.' She used a finger to hook a soggy piece of biscuit from her tea. 'Oh, blow, that always happens. Now, let's talk about Brian and your dad shall we. After all, it's why I phoned you in the first place.'

'Yes, Mum, sorry.' Margaret sipped her tea. 'Well to start with, I can see Brian's not well, but Dad looks fine.'

'Does he? The doctor says it's his heart, but will he listen? No. I've had to convince him you're only here because John lost his job and got you thrown out of your house.'

'That's true but –'

'But nothing. Dad *does* need help although he won't admit it. And I could do with a hand too. What with Brian and my job at the Big House, I don't know if I'm coming or going half the time.'

'Big House? Why do you still call it that?'

'No idea. Habit I suppose. You started it when you were a child.'

'Oh, I see. Fame at last.' Margaret smiled and sipped her tea. 'Tell me all about poor Brian. It was such a shock to hear he was alive. I want to help all I can.'

'I can't tell you everything because I don't know myself. What we do know is, he was picked up for vagrancy a couple of years ago about half a mile from here. Once they had him in the police station, they soon realized he wasn't…' Patricia lowered her voice and tapped the side of her head. 'You know, wasn't the full ticket.'

'Then what happened?'

'It was the day we were all looking for Mary. The police were busy, so Brian was quickly admitted to hospital. After a few weeks the Matron decided he didn't need to be there, but as he had nowhere else to go she found him a job, helping in the wards. She was right when she told us he suffers with terrible nightmares. But the hospital doctor prescribed some tablets which have almost got them under control. Even so, he still has the occasional bad night.'

'And now he lives with you and dad. Poor Brian.' Margaret put a hand to her mouth. 'Oh! I didn't mean it like that. I'm sorry, Mum.'

'Don't be silly. Anyway, I need you here to help me.'

'And it's what we came for. You can leave Brian to me now. You concentrate on looking after dad.'

Chapter 9

The smell of wood smoke served Frank as a calling card. He had been told many times, "Cleanliness is next to godliness," but still it was difficult to decide where his grubby neck finished and soiled clothes began. He willingly did odd-jobs in return for food and drink, but the call of the open road always enticed him away from the charitable works of others.

The police had realized long ago, arresting him for vagrancy was futile, the desk sergeant's maxim about old dogs and new tricks proved to be correct.

The inhabitants of the village kept an eye out for him. Not because they feared this travelling man, but to see if he ever rode his rusty bicycle. Children were fascinated by tin cans hanging from the handlebars and bundles of rags lashed to the frame. Tyres had become a luxury. Raucous metal rims now announced his presence before he came into view.

He shamelessly sifted through the contents of dustbins in daylight. The villagers turned a blind eye, they had accepted this stranger in their midst.

Walking beside his trusty steed, Frank entered the village. Outside the pub he patiently encouraged anything left in glasses to join his bottle.

Lifting the lid off a dustbin his eyes lit up. Today could be his birthday, as could any other day. He had no idea. But the sight of fish paste and watercress sandwiches lying amongst limp balloons and half-burnt miniature candles were a gift as good as any he could wish for. Dirt-encrusted hands reached in for the manna that had escaped a horde of locusts dressed as children.

His early morning round complete he trundled his treasures towards the woodland bordering one side of Oakwood House.

Lifting his bicycle, Frank worked his way through fallen stone blocks covered in moss. Many years ago, an oak tree toppled part of the wall surrounding the grounds of Oakwood House.

Squeezing between this rough barked colossus and the defences it had breached, he headed through the trees towards his camp.

He stopped as the sound of children's laughter filtered through the woods. He quickened his pace. The squeak from dry bearings sent a startled squirrel darting up the side of a silver birch.

A young girl ran down the woodland path to greet him. 'Captain,' she shrieked.

Frank moved his free arm to cross his waist, and bowed. 'Top of the morning, missy. Why aren't you at school?'

'It's the school holidays, silly. I thought pirates knew everything.'

'Ahh, that we do. I was just teasing.'

The girl took hold of his hand.

'Who's with you?' he asked. 'Is Cynthia here?'

'Yes. And Bridget. We want another story.'

'And so you shall, my little beauty. And so you shall.'

The three children sprawled on the ground and watched, spellbound, as Frank used the broken leg of a chair to fight Slippery Sam. 'Take that, you dirty dog, and that. I'll teach you not to cross swords with Captain Black Bart.'

'Get him, Captain,' Cynthia squealed. 'Don't let him escape this time.'

Drawing back his weapon he thrust it forward. 'Got you, you scurvy knave. Now beg forgiveness or you'll walk the plank.'

'Yes. The plank! Feed him to the sharks.' Bridget clapped her hands together. 'Go on. He deserves it.'

Frank tugged at his matted beard. 'Not so fast. I've a mind to let him go. Sam's a pirate, same as me. We got to stick together, ain't that so?' He bowed to his invisible adversary.

'Don't let him go again, Captain. He'll come back and kill you.'

'Slippery Sam can try. But I'm more than a match for his kind.' He bent down and picked up a *Beano* comic. 'Aha, look here, me hearties,' he said conspiratorially. 'Sam's dropped a new map showing where he's moved his treasure to. I'm off to look for it, so I am.' He walked away from his camp into the trees.

'Wait for us. We'll help you search.'

Frank stopped and glanced back. 'No, I'll go alone. His skeleton army may be guarding it.'

'We don't care. We're not scared.'

'Just one of you then. I need two people to guard my camp while I'm gone. And don't forget you've all sworn a pirate oath never to tell.'

The scourge of the Seven Seas waited while the girls argued about who would accompany him in his search for buried treasure. It was a game the youngsters had played before.

*

At the dining table in Oakwood House, Carl Lyonaisse pushed a plate away, the willow pattern still largely hidden by two eggs, rashers of crisp bacon, and mushrooms picked while the dew still kissed their virgin skin. Taking an Irish linen napkin from his lap he placed it on the table. The butler dipped his head deferentially as Carl left the room.

Slowly mounting the stairs, he paused as he heard his wife sob. He walked towards the sound he had heard many times before. Without knocking, he entered Mary's room.

Elizabeth sat on the carpet, one arm around the empty chair, her other hand wiping tears from her cheeks. The sight of the teddy bears seated serenely around the table and his wife grieving brought a lump to Carl's throat. Crossing the floor, he put a hand on her shoulder. 'Please don't, my love. Upsetting yourself like this won't bring her back. It's been two years since we buried our Susan and three years since Mary disappeared. All the tears in the world can't change anything.'

'I know. Sometimes I feel they are still here. Both of them loved this room so much.' She turned her wet face up towards him. 'Do you still believe someone may have taken Mary?'

Carl pulled a handkerchief from his pocket. Wiping away Elizabeth's tears, he dabbed his own eyes. 'We may never know. But one thing's for sure, I'll keep my promise to you. We'll always leave this room just as it was.'

'Yes.' She tried to smile. 'Until our little angel comes back.'

Carl looked away. 'That would be a miracle.'

'The miracle I pray for every day.' Elizabeth laid her head on the chair and sighed.

Taking her hand, he tried to encourage his wife to get up.

'Don't worry, I'll be down shortly,' she whispered.

Chapter 10

In the village, a poster pasted on a wall gave Alan Reardon hope life may still exist somewhere. Colourful artwork of a man stripped to the waist, arms held out in the form of crucifixion while standing up on a motorcycle, invited the public to: "Come and see the Wall of Death Riders!"

The flyer also boasted wild animals, scantily clad girls and a Wild West show. And if all this were not enough, an amusement fair had joined forces with the travelling circus. The lure proved irresistible. A short train journey held the promise of transportation from boredom to excitement.

*

Steel wheels clattering over joints in the rails provided a noisy accompaniment to the rhythmic swaying of the train carriage. Alan watched the passing farmland through the open window. He smiled as cows lifted their heads and wandered away from clouds of smoke descending onto their field.

Next minute, it was Alan's turn to experience smoke from burning coal. Jumping up, no mean feat in his tight trousers, he yanked on the leather belt and let the window fall with a satisfying thud inside the carriage door. He felt for his seat in a world suddenly deprived of light. Thanks to poor maintenance, or vandalism, the carriage lights did not do their job as the train thundered into a tunnel.

As it emerged from the darkness he reached out and released the belt from its retaining stud and pulled hard. With the window open once more he used his hands to encourage the ethereal invader to leave by the same way it had entered.

*

Leaning out from his lofty vantage point, the driver of the train waited for the guard to wave his green flag. The fireman shovelled on more coal. Steam hissed. Orange specks danced in the smoke as it billowed upward.

Slamming the carriage door behind him, Alan carefully brushed spots of soot off his powder blue drape jacket. Using a window of the "Ladies Only" waiting room as a mirror he slid a comb through a hairstyle made possible by a generous application of Brylcreem.

Handing over his train ticket Alan waited for the man to clip it.

Leaving the station, he sauntered amongst groups of people walking in the direction of the circus. The seductive smell of vinegar-soaked chips floated on the air, sending his saliva glands into overdrive. A young couple shared a meal, eager fingers diving into scrunched up newspaper.

*

Hand-painted light bulbs struggled to make their statement against a sky being painted pink by the retreating sun.

Golden horses, eyes staring wildly ahead, rhythmically bobbed up and down to the sound of a steam organ. Reaching out on legs that would never know the feel of grass beneath their hooves they galloped on, tirelessly carrying riders round and round.

Children clutching mats, shrieked as they spiralled down the Helter-Skelter.

In their efforts to impress girls, men hurled battered wooden balls at coconuts.

Mothers helped toddlers hook plastic ducks drifting aimlessly in a moat surrounding a fairy-tale castle.

The warm smell of candy floss competed with burgers and fried onions.

Alan was impressed.

Pulsating rock 'n' roll music attracted him through jostling crowds to the Dodgems.

Elvis had just finished telling his hound-dog its true worth as bumper cars ground to a halt. Youths with their girls rushed across the battle-scarred floor to claim their rides. The smell of electricity hung in the air.

Alan watched these modern-day charioteers race around the track amidst a shower of sparks descending from the wire mesh above.

Crepe soled shoes and shirts with upturned collars replaced ancient Roman sandals and rough tunics. There was bone shuddering, teeth rattling collisions, but no combatants waited the life-or-death decision from Caesar. He considered riding alone but dismissed the thought. Challenging young men in this sex fuelled ritual would only invite trouble.

It was time to find a girl he could call his own.

*

Alan peeled back the wrapper of a choc-ice and bit into it. The sudden coldness sent a shockwave through a tooth that should have been removed ages ago. He spat and threw the offending treat to the ground. The girl, selling ice cream and toffee apples, smiled. 'Bit cold, was it?'

'Ha, bloody ha.' He wiped his mouth with the back of a hand. 'That's not funny.'

'Sorry.' She came from behind the counter of her kiosk holding a toffee apple. 'Here, have this on me to make up for it.'

'You can stick…' Alan stopped as the girl stepped into the glare of overhead lights. His mouth opened but for once he lacked the ability to speak. She could have been the fantasy he teased his body with as he lay alone in bed at night.

Shoulder length hair framed her face. False eyelashes emphasised hazel eyes. Baby-pink lipstick accentuated plump lips. Face powder failed to hide a sprinkling of freckles. Her smile rivalled Marilyn Monroe.

Alan swallowed as he gazed at a polo necked sweater being pushed to its limits. A mauve mohair pencil skirt ending just above her knees allowed nylon stockings to show off slender legs. Practical flat shoes, probably insisted on by her mother, did little to spoil the image.

'Do you want it or not?' She thrust the apple towards him.

Alan grimaced. 'No. I don't like toffee.'

'Please yourself.' She turned to go back into her kiosk.

He reached out a hand. 'Wait. What's your name?'

'Rumplestiltskin. What's yours?'

'Alan. Now, don't mess about. Tell me your name.'

Twisting wax-paper around toffee-coated apples the girl carried on replenishing her stock. She licked her fingers. 'It's Sheila…and I hate it. Who ever thought of calling me that? You happy now?'

'It's not a bad name. I like it.' He eyed her up and down. 'Do you fancy doing anything when you finish work?'

She ignored him and opened the ice cream box. The generator at the rear of the kiosk coughed black smoke as more power was coaxed from it. She sorted through the stock, slid the lid back in place and wiped cold hands on a towel.

Alan turned away.

'I don't mind,' she said. 'Where are you thinking of taking me?'

'Anywhere you like. What about the Caterpillar? Or maybe the Wall of Death? You choose.' Alan struggled to get a hand into one of his trouser pockets. 'I think I've still got about ten bob.'

'I don't fancy any of those. I grew up in this fair. It's boring.' She mimed a yawn. 'I like the circus we're travelling with, especially the lions, but I've seen it all loads of times.'

'Oh, shame. I'd like to have seen the Wall of Death riders.'

Reaching up, Sheila wiggled a sign onto two hooks, *SHUT*. The filament inside a bulb glowed for an instant after she turned it off. A moth courting the light spiralled off into the dusk. 'How about the flicks?'

'Okay, is it far?'

'No. She said it's only a couple of miles. We can walk it.'

Alan looked down at his crepe soled shoes. 'In these?'

'Why not? Or I can always borrow my dad's hobnail boots if you like. He–'

'No thanks. I'll manage.'

*

Piles of bricks and burnt timber littered the ground. Rubbish and weeds adorned this evidence of the Blitz, softening the destruction. Sheila clutched Alan's arm and pointed to a black cat walking along the top of a wall. 'They're supposed to be lucky, aren't they? Black cats? Looks as though these houses could have done with a bit more luck.'

He frowned. 'I didn't realize places like this copped it in the war. I thought it was just cities like ours.'

'Did your house get bombed?' She sounded concerned.

'Not really, but the roof caught light during one raid, bloody incendiaries. We were lucky, the Germans turned a lot of our road into rubble.'

'Honest?'

'Yes. When we were kids, we thought it was normal to find places like this to play on. Cowboys and Indians, doctors and nurses, you know the sort of thing.'

Sheila shivered. Putting an arm around Alan, she pulled him close. 'I was evacuated. Me and mum stayed with an aunt somewhere. It must have been awful for you.'

'Huh! It was, but just you wait until the next one starts. Atom bombs. That's what we're in for, *bloody* atom bombs. Just wants one nutter to push a button and we're all for it.'

'Don't.' She glared at him. 'You're scaring me. They won't…will they?

'The Americans used a couple to wipe out loads of Japs, so why not the Russians? We should make the most of things. There's no future for us or anyone else. Not if they start chucking those things about.' Alan stepped off the pavement and lashed out with the side of his foot. A tin can left the gutter and flew through the air before rattling down the empty street.

'I heard there's an even worse one,' she said. 'The hydrogen bomb.'

'Yes, I've heard of that too.' He looked down at his shoes. 'My dad moans at me, about my clothes, the mates I used to knock about with and now my music. What a load of shit. He ought to be moaning about the politicians who can kill us all. Not what style my hair is.'

'I like your hair. What do you ask for when you get it cut?'

'Easy. Tony Curtis and a D.A. That's polite for duck's arse. Oh, and I always get something for the weekend.' He grinned.

'You must earn good wages. Those nice clothes. Fancy haircuts and smart shoes. I bet –'

'I get by. Dad's always on at me to give more towards the housekeeping but he don't know half of what I get my hands on.' He touched the side of his nose. 'Better not to ask. But that was before they moved down to the dump where we live now. Not much chance to duck and dive down here.' Taking out his comb he stroked it through his sideburns. 'I haven't had to try the local barber yet, but I bet he only does short-back-and-sides.'

*

Sheila and Alan held hands as they left the cinema. He pointed as they passed the lobby photos.

'He had the right idea. His parents didn't understand him either.'

'James Dean you mean? He's cool.'

'Yes. *Dead* cool.'

She pulled away from his embrace. 'That's not funny.'

'No? Still at least he didn't die as an old man lying in his own piss. Urghhh, I don't want to get old.' Alan spat. 'One thing's for sure, I can't see me and my mates racing like cars, doing a chicken run. There was only one in the road where I lived. It belonged to the doctor.'

'It must be great to live in America,' she said, wistfully.

'Want a fag?'

Sheila frowned. 'No, I tried it once, I don't like them.'

'Please yourself.' He cupped both hands around a cigarette, flicked his lighter and drew hard. Smoke drifted between them.

She coughed and flapped a hand at it. 'Take me back, please. It's getting late. Mum will be wondering where I've got to.'

*

Laughter, applause and an enthusiastic circus band disturbed the silence of the night. A woman rushed a small boy out of the entrance to the Big Top and stood watching as he retched to restore normality to his overloaded stomach.

Alan leaned back against the Ticket Office and pulled Sheila close. She put her arms around his neck and nestled her head on his shoulder. The velvet collar of his jacket lost its sheen as her face powder rubbed off. But Alan was more concerned about the discomfort he was feeling as drainpipe trousers sought to constrain his lust.

Sheila could feel his excitement rising and rubbed her body against him. He turned his head, found her mouth with his and kissed her. Not the tentative exploring kiss they had shared in the darkness of the cinema. This was a kiss to drive teenage hormones out of control. She pulled away and sucked in the night air.

He took her hand and held it against his problem. She shook her head. 'No chance. I'm not like that.'

'Oh, great. What am I supposed to do now?'

'Start running to catch the last train?' She kissed his cheek and gently pushed him away. 'Go on, you don't want to miss it.'

'Can I see you again?'

'I hope so. But how?'

He pulled a folded envelope from his pocket. 'Here, take this. I wrote my Nan's phone number on it in case I needed to call home. You can always leave me a message. She lives next door.'

'Thanks. I'll see when mum and dad can spare me and then call you. There's a phone-box not far from where we're camped.'

As he walked towards the train station, Alan continued to turn and wave even though he was not sure Sheila could still see him.

A motor bike with a girl in a sidecar passed him in the lane. He watched it disappear from sight. 'Pity I didn't get to see the Wall of Death,' he muttered. 'Wonder if anyone's ever tried it with something like that?'

Chapter 11

Mr Lyonaisse plucked a blood-red rose. Holding it close, he inhaled deeply, its scent brought the hint of a smile to his troubled face. After detaching several thorns, he threaded the bloom into the button hole of his lapel and continued his morning stroll.

Douglas sat on a garden bench with his feet up on a wheelbarrow piled high with weeds. He lit his pipe and admired his morning's work. The sound of footsteps on gravel caused him to look up.

'Morning, sir.' He touched the peak of his cap.

'Good morning. No, don't get up. I'll join you in the sun. Good for my bones.'

'Just taking a break, sir.' Douglas pointed towards the barrow. 'Seem to grow faster than ever these days. They must thrive on this new weed-killer. That, and all this rain we've been having.'

Mr Lyonaisse smiled and took a folded newspaper from his pocket. 'I thought you may like to see this. Seems your son was luckier than we all thought when you brought him back here.'

*

A spade bit into the grass as another trench began construction in the meadow. Piles of topsoil soon lined the gaping wound in the field. Wild flowers lay scattered. Doomed to wilt and die.

Taking off his jacket, Brian tossed it to the ground, rolled up his shirt sleeves and started to dig.

He was up to his waist when Douglas spotted him and wandered over with Rex at his heels.

'Hello, son. You look busy.' Douglas removed his cap and scratched his head. 'They're not coming back, are they?'

Brian dropped the spade and looked all around. His eyes opened wide. Fear transformed his face. 'Who?'

Douglas frowned at the consternation his simple question had evoked. 'The Cub Scouts. They were here last month, don't you remember?' He stared down into the trench. 'I had the job of filling in the last lot, now I see you're digging another one.'

'Oh...I see. Digging another...?'

'Trench toilet, aren't you?'

'No, it's a shelter. An atomic-bomb shelter.' Brian picked up the spade and jabbed at the earth. 'No good painting windows white, that won't do it.'

'I'm not sure I know what you're on about, but it's time for lunch. Are you ready?'

'No. Not yet. I've got to finish this.'

'I shouldn't worry too much. The newspapers don't know what to fill people's heads with next. There's not going to be another war.'

'That's what they said last time.'

'Okay, maybe they did. But it's different this time. If the Russians attack us, they'll all get bombed too.'

'Which is what happened to Germany. But it didn't stop them from doing it.'

'Hmm, I see your point. Why don't I ask Mr Lyonaisse if you could use one of his cellars?'

Brian scowled. 'No. I've seen what happens to people in their houses. This is safer. They don't bomb fields.'

Douglas shook his head. 'Okay, son...you win. I'll ask your mother to keep your lunch warm. Come on, Rex, let's get back home.'

*

Patricia pushed rashers of bacon around the frying pan. She turned as Douglas entered the kitchen followed closely by Rex. 'Where have you been all this time?' She peered through the window. 'And where's Brian? Isn't he with you?'

'No, love. I spoke to him. He's digging a trench in the meadow. I told him–'

'Digging? Why?'

'Beats me. He says it's a shelter.' Douglas spread margarine on slices of bread. 'Any tea, love?'

'Yes, it's in the pot, help yourself. Can you manage all these rashers? I can't keep them hot any longer.' She brought the pan to the table and scooped bacon onto his plate. 'Why is he digging a shelter? What's it for? He'll need a jolly good roof on it if the weather forecast is anything to go by.'

'I take it there's more rain on the way then?' He placed the rashers between the bread. 'Still, looking on the bright side of things, I haven't had to water the lawns much this year. Anyway, I didn't like to ask too many questions, he already seemed upset.'

'Oh dear.' She wrung her hands together. 'I do hope he's all right.'

'He'll be okay, and the exercise is probably doing him good.'

'Do you think I should have a word with Margaret? I could ask her if John or Alan would help Brian.'

'No. Let's leave him to it. He's not doing any real harm, and I can always fill it in if there are any complaints from the Big House.' He poured a cup of tea. 'Speaking of which, I've got some news for you. Mr Lyonaisse showed me something in the paper.'

Patricia joined Douglas at the table. 'When Brian decides to come home, I'll cook his lunch.' She shuffled her chair closer. 'So...what was it? Tell me. What did he show you?'

Douglas put his sandwich down. 'It was a newspaper article about a coach crash, an outing from the hospital where Brian worked.' He reached over the table and held her hand. 'I didn't say anything to him just now, and we mustn't tell him. Some of the people he knew at the hospital have been killed.'

'Oh! Surely not, how terrible.'

'There were photos. One showed a coach lying on its side halfway down an embankment. The other was of staff and patients all posing at *last* year's outing. The paper had put rings around the faces of those who went this year and died in the accident.' Douglas swallowed. 'Brian was standing next to one of them.'

She put a hand to her mouth. 'Oh my God...I dread to think –'

'I know. We've been very lucky.' He reached across the table and grasped her arm. 'Remember, my love, not a word to him.'

Patricia sighed. 'And to think I was worried about Brian and his shelter. From what you've just said there must be a few mothers wishing their sons could be doing just that.'

Chapter 12

Over a hundred miles away, Edward Stanton, a man in his mid-fifties stared incredulously at photos in a newspaper. His right hand remained frozen in the air above a cup. Dropping the tea-spoon he jumped up from the dining room table and rushed to his sideboard.

Searching the drawers, he found his magnifying glass amongst the Stanley Gibbons postage stamp catalogues. Picking up two framed photographs from their prominent positions on the sideboard, he kissed the one of a radiant young bride. Returning to the table he propped up the picture of his son's platoon.

Forcing his hand to stop shaking he ignored the photo of the crashed vehicle and concentrated on the other one. The description beneath identified it as having been taken the previous year. He moved the magnifier over the poor-quality images. A face jumped out at him.

He moved his attention back to the framed photograph. A young man wearing a peaked cap, crisp uniform and a cane tucked beneath his arm stood in centre place amongst his companions.

Edward held the glass over the newspaper once more.

The same man was amongst men and nurses posing in front of a coach outside the hospital.

The magnifying glass clattered on the table. 'It can't be…he's dead. They all are, God rest their souls.' Tears ran down his cheeks as he turned his face up toward the ceiling. 'William, what the hell's going on?'

Bewildered, he went back to the sideboard and this time returned with a scrapbook.

Newspaper articles, with pencilled dates, covered the progress of the Allied forces in the battle for Italy.

Alongside one was a letter from the War Office telling them their son, William Stanton, Private, had been killed in action. A list of casualties in another article revealed he had been lost with his officer and most of his comrades. Another small cutting, dated after the end of the war, concerned an investigation into their fate.

According to this report, one of only two survivors of the action had spoken to an officer of another regiment shortly after the attack. He had raised questions concerning the absence of his captain during the fatal engagement. The soldier who made the allegations died later in the war, but his diary had been sent anonymously to their news-desk.

The diary entries, regarding a captain who may have been responsible for the subsequent loss of his platoon, were enough for one reporter to try and establish the truth.

During his investigations, their reporter carried out interviews with men who had fought at Monte Cassino. He was told of stories circulating at the time about a missing officer. Some said he was wanted for desertion, others that he died with his men. Their reporter finally abandoned his quest when the War Office refused to corroborate any details.

Edward slammed a fist onto the table. 'I never believed the papers.' The table shook as he kicked out. 'The War Office reported them as killed in action. He can't be alive.' He took the newspaper to the window, pulled the net curtains aside and checked again. 'But it *is* him. I'd bet my life on it. If he'd stayed with his men maybe it would have turned out differently. The cowardly bastard *must* have abandoned them. He doesn't deserve to live.'

A few days later, after mowing lawns and tidying flower beds, cancelling newspapers and milk deliveries and scouring *Dalton's Weekly* for holiday lets, he was ready for his journey.

Packing a suitcase, he paused and held up the photo of his son's platoon. 'I swear on my life I'll set things right, William.' Wiping tears from his eyes he buried the framed picture amongst carefully ironed shirts.

*

Edward Stanton bit into a crusty roll. Raw onion overpowered cheddar cheese.

The roadside café was a welcome break from the drive.

Long journeys were a thing of the past since the loss of his wife. Before she died, trips to the seaside or Lake District were undertaken whenever the opportunity presented itself. The key to all the AA boxes dotted about the country bolstered confidence in his Hillman Husky. With their trusty Thermos flask filled to the brim with tea, along with a wicker basket containing everything needed for a picnic, the world had been their oyster. Those had been days of mixed emotions. The joy of visiting new places, rambling through country lanes, watching wildfowl on water, had often been spoilt by the ever-recurring memories of their lost son. Seeing trees welcome the spring with fresh buds, knowing he would never share their experience, brought on undeserved pangs of guilt.

Idly, Edward stirred his tea, chasing small clumps of cream around a chipped mug. Sweeping spilt sugar off the table with one hand, he reached into his jacket pocket with the other, pulled out a map and spread it on the table. Tracing the pencil line marking his route he breathed out deeply as his finger stopped around the halfway mark. 'Not bad, soon be there.'

Pushing the plate away he picked up the map and hurried back to his car.

A fly arrived to scavenge the sugar particles left behind.

Close to his destination, Edward stopped in a village shown on his small-scale map. The man in the newsagents gave him directions for the last stage of his journey.

*

In the hospital, after explaining to the girl behind the desk why he wished to speak to her, Edward sat in reception and waited for the Matron.

As she approached, the smell of Dettol, not perfume, wafted around her crisp, starched uniform, black stockings and polished shoes.

Edward stood up to greet her. 'Good morning, Matron. Thank you for seeing me.'

'And you are?' She held out a hand.

'Mr Stanton. I did tell your receptionist.'

'Pleased to meet you, Mr Stanton. Now…what can I do for you?'

Edward fumbled for his wallet. 'I won't take much of your time. I'd just like to ask about this.' He thrust the newspaper article towards her.

Glancing at it, she said, 'The accident? What can I tell you? Not much more than you've read I'm afraid. We are all in shock, those poor young men, as if they hadn't suffered enough.'

'No. Not the accident, the photo taken last year. I think I know one of the men.'

'Oh? Which one?' She took the folded page from him and stared.

'Him.' He reached out and pointed.

'Billy?'

'Billy? Is that his name? I must have made a mistake.'

Matron smiled. 'Sorry. We knew him as Billy when he first joined us, but now we know it's Brian. Brian Miller.'

Edward gasped. 'It *is* him.'

Matron looked surprised at this outburst. Handing the paper back she said, 'You know Brian? Is he a relative of yours?'

'No, he's a family friend. Is it possible to speak to him, please?'

'You're too late. He doesn't work here anymore. He's gone back to live with his parents.'

'Damn! Oh, please excuse me.' His cheeks reddened. 'Do you have their address? I've travelled miles to meet him, don't tell me he's moved miles away.'

'No, you're in luck, he's living close by. But I'm not sure I should give you his personal details. It wouldn't be right.'

'I see. Well, I've come to find Brian so I'm not about to give up now.'

'I understand. Sorry I can't be of more help to you.' Matron glanced at the clock on the wall. 'I have to get back to the wards.' She turned as she walked away. 'If you write to him, I can forward your letter.'

'Thank you, I may do that.' Edward frowned. *I'll ask around in the village. If he's local someone's bound to know him.*

Matron smiled. 'Good luck. I'm sure he'll be pleased to hear from you.'

'Not half as pleased as I will be when we get to meet,' Edward said, with just a hint of menace in his voice.

Chapter 13

Tommy Green flicked through the pages of the dog-eared comic. '*Superman's* all right,' he agreed, 'but it's not worth swopping for this *Batman*.'

The boy standing in the open doorway frowned. 'Give us it back then. I can always take it to school when we go back next term.'

'And get it confiscated by Killer Edwards? He must have more comics than any of us by now.' Tommy laughed and held his hand out. 'Go on then, I'll swop you. But I'll have one of those *True Crime* ones to make up the difference.'

'Okay. It's a swop.'

Comics were exchanged, hands spat on and shaken to seal the deal.

'You coming out? It's not raining now.' Tommy pointed down the street. 'We could go scrumping. The posh lot who just moved in at the bottom of your street don't seem interested in picking anything.'

'I can't. I've got to stay in for two days.' The boy assaulted one of his nostrils with a finger. 'Weren't my fault she put her silly vase near the edge of the mantelpiece. If it hadn't been raining, I could have flown my Spitfire in the garden.'

'Did it smash?'

'Not really. Tore the tissue a bit and broke one of its wings. But I soon mended it. I've got loads of spare balsa wood.'

'I meant the vase.' Tommy grinned. 'Okay. I'll see you later.'

*

Tommy ran towards the high wall and launched himself into the air. Grabbing the top, he heaved himself up, the toes of his shoes scraping the bricks.

The trees in the garden had once been carefully tended. Now they stood neglected, fallen fruit rotting on the ground. But the flower beds had not shared their fate, not a single weed desecrated the freshly hoed beds.

A protruding nail spoilt what should have been an easy drop into the garden for Tommy. A sound of fabric tearing meant trouble at home. Hard earned money had paid for his trousers and a leather belt would exact retribution for this careless act.

The flowers broke his fall. In return he changed the plants from display to dismay. It was obvious, even to him, they were never going to win any prizes. He lay still for a moment, gazing up at the sky.

Picking himself up he brushed his knees, smearing blood on one of them in the process.

The fruit tree was no match for the young harvester. He was soon lodged high in its branches, filling his sleeveless knitted jumper full of apples. The woollen garment was the last thing he needed to wear in the present weather but his mother had insisted. Tucked into his trousers, it made the perfect receptacle for stolen apples.

Dropping to the ground, he fell over and rolled on the grass. A man loomed over him and a hand reached out. Tommy scrambled to his feet and ran. Reaching the wall, he jumped but missed getting a handhold. He turned and kicked out. The man clutched his shins as Tommy jumped again. This time his fingers grasped the coping stones and he pulled himself up, swung his legs over and dropped to the ground. Grasping the front of his bulging jumper, he ran.

*

Leaving the tobacconists, Brian unfolded the sketch his mother had given him. The amateurish drawing had all the relevant landmarks needed for him to find his way to the shop and home again. Village green, church and High Street were all carefully marked with arrows to provide a circular route.

The shops were soon left behind as he strode along a footpath clutching a tin of pipe tobacco.

*

Edward Stanton opened his mouth in surprise as he saw Brian leave the tobacconist's shop. Hardly able to believe his luck, he hurried towards him.

Tommy was breathing hard as he ran. Edward stepped aside as he saw the boy. But it was the wrong choice. The pair collided and Tommy was knocked backwards as he ran into the man trying to ward him off. Apples spilled from his jumper and into the gutter.

By the time Edward got to his feet, Brian had disappeared from view.

*

Brian paused at a gate leading into a field of waist-high wheat. The footpath sign pointed in the direction of the churchyard. But he could see from the crudely drawn map his mother had drawn, a small diversion would take him past the church, into the meadow and enable him to visit his shelter before returning home. He decided to take the detour.

Minutes later he stood looking at a copse of trees. It was not on his map and he realized he had strayed off course. He knew his general direction was still correct and made the choice to cut through the trees rather than retrace his steps.

He made his way down a neglected path. Thorns snatched at his clothes from either side as he forced his way through. He was about to give up when something caught his eye. A cherub, tainted with spots of yellow and green lichen, lurked in the shadows.

Carefully pulling the barbed bushes aside he saw the outline of a grave. Chamfered edged stones, marble chippings and a small headstone. He spat on his handkerchief and wiped the grime from lead letters and numerals revealing two names. The years of birth differed, but the dates of their deaths were identical.

September 15th 1954.

Brian scratched his head and turned back the way he had come.

*

Back in the High Street, the indicator of Edward's Hillman Husky obediently blinked before the car turned to the right. He was about to make a third circuit of the town in the quest to find a man he held responsible for his son's death.

*

In the kitchen Douglas Miller wrestled the lid off the tobbacco tin. 'Thanks for this, son,' he said. 'Did you use mum's map?'

'Yes. Thank you for asking.'

'Your trousers are a bit muddy, and you've snagged the arm of your jacket. Did you have a fall?'

Brian looked down. 'No. I tried a short cut.'

'Did you? Why didn't you stick to the map? That's what we agreed.'

'I wanted to visit my shelter.'

'Oh…never mind. At least you got back home safely.'

'Can I ask you something?' Brian pulled at an earlobe.

'Of course, you can. I can see you're puzzled. What is it?'

'I found something.'

'Did you? What?'

'A grave.'

Douglas laughed. 'I expect you did. There are enough of them in the churchyard.'

'This wasn't in the church. It was hidden in some trees.'

Filling his pipe Douglas stared at his son.

'Are you sure?'

Brian stared up at the ceiling. He cleared his throat. 'Yes. There was an angel.'

Douglas frowned as he put a match to the bowl of his pipe.

'A very small one,' Brian said.

'Was there a headstone? Do you remember the name on it?'

'Yes.' Scrunching his eyes Brian concentrated hard until he recalled the names and dates.

Clutching three bottles of milk to her breast, while holding a fourth in her free hand, Patricia used her ample backside to push open the kitchen door.

'Tell your mother what you just told me,' Douglas said, one hand resting on the back of a chair.

Despite his mother's obvious impatience, Brian insisted on recounting his entire walk before giving her the details of the hidden grave.

She gasped. Her arms dropped to her side. Four bottles crashed to the flagstone floor. Glass exploded. Brian dived under the kitchen table.

'Incoming! Take cover!' His fingers raked the flagstones.

'It's all right, son. There's nothing to worry about. Come on out.' Douglas reached down. Turning his head he asked, 'Have we still got the bit of brandy I saved from Christmas?'

Patricia put the mop back into a bucket. Standing on a chair she reached into the far recess of a cupboard, found a small bottle and handed it to Douglas. He poured a measure into a cup and handed it to Brian. 'Here, drink this. You'll feel better.' As the shaking came under control, he took the glass from his son. 'Okay now?'

Brian ran his tongue across dry lips. 'Yes. Thank you.'

Furrows appeared on Douglas's brow. 'Now, tell us again, are you sure that's what you saw?'

'Yes.'

'And the names were definitely Barry and Susan Bridlington.'

Patricia's hand shook as she held smelling salts to her nose.

Brian took a biscuit from the brass bound barrel. 'Yes. Why?'

The effect his news had on the people claiming to be his parents bemused Brian. He was no stranger to death. He had seen the *Grim Reaper's* scythe cut down men of all ages, along with women and children. Night and day he was tormented by stark images, insisting he re-live his actions. Visions of loose earth half covering cold flesh, sightless eyes accusing him.

'Because Susan was the Lyonaisse's daughter. She was married to Barry. Surely you must remember them?' He turned to look at Patricia. 'I think I'll walk up to the Big House.'

'Do you think you should?' The colour was beginning to return to her face. 'I really thought they'd emigrated. Now this…how sad.'

'Here, drink your tea, before it gets cold.' Patricia pushed a cup towards Brian. 'You seem miles away. Are you feeling all right?'

He dipped a hand into the biscuit barrel. 'Yes, I'm fine. Thank you for asking.'

'Would you like to go with your father?'

'No.'

Douglas crossed to the kitchen door and took his jacket off one of the pegs. 'Won't be long, love.'

*

Elizabeth Lyonaisse set the tray down. 'Here you are,' she said. 'Now I'll leave you two to talk in peace. Cook was very busy so I brought this up myself.'

Her voice sounded vague. Her mind was elsewhere. Today was the day she chose to refresh the food and drink in what was now known simply as Mary's Room. She would willingly give all she had to hear Susan's laughter once more as she watched Mary serve her teddy bears with biscuits and orange juice. She longed to feel the warmth of Mary's tiny body clinging around her legs. Or to sit by her bedside as Susan read her a story. Elizabeth brushed the threat of tears from her eyes.

'Thank you.' Douglas touched his forehead, a reflex action.

'Yes, thank you, my dear.' Carl watched his wife leave the room then turned to his visitor.

'What can I help you with? Do you need something for the garden?'

'No, sir, everything's coming along fine. Those new bedding plants –'

'Sorry to interrupt you, Douglas, but I do have a lot to do this morning.' He pulled a pocket watch from his waistcoat. 'Could this possibly wait?'

'It could, yes. But I only need a minute or two. Something's happened and it's a bit of a mystery.'

'Oh?' Carl Lyonaisse looked bemused as he stirred his tea. 'What is it? Are those wretched dormice back?'

'No, sir. Nothing like that.' He explained his wife had drawn Brian a map to help him walk to the village on his own.

'Where's all this leading?' Carl drummed his fingers against the side of his chair. 'Surely a trip to the shops doesn't warrant all this fuss?'

Douglas took a deep breath. 'No, I'm sorry, sir. But it's how he found the grave.'

'A grave? What are you on about, man? Of *course* there are graves, there's a churchyard.'

'Which is exactly what I said. But this one is not in the church. It's inside a copse of trees on your land.'

Carl's face paled. He bit his lower lip and frowned. Fingernails dug into the leather covered arms of his wing-back chair. 'So…it's been found…I had hoped our secret was safe.'

Now it was Douglas who looked surprised. 'You *know* about it, sir?'

'Yes.' Carl gave a deep sigh as he gently shook his head from side to side. 'I can see I'm going to have to confide in you. But what I'm about to tell you remains in this room. Understood?'

'Yes, sir.'

'It *is* our Susan…and Barry. We told everyone they had gone to Australia. Lots of people do you know, so it seemed plausible at the time.' Carl's voice faltered. 'Elizabeth had joined them at their place in Norfolk for a short holiday. She thought her visit may lift their spirits after losing Mary. Then one morning she found them in the boathouse sitting in their car. A hose, connected to the exhaust pipe, had been run through the window. The engine was running. A year to the day after losing Mary we lost our daughter. And Barry of course. As soon as I heard I rushed up there to be with Elizabeth.'

Douglas stared in amazement. 'Suicide? That lovely young couple took their own lives? How terrible!'

Carl took a deep breath then sighed. 'Yes, it grieves me to say it, but they did. Elizabeth insisted I had their bodies returned and buried in secret on the estate. We settled for the grave-site your son found. It's on our land so I *had* hoped it would remain hidden.' Tears filled his eyes. 'I wish I could forget the day of the funeral, but I can't. To keep the knowledge of their deaths secret, the only people to attend were Elizabeth and I, and an itinerant Irish labourer who dug the grave. Oh, and the vicar. He did appreciate the new bells. I trust your son won't tell his story to anyone.' He licked his lips again. 'As you know, suicide is a crime, so we encouraged people to think they had emigrated. Better that people don't know the truth. Family name, respect in the community, that sort of thing.'

'You can rely on us, sir. Your secret's safe. I just don't know what to say…about your loss. I know how we felt when we thought we'd lost Brian.'

'Good man. I appreciate your loyalty.'

Chapter 14

With the exception of fresh Y-fronts and fluorescent green socks, Alan was naked.

Holding a shoe over the kettle's spout he moved it back and forth through the steam while teasing the blue suede with a brass-wire brush. Satisfied, he turned his attention to the second shoe.

Dampening a tea-towel he wrung it out before taking it to the ironing board where his drain-pipe trousers lay waiting. Spitting on the iron to check it was hot enough to use, he spread the damp cloth on the garment. The iron hissed as he applied it to the moist cloth, sending clouds of steam into the air, filling the kitchen with a smell of scorching cotton.

Alan was taking great pride in his work this morning. His usual method of pressing trousers by placing them beneath the mattress when he went to bed would not do this time. The creases had to be sharp enough to satisfy a sergeant-major. Today was special. Sheila had been given a rare day off from her duties at the fairground.

Taking the warm trousers, crepe soled shoes and a red and black striped shirt his mother had ironed for him the night before, he went back up to his bedroom.

As he dressed, he imagined what it would be like to be married to Sheila. Living in a home that *meant* something. Sharing love, not resentment. Taking pleasure from walking to the shops with his wife. Perhaps buying a pet, a cat maybe, something always denied to him by his father. Simple pleasures. Not too much to ask.

Gold coloured cufflinks and a black and white knitted tie resembling a zebra-crossing completed his image. Another record dropped on the auto-changer and Elvis sang, *Baby, let's play house.*

*

Sheila met him on the station platform. Alan ran towards her and they met in a lover's embrace. He picked her up and swung her around. She clung onto a wicker basket with one hand while holding him onto tightly with the other. Putting her down he said breathlessly, 'I am glad you came. I thought you might change your mind.'

'I said I'd be here, didn't I.' She kissed him gently.

'People say a lot of things. My dad's always saying he'll chuck me out but I'm still here.' He frowned as he remembered the last big bust-up. 'Mind you he came close to it when he had a go at me about those cinema riots. How am I supposed to know why these things happen?'

Cinema operators far and wide had asked the same question while surveying rows of broken seats after screening *Blackboard Jungle*. Alan's mother had joked perhaps Bill Haley had a side-line replacing cinema seating. Her effort to defuse yet another argument between father and son failed.

Alan curled his hands into fists. 'He doesn't understand anything. Just because his lot won the war, he thinks everything should stay the same as it was.'

She took hold of his hand. 'Don't get upset. I've been looking forward to today.'

'Sorry.' He looked at the basket. 'What's in there?'

'A picnic.' Sheila smiled. 'I made the sandwiches myself. Not the cake though, mum made that. And there's ginger beer.'

'Ginger beer? That's for kids. I only drink *real* beer.' Seeing the look on her face he wished he could retract his words. 'Only kidding,' he said, 'I love ginger beer.'

Her smile returned.

Inwardly, Alan breathed a sigh of relief. Talking with girls had never been easy for him. He missed the good-natured banter of his mates. They had always given as good as they got. No offence meant or taken. With girls it was like walking on eggshells.

Sheila was not finding the forging of this new friendship any easier. She too felt at ease with the familiar girls and boys she toured the country with. Some of these boys tried to change her virgin status, but so far she had managed to resist their efforts.

But this was her third meeting with Alan, and she was beginning to doubt if she could trust herself with him. *He's a bit strange,* she thought. *He can be moody at times and gets angry about his father. But he's different from the fairground boys. And he's always so smartly dressed.*

Her emotions churned within her. Nature was pulling her one way, but her sense of what was right fought against her natural desires.

Holding hands they left the station, Alan proudly carrying the picnic basket. 'Where are we going?' he asked. 'I don't mind. I've been saving up. I've got just over four pounds.'

'You won't need that, walking's free and we've got the picnic. There's a park not far from the station. I took a short cut through it to get here.'

'Good thinking.' Releasing her hand, he transferred his arm to around her waist. The basket bumped against his leg. He struggled for a while, but eventually accepted defeat. Removing his arm from her waist, he held her hand again.

*

'Those sandwiches were great. I'm glad you remembered the salt,' Alan said.

'You're as bad as my dad,' she sniggered. 'He smothers his hard-boiled eggs in salt. What did you think of the cake?''

'Bloody lovely, if you'll excuse my French.' Draining the last of the ginger beer he wiped his mouth with a handkerchief before offering the cotton square to her.

'Can I keep it? As a souvenir of our lovely day together?'

Alan laughed. 'Of course, you can. An aunt gave me a box of them last Christmas but it serves me right. I suppose it was because I moaned about always getting socks.'

Sheila folded the handkerchief and placed it carefully into her handbag. 'Thanks. I'll sleep with this under my pillow tonight.' She leant over and kissed him gently. Their lips parted then joined again. Firmer, filled with passion. Running a hand through her hair he pulled her closer. The lovers embrace plunged them into a place where time stood still. The warmth of her skin, and the perfume she wore, delivered a message. Male testosterone rose to accept it. She pulled away. 'We mustn't,' she gasped. 'I want to, but I'm saving myself until I get married.'

'That's okay, I'll marry you.' He pulled her to him and sought her lips. She pushed him away.

'No. Please don't. I think I love you, but I want to wait.'

'Shit!' He changed his position, seeking to relieve the pressure brought on by their shared intimacy.

*

During the slow walk back to the station they discussed their future together. Alan was eager to get engaged, to begin saving for the wedding. 'We should get married as soon as we can,' he said. 'I saw a Civil Defence film about the next war. They said we'll get a three-minute warning. Just time to stick your head between your legs and kiss your arse goodbye.'

Sheila frowned. 'Don't be so crude.'

She shared his dreams but was more pragmatic. Although she aspired to the life of a housewife as shown in glossy magazines, she knew real life was more complicated. She had seen how hard it had been for her own parents.

*

As the train steamed into the station Alan and Sheila loosened their hold on each other. Alan stood with his hands resting on her waist. He stared into her eyes. 'I love you,' he murmured. 'I want to marry you. Look after you. Get somewhere for us to live.'

'But we're not old enough. We can't. Not unless both our parents agree. And there's no chance my mum would.'

'My bloody dad *would.* He'd be glad to see the back of me. Miserable old git.' He leaned forward and kissed her. 'Anyway, I'm going to start saving for our wedding.'

Carriage doors slammed. The guard raised his green flag and put a whistle to his mouth. The train lurched forward. Alan whirled around and pulled open a carriage door. Jumping inside he struggled with the window as the engine picked up speed. Sheila ran along the platform, touching fingers to her lips, blowing kisses.

Despite the notice above the door warning against such actions, Alan leaned out. 'See you on your next day off,' he shouted.

She was still waving as the train snorted away. Great plumes of black smoke, speckled with occasional orange sparks, drifted over the embankments on either side of the line. The train disappeared from her sight. Picking up the empty basket, she set out on the lonely walk back to the fairground.

*

Alan paced up and down in the kitchen. His mother sipped tea as she waited for him to tell her the cause of his agitation. Past experience had proved to her patience was indeed a virtue when dealing with him at times like this.

'I want to do extra hours. I'm not getting enough dosh.' Alan tried to thrust his hands into tight trouser pockets and failed.

Margaret stared at him. 'Why? You always moan your dad makes you do too much. And don't use that word, it's common.'

'Okay. I need more *money*. Better?'

'There's no need to be rude. And you still haven't answered my question.' She turned and put her tea-cup into the kitchen sink.

'Just trust me, I've got my reasons. Will you have a word for me? Please, Mum. I really want to work more hours.'

'Good. I'm glad to hear it. I always tell your dad you aren't lazy. It was the jobs they found for you down at the labour exchange. I knew they weren't suitable.' She smiled.

'Gardening's not great either, but it'll have to do. There's no other jobs in this God-forsaken place is there. Why can't we move back home? I hate it here.'

'We have to stay. Your nan needs me. And your dad doesn't like it any more than you do. You should hear what I have to put up with from him.'

'Perhaps you two should get a divorce. You don't get on, so what's the point?'

Margaret stared up at the ceiling and sighed. 'I have thought about it, believe me. I really have. But I made my vows and so I'm stuck with him.'

'When I marry, I'll make sure she's the right one. I don't want to end up like you.'

'I thought your dad *was* the right one. Just goes to show how wrong you can be. Anyway, enough of that. Leave it to me, I'll see what I can do about getting you more work.' Her eyes twinkled as her expression changed. 'I think I'd better wait until he's sitting down. I think it's going to be a bit of a shock for for your dad.'

'Thanks, Mum.' Alan looked puzzled.

*

'So…your mother says you want more hours. What are you after? Not more of those bloody records I hope.' John Reardon glared at Alan. 'If I have to tell you once more to turn that racket down, I'll sling them all in the pond.'

And you'd be close behind them, Alan thought. 'Actually, I'm saving up to get married.'

'Married? Who'd want a lazy bugger like you? What's the name of her guide dog? Or have you put some poor sod in the family way? Is that it?'

'No, it's not. You leave Sheila alone, she's not like that.'

'Sheila? Not heard her name before. Where did you meet her?'

'What's it got to do with you?' Alan scowled. 'Now, are you going to sort me out more work or not?'

'I can get you plenty of hours. The sooner you sling your hook, the better I'll like it.' John rammed a garden fork into the earth with the force and venom of a soldier burying his bayonet into the enemy. 'Go and change out of those poncey clothes of yours.'

Alan scowled. *Better than that demob suit you wear. Give me a drape any day.* 'Okay. I'll just grab a cuppa then I'll be back.'

'And I'll believe that when I see it. You've done nothing but skive since we got here.'

'No, I haven't, I've been helping Mum.'

'Huh! Go on, hop it, before I change my mind.'

*

The next few days surprised John Reardon. He took advantage of his son's enthusiasm to reduce his own efforts.

Douglas Miller was delighted. He preferred an eager worker, to one who laboured against his will.

Alan cursed the blisters on his hands, but delighted in counting money accumulating in the jam jar hidden in his bedroom.

Chapter 15

Brian patted the final piece of grass into position. The resulting hump, with its wooden hatch secured by a sliding bolt and padlock, seemed out of place in the gently sloping meadow. Planks, surplus to requirements and showing signs of having been attacked by woodworm, were tossed into the wheelbarrow. Wiping both hands on his trousers he pushed the barrow back towards the shed where his father stored all manner of things.

Inside the storage shed, the smell of creosote filled the air. Jam jars containing collections of screws and rusty nails jostled for space amidst hurricane lamps and stiff paint brushes languishing in turpentine. On the floor, sacks that once held flour now bulged with firewood and logs.

The one wall not shelved was perforated with six-inch nails supporting garden forks, spades, shears, trowels, dibbers and assorted bundles of garden twine. Two lawnmowers and a collection of rakes stood next to a stepladder speckled with paint.

Brian searched this gloomy treasure-trove. Finding an empty ink bottle, he used a hammer and a large nail to knock a hole into the metal screw-on lid. Using secateurs, he cut short lengths from a discarded washing line. Minutes later, clutching a bottle of methylated spirits and a box of Price's candles, he closed the shed door and headed towards the meadow.

*

Startled rabbits ran as he approached the mound in the field. Releasing the padlock, Brian lifted the hatch and stepped down into the darkness. The smell of recently dug soil greeted him. Feeling inside a recess he found his matches, wrapped in grease proof paper.

The match produced a line of small blue sparks as it scraped down the side of the box before spluttering into life. He lit a candle and by its light assembled what was to be a lamp.

Methylated-spirits substituted the blue ink that had once filled the bottle. Setting his new light on a rustic table he sat on a pile of old blankets and checked the contents of a wooden crate. The smell of oranges lingered in the wood. A paper label bore a coloured picture of a foreign land.

'One tin of Spam, three baked beans.' He shuffled the tins around. 'Tin of condensed milk, two packets of tea, bottle of Camp coffee. Sugar. Four packs of toilet paper.' Brian placed a tick against the items on his list. 'Not bad,' he muttered, 'soon have enough supplies. But I must get a torch and some drinking water.'

*

That night, back in his room, Brian sat bolt upright in bed, clutching a sweat-soaked sheet. Images from deep within his mind hovered in front of him. A young girl, mouth open, her screams frozen in time. Accusing eyes. Earth raining down on bodies.

He yelled out as fear and panic gripped him.

In the adjacent room, Patricia Miller tore back the blankets and leapt from the bed. In her haste she knocked a cup off the bedside table. It smashed on the linoleum. Her false teeth lay amongst the pieces of china. Douglas Miller mumbled, grasped the covers and heaved them back.

'It's Brian,' she said. 'I'll go. You get back to sleep.' Bending down she rescued her dentures from the wet floor, wiped them with the bed sheet and eased them into her mouth. Quickly putting on her dressing gown and slippers she made her way to the adjoining bedroom.

Gently knocking, she opened the door. The lamp on the bedside table cast Brian's shadow onto the wall beside him. In the low light his face matched the crisp white pillows. Patricia put a hand to her mouth. 'Brian, my love, it's me. Did you have one of those nightmares?'

Brian fidgeted, his eyes constantly moving from side to side. A nervous twitch distorted one side of his face. Beads of sweat glistened in the glow of the bedside light. He held the bedclothes up to his chin. 'Yes. Sorry I woke you.'

Patricia sat on the bed and dabbed his forehead with a handkerchief. 'Don't worry, I'm fine. It's you I'm concerned about. Can't you tell me about these nasty dreams you have?'

'No. I don't want to talk about it.' He slid down beneath the bed covers, fingers screwing up the sheet.

'It's okay. Don't worry, just try to rest.' She placed a hand on his damp hair. 'Would you like me to stay with you?'

'No. Please go back to bed. I'll be all right.'

'Are you're sure?'

'Yes. Thank you.'

She stood up. 'There's just one thing while I think of it. Your father and I are worried about the amount of time you spend in the big hole you've dug in the meadow. It's not healthy hiding away in the ground.'

'It's something I have to do. Sorry.' Brian turned over to face the wall.

As the door closed behind her, the metallic click of the catch caused Brian to sit bolt upright. One hand reached beneath the bedclothes seeking the pistol he no longer had. 'Oh, God,' he said. Licking his dry lips, he swallowed. 'I can see faces. Go away! It wasn't my fault.' Pulling the covers up over his head he sat shaking so hard the headboard beat out an accompanying tattoo on the wall.

'Is he okay?' Douglas asked as he felt his wife get back into bed.

'Not really.' She gave a deep sigh. 'I wish he could tell us what's troubling him. Perhaps we could help. And I'm going to make sure he's taking his tablets, perhaps he's missed some.'

'The matron said we had to be patient. There are a lot of poor devils worse than Brian. God knows what they went through during the war.'

'I suppose you're right, dear.' She put a hand out and patted the mound of blankets next to her. 'Thank goodness you were too old to be called up. Otherwise, I may have had two of you to worry about.'

'I did my bit in the Home Guard.' Douglas yawned. 'That was bad enough. Come on, let's get back to sleep. I've got a lot to do tomorrow.'

'And I've got a smashed cup to clear up before I do anything else.' Reaching out she placed her dentures on the bedside cabinet. 'Goodnight, dear, sleep tight.'

In his room Brian paced back and forth. Kneeling, he looked beneath the bed. Standing to one side he pulled aside the curtains and peered furtively down at the gardens. His pyjama jacket stuck to his skin, the sweat becoming cold.

He pulled the mattress from the bed and leant it against the iron frame. Taking the blankets, he crawled into the shelter he had made. Pulling both knees up to his chest he grasped them with both hands, terrified of the demons from his past returning to exact their due. He shivered. *This isn't helping. They're still here. I can feel them. I need fresh air.* Dressing quietly, he picked up his shoes and carried them down the stairs to the front door.

*

Dew from the grass glistened on his highly-polished shoes as Brian crossed the meadow. The sun was still below the horizon, forcing the sky to change colour, encouraging the few remaining stars to depart. Birds welcomed the new day with their songs.

He stumbled through a sea of wild flowers. He appeared to be sleepwalking or suffering from the effects of drinking too much. But he wasn't. He was exhausted by a lack of sleep brought on by a troubled conscience.

Bending down, Brian unlocked the padlock and swung back the hatch door letting it rest on the grass. Descending into the darkness of his dug-out he groped for his matches. The homemade lamp spluttered but soon brought a little light into the gloom. He closed the hatch and sat on the planked floor. After a while he ised his hands to conjure up silhouettes on one wall. The flicker of the lamp's wick added movement to rabbits, goats, and flapping birds.

He yawned. His fingers scraped against the roof boards as he stretched both arms above his head. Dust motes floated in the air, visible against the glow of his lamp.

Suddenly, something caught his attention. In the darkness he saw nebulous figures coming towards him. First a child. Then soldiers. He scrambled to his feet; hands held out to fend them off.

He turned away. His nightmares had returned. With eyes closed, he screamed, pushing at the hatch. As it swung open, he gulped at the cool air. Up above, stars continued to punch holes in what remained of the night sky. Inky blackness turned into watery grey, tinged with the hint of orange. Scrambling out he ran. His feet slid on the wet grass and he pitched forwards. The meadow rushed up to greet him. For a moment he lay still, relishing the feel of cold wet grass against his face. Then he remembered the faces. Using his hands and arms he levered himself up and ran.

Trees loomed ahead and he realized he was heading away from the houses. Hesitantly he turned and retraced his steps towards the glow from beneath the earth.

Holding his breath, he crept toward the open entrance of the shelter. Lifting the hatch from the grass, he slammed it shut, hastily slid the bolt into place and snapped the padlock. Inside the excavation, a sudden rush of air extinguished his homemade lamp.

Stopping to check he was heading in the right direction; Brian made his way towards the ghostly shapes of the houses.

Chapter 16

Carl relaxed in the room filled with books collected by his father.

The high-winged chair hid him from casual gaze, one hand resting on a chair arm, fingers fiddling with the brass studs holding supple green leather in place. The pages of the illustrated encyclopaedia rose and fell as Carl sought to improve his knowledge of the world. He leaned forward, peering around the chair as Elizabeth knocked and entered.

'Sorry to interrupt, dear. I know you value time on your own, but you have a visitor. I asked him to wait in the hall and cook is making a pot of tea. I told her to bring the Scottish shortbread, after all, he's come all the way down from London.'

'Who has? I'm not expecting anyone.'

'He gave me his card.' She coughed as she offered it to Carl. 'He's from your company.'

'Not mine anymore, my dear. More's the pity.' He studied the business card and extinguished his cigar. 'Hmm, I'd better go down and greet him. He's obviously made a great effort, it would be rude to keep him waiting.'

'Would you like me to open a window?' Elizabeth put a hand over her mouth. 'It's getting a bit hazy in here.'

'No thanks, it's fine.'

'As you wish.' As she left the room, she breathed out audibly.

As Carl descended the staircase the man in the hall came towards him and held out a hand. 'Nicholas, Nicholas Steed,' he said. 'My secretary phoned to –'

'Did she? I didn't get any message. But it doesn't matter. Let's go to my den, I'll make sure we're not interrupted.'

Carl spent the next couple of hours answering questions and offering suggestions. The two men shared a common interest in the continuing success of the company. Nicholas to ensure his high standard of living would be maintained, Carl to protect the value of the shares he held.

'Thanks, Carl. You've been a great help. As I said, I've only recently bought into the company. As it's all a bit new to me, my partner agreed it was important I get it straight from the horse's mouth.' Nicholas returned the papers to his briefcase and snapped the lock. 'It's cleared up a few problem areas. I hope you didn't mind me calling in like this. As I said, I did tell my secretary to phone you –'

Carl shook his head. 'Think nothing of it. Reassuring to know the firm is in good hands. The decision to sell was one of the hardest I've ever had to make.'

His visitor smiled. 'I understand. All those years building it up, then the heart attack. That's what I call real bad luck.'

'Not surprising though was it. How do you think you'd cope with the loss of your grand-daughter?' Carl frowned.

'I shudder at the thought. Would you think me rude if I was to ask what happened? It's been mentioned in the office, but nobody seems to know the full story.'

'No, it's quite all right. I've been told not to bottle things up. Talking about it is supposed to help.' Carl took a cut-glass decanter from the tantalus and poured a brandy. 'Will you join me?'

Nicholas shook his head. 'No, thanks. I drove down from London don't forget.'

'Quite right.' He raised the short-stemmed balloon glass. 'It was our wedding anniversary. Elizabeth and I were enjoying champagne and salmon canapés on the lawn. It all seems like yesterday.' He sipped at his drink. 'Our daughter paid us an unexpected visit with her husband and our grandchild, Mary. She would have been nearly eight years old by now.'

'How are they coping with their loss?'

Carl breathed in deeply and sighed. 'Please…don't ask.' He swirled the brandy around his glass as he gathered his thoughts. 'As I was saying, the two of them joined us for drinks. Mary went up to her room. We thought nothing of it as she always played there when visiting. She loved those teddy bears.'

'My boy does too.' Nicholas smiled.

'We all took turns to check on Mary, but when my wife went, she wasn't in the room. The four of us searched the house from top to bottom. We thought maybe she was playing hide-and-seek with Mrs Fluffy, her favourite teddy.' He paused. 'We checked all the places where she had hidden before. By then we were beginning to panic so I roped in my gamekeeper and gardener to help scour the grounds.'

'How *frightening* for you. Then what happened?'

'It became obvious the search needed to be widened so I phoned the police.' Carl paused while he sipped his brandy. 'I expected George, our local bobby, but as luck would have it he was not on duty. He'd broken a leg falling off his bike when a dog ran into the road.' Opening a mahogany box, he offered it to his visitor.

'No thanks.' Nicholas shook his head. 'My wife detests the smell of those.'

'Shame.' Carl struck a match and puffed at the Havana. 'The police did all in their power, but nothing was ever found. Mary had just vanished.'

'Do you think she was taken? Did the police question anyone?'

'Oh yes, they were very thorough. Douglas, my gardener, took offence when he was interviewed and was most indignant when they insisted on digging up parts of the garden.' Carl's expression changed. 'And the police made a lot of MacIntyre's statement, when he told them he thought he saw Mary near the woodland. MacIntyre's my gamekeeper by the way. He said the child was a long way off so he couldn't swear it was her. Of course, he didn't know at the time she was missing.'

'That's a great pity. If he had, he could have brought her back.'

'Yes, maybe. But I don't blame him, the local children tend to treat the woods as their own. They don't do any harm. He was very fond of Mary, used to carry on her his back and take her for walks. Her disappearance hit him hard.' He lowered his voice. 'Poor chap took to drink for a while. Not a good idea when you're handling guns every day. I turned a blind eye of course and he soon got over it. The drinking I mean, not Mary.'

'What about the locals? Were any of them suspects?'

'Not really. Frank was taken down the station, he –'

'Frank? Who's Frank? I haven't heard him mentioned before.'

'He's our local tramp. He bags a few rabbits from time to time, does odd jobs, that sort of thing.'

'Oh, so did the police charge him?'

'No. They never charged anybody. They say the case is still open, but without any new information there's not much they can do.'

'I suppose not. What you and your family have been through I find hard to imagine. Have you thought about hiring a private detective?'

Carl sighed. 'I've tried two. The first one made a great show of investigating people such as the man in the village who insists on wearing a raincoat whatever the weather.' Carl almost managed to smile. 'I think the detective and him may have had something in common, if you catch my drift.'

'Oh, I see…I think. Anyone else?'

'Not really. As I said, both the men put on a bit of a show but neither of them had anything to offer for their efforts at the end of the day.' Carl leaned towards his visitor. 'Mind you, I could have told the second one there wasn't much chance of finding out what happened to Mary by spending hours in the local pub.'

It was Nicholas's turn to smile. 'In fairness there is something to be said for listening to conversations in public houses. I've picked up business like that in the past. But I take your point. It does seem an unusual way to go about finding a missing child.'

'That's why I gave him his marching orders.' Carl paused, appearing to be lost in thought. 'There was another strange thing happened the same week. The police picked up a man for vagrancy, realized he was mentally ill and had him committed to a local hospital for servicemen.'

'And?'

'And he turned out to be my gardener's son. They received a telegram telling them he had been killed during the battle at Monte Cassino.'

'But why didn't the police recognise him? Surely he must have been known to them if he lived here before the war?'

'Ah, you're right. And if George had been on duty he would have done. He knew the family well. But his broken leg led to Brian, he's my gardener's son, being incarcerated. It took a hospital cleaner to set the ball rolling and get him re-united with his family recently.'

'How extraordinary.' Nicholas stared at Carl. 'I've got a very good friend, Victor, who I *think* was at Monte Cassino. I wonder–'

'Elizabeth is really excited,' Carl interrupted. 'She believes if Brian was found alive after all these years, there must be a hope of finding Mary.'

'Do you share her feelings? I mean, about finding your grand-daughter?'

'I wish I could…but I'm afraid I don't. Neither did our daughter, or her husband, towards the end. But that's another story which I'd rather not go into right now.'

'That's understandable. Besides, it would be rude of me to pry.' Nicholas stood up and brushed at the creases in his trousers. 'I think it's time to be off. Thanks for seeing me, I do appreciate it.'

Carl pushed himself up out of his chair and shook hands. 'Thank you. If there's anything I can help with, please don't hesitate to contact me.'

'Excuse me asking, but I'm curious. What is Brian's surname? I'll be meeting up with Victor soon. Who knows, maybe he knew him during the war.'

'Miller. Brian Miller. Seems to be a long shot, but if he does know him it could help unravel the mystery.'

Chapter 17

Edward Stanton kept Brian in sight as he followed him along the footpath. Every day for a week he loitered around the tobacconist's shop. Today he was rewarded. Turning his coat collar up, he strode on. 'You'll pay for William's death, Miller,' he muttered. 'The hangman can take me for all I care.'

Brian stopped. He ran his finger down the dotted line on the map. He had collected his father's tobacco many times, but still lacked confidence. He stared at the church spire, then back to his map. Satisfied, he folded the drawing and put it back into his trouser pocket. He continued his walk; unaware he was being followed.

Crossing the meadow Brian headed for his shelter. Keeping a grip on the bag of shopping he bent down and lifted the entrance hatch.

Edward stood at the edge of the field and stared in amazement as his quarry disappeared beneath the ground. Scratching the side of his head he strode through the grass. 'What's he up to? This I've got to see.'

As he slowly walked forward, he resisted the urge to walk on tip-toe.

Edward stared down at the ends of boards resting on the grass supporting a mound of soil topped with turves. Evidence woodworm activity may have weakened these wooden slats gave him an idea. Bending down he swiftly shot the bolt securing the entrance. Stepping up onto the piled earth, he jumped up and down.

Inside the shelter, soil filtered down through cracks between planks forming the ceiling. Brian heard them creak and moved towards the entrance. He was too slow. With a sound resembling a line of ceremonial rifle shots, the wooden ceiling gave up the struggle. The falling timbers, driven down by the weight they were intended to support, crashed onto Brian, forcing him to the ground. His methylated spirit light was extinguished. Dirt and dust forced their way into his eyes, ears and nostrils. Panic gripped him. Desperately clawing at the floor, he shouted, 'Incoming! Take cover!'

Hearing Brian's cries, the man jumped harder. The mound collapsed beneath this assault, causing Edward to fall to his knees. Quickly regaining his feet, he jumped again. 'Die, you bastard, die like my son did. I hope you rot in hell.' Tears ran down his face, joining beads of sweat. His initial outburst changed to controlled anger. He methodically stamped back and forth until the man-made hill was no more than an untidy blot on the surrounding meadow.

Breathing heavily, Edward sat on the grass. He grimaced at the dirt embedded into his polished brogues and on his trousers. Taking a handkerchief from his pocket, he spat on it and tried to reverse some of the damage. Glaring at the patch of ground, pock-marked with deep foot prints, he sighed. 'Now you know how it feels. I hope you suffer for a while before you die.' Getting to his feet he looked around. Satisfied there were no witnesses he headed back to the village.

Inside the shelter Brian struggled to breath. His stash of tins had halted the onslaught from above but not before the broken slats had pinned him to the floor. He could taste dirt as he sucked air contaminated with dust, deep into his lungs. As he lay in the dark, he was not alone. Images surfaced from deep down in his memory. The nightmares he suffered during his sleeping hours were back. He tried to scream but no sound came. He spiralled down into an exploding vortex of colours; his ears filled with the sound of pumping blood.

*

Alan was deeply engrossed in his magazine as he walked the Miller's dog through the meadow. The New Musical Express top twenty singles chart mattered to him. He missed the excitement of visiting record shops with his friends, crowding into sound booths to listen to the latest releases before parting with his dole money.

The newsagent in the village had agreed to order the magazine for him, but on the strict understanding it was to be paid for in advance.

Rex sniffed the grass, pushing at its roots, scraping the ground with his paws. The Miller's collie knew nothing about the vagaries of pop stars and their careers but he could have told his human companion which animals had passed that way. The meadow was an open book to him.

The rabbit hole took Alan by surprise, one minute he was checking the new entries to the charts, next he was studying grass close up. Rex ran back and licked his face.

'Get off! Urggh!' He used a hand to wipe the dog's saliva off his cheek. Getting to his feet he looked around to see if anyone had seen his fall. 'Go and chase rabbits or something.' Picking up his magazine he shook off a beetle. 'And you can bugger off too.'

Brushing his trousers, he stared across the meadow. 'That's funny,' he said, taking a few steps forward. 'Looks like batty old Brian has filled in his hole. Wonder why? He says it's his shelter, but I reckon he plays with himself in there. I bet he's got a load of dirty books he doesn't want anyone to see. Come on, dog. Let's go and see if he's done a good job.'

With Rex at his side, he ambled over the grass. Suddenly the collie raced ahead through the grass. Alan hurried after him. 'I *thought* I heard something. Go on, Rex, find it.'

Reaching the patch of trampled ground, he stood with his mouth open. Rex dug at the soil, paws working like pistons, dirt and stones flying through the air. Alan bent down and pulled at turves and clumps of earth. 'Is that you, Brian? It's me.' Seizing the end of a piece of exposed timber he strained to pull it free. A muffled voice stopped him. 'Don't. Please…don't.'

'What the *bloody hell* happened?' He knelt and placed an ear to the ground. 'Stay there, mate, I'll go and get help.'

*

'Quick, Dad,' Alan gasped, 'Get some shovels.' He stood in the doorway, his chest heaving.

'Do what, you daft sod. Get out of the light. I'm filling in my football coupon.'

'But it's Brian, he's buried! I've tried, but I can't get him out on my own.' He glared at his father. 'Bollocks to you then. I'll go next door.'

'That's right, you do that. See if they fall for your stupid idea of a joke. And watch your *bloody* language.'

'Nan, Brian's in trouble! His shelter's collapsed!' Leaning against the door frame of the Miller's house he pointed towards the meadow.

'Douglas,' Patricia yelled. 'Something's happened to Brian!'

Douglas fought to tuck his shirt in as he half ran, half stumbled down the stairs. 'What's going on? What's happened? Is he all right?'

'No, he's in deep shit, oops, sorry Nan, I mean he's in trouble. That shelter of his has fallen in on him.'

Douglas pushed past his wife and Alan and headed towards his shed. 'Don't worry, love, I'll get a spade,' he yelled.

Alan shouted back. 'Leave one out for me. I'll be there in a minute.' He took several deep breaths. 'Can I have a drink first please?'

Alan drank the cup of water and wiped his mouth with the back of his hand. 'Thanks, Nan, I needed that.'

Douglas grabbed the spade leaning against the shed. 'Don't worry,' he shouted back over his shoulder. 'We'll save him.'

*

As he ran towards the collapsed shelter, Alan could see MacIntyre, Douglas and Rex digging as if they were all possessed. Only the rear end of the collie was visible.

Reaching them, Alan leaned on his spade and sucked in great gulps of air. 'Any luck?' he gasped. 'Christ, the last time I ran like that, there was a load of coppers chasing me.'

Douglas trod down hard on his spade, lifted another load of soil and tossed it to one side. 'And you'll soon be seeing another lot. This wasn't an accident.'

Alan rolled up his shirt sleeves. 'What? Surely you don't think I had anything to do with this?'

'Of course not. But *somebody* has done their best to kill Brian.' Dropping to his knees he tore at the ground with his bare hands. 'Mind where you dig,' he urged. 'Try to leave some of these footprints, they'll be wanted for evidence.'

'Don't waste time doing it like that,' Alan said. 'Keep using your spade.' Turning to resume his own efforts he watched Rex withdraw from a hole he had been excavating. The dog lay on its stomach, front paws extended. Suddenly a human hand appeared; fingernails torn and bloody. Alan gasped. 'Look, Brian's still alive. Good old Rex.'

The gamekeeper ran around, bent down and grasped the protruding hand. 'It's okay,' he yelled. 'Hold on, we'll soon have you out.'

Alan grinned. 'At least we know he can breathe now.' He patted Rex's head. 'Good dog. There's a *good* dog.' Rex's tail swept loose soil from side to side.

'Come on, Alan, let's concentrate on where the entrance was,' Douglas said, his chest heaving. 'We don't want to make this worse than it already is.'

Alan stared into the ashen-face. Dirt did nothing to hide the man's anguish. 'Fine,' he said. 'But you don't look too good to me. We'll carry on digging while you go back and phone the Old Bill. And take it easy, don't run. And don't worry, we'll have him out in no time.'

'I think you're right.' Douglas took a deep breath. 'You've got more strength than me. Thanks. I'll leave you both to it and be as quick as I can.'

'Good. But remember, Granddad, *don't* rush.'

Douglas ran a finger around his collar as he hurried away.

'And tell Nan to put the kettle on,' Alan called after him. 'I could murder a cuppa.'

*

Alan looked up as Douglas returned with the police and fire brigade, relieved the burden of rescue was about to be shared.

Douglas stared at his son, still trapped up to his waist in the excavation. 'Are you hurt? Have you broken anything?'

'No.'

Douglas reached out to Alan. 'Well done. Looks like you got him out all on your own.'

'Almost,' Alan gasped. 'MacIntyre left me to it while he went off to see if he could catch whoever did it. I told him it was okay to go. All this digging's bloody hard work and he wasn't really much use with a spade.' He sank to the ground and lay back, staring up at the sky. 'Thank God the cavalry's arrived, as my mum would say.'

*

George continued writing. 'So, you're sure you heard a voice?'

Shuffling his feet on the kitchen floor, Brian nodded.

'But you didn't hear what was said. Is that correct?'

Brian shook his head. 'No. Sorry.'

Douglas reached out and put a hand on his son's arm. 'Don't be sorry. None of this was your fault.'

'Do you know of any reason why someone would do this?' The sergeant paused. 'It's obvious it *was* a deliberate act. We just need to know why. If we have a motive then we stand a chance of apprehending the perpetrator.'

Brian's eyebrows lowered as his face screwed up. 'Pardon?'

'He means,' Douglas intervened, 'they need to find out why anyone would try to kill you.'

'I don't know. Sorry.'

'Can we leave it for now?' Douglas frowned. 'Brian's confused. What he needs right now is a hot bath and some clean clothes.'

'Yes, I think I have sufficient for the time being.' He turned to leave. 'But if either you or your son remember anything that may assist us with our enquiries then –'

'Certainly. Thank you. If we do, I'll come down and report it straight away.'

George closed his notepad and slipped an elastic band around it.

*

'Finished mucking about?' John Reardon glared at Alan.

'At least he did something useful,' Margaret said. 'More than I can say for you.'

'You said it would be quiet down here in the country,' John retorted. 'Huh! Some hopes. First a kid goes missing from here, and now there's nearly been a murder by the sound of it. It was safer back in London.'

'Well, you know where it is, why don't you go back?' Margaret scowled.

'If I could get a job I bloody well would. This gardening malarkey will be the death of me.'

'I can but live in hope,' Margaret muttered under her breath.

Chapter 18

Alan stared out of the carriage window; his vision of the countryside occasionally interrupted by clouds of smoke from the train. Putting a toffee into his mouth, he flicked the screwed up sweet-wrapper onto the opposite seat. Glancing at his hand he was horrified to see his fingernails harboured large amounts of dirt. 'Shit! It's all that bloody digging. I can't let Sheila see these.' Taking a comb from the top pocket of his drape jacket, he used one of the end teeth to prise out the grime and wipe it onto the seat beside him.

A man hunched up against the door glared at Alan. He opened his mouth to protest…but changed his mind. Instead, he stood up, took his raincoat and umbrella down from the sagging string rack and stepped into the corridor to seek a seat elsewhere.

*

Alan swaggered along the platform. Sheila rushed forward to greet him. 'You're late,' she said, 'I thought you'd be here ages ago.'

'Train got held up for some reason. I think some stupid cows got onto the track.' He held out a box of chocolates. 'Brought you these, Black Magic, hope you like them.'

'They're lovely, thank you. This is the first time a boy's bought me chocolates.'

Alan looked down at his feet, swallowed, and then cleared his throat. 'Hmm. Actually…to tell the truth, I didn't buy them. I got them for helping rescue my Uncle Brian.'

'Who's Brian?' Sheila frowned.

'It's a long story,' he said, putting his arm around her waist. 'Let's start walking and I'll tell you all about it.'

*

'He was actually buried alive?' Sheila gasped. 'I can hardly believe it. Who would do such a thing?'

'Beats me. The police thought at first it was probably kids. But when they arrived and saw the size of the footprints it soon put paid to that idea.'

'And you dug him out? On your own?'

'No. I didn't say that. I said I helped his dad. But I did do most of the work. His dad's got a dodgy ticker.' Alan placed a hand on his chest. 'He was struggling so I made him go and phone the Old Bill.'

'So, you're a hero. I'm proud of you.' She looked him up and down. 'Hard to imagine you digging, dressed like you do.'

'I never had this clobber on. Not for walking the dog. And do you think I could dig in these?' He pointed to his shoes.

Sheila laughed. 'I see what you mean. You don't see many labourers wearing blue suede shoes.'

'That's true.'

'What have the police done about it? Have they caught anyone yet?'

'Do me a favour. Our local bobbies aren't exactly Dixon of Dock Green, or Sherlock bloody Holmes.'

'That's not very nice. After all, they did buy you some chocolates for helping out.'

'Did they boll – I mean, no they didn't. My nan and Brian went into the village and got them for me.'

'Well, they're very nice whoever bought them. Thank you. It was a nice thought.'

'I tried to get you some black stockings, but you should see what the shop in the village sells. On second thoughts, perhaps you shouldn't. I couldn't believe people still wore old-fashioned things like that.'

'Black stockings? How did you know if I'd like those?'

'I didn't. But I do.'

Alan took his arm from around her waist and moved away before she could react.

'Oh, do you. I suppose you buy them for all your girlfriends.'

'No, I don't. I haven't got any other girlfriends.' He put his arm back and pulled her close. 'There's only you.'

Sheila smiled. 'I was only kidding. I'd like some black stockings.'

'You wait until we're married. I'll buy you loads of things.'

'Married? Don't be silly. Let's just enjoy today.' Taking hold of his hand she squeezed. 'I heard last night we may be moving on sooner than expected. *We've* been doing well but ticket sales at the circus haven't been great, so they've decided to move on. Which means we'll have to pack up too.'

'You can't! How am I supposed to see you?'

Sheila blushed. 'I don't know. I have to go where my parents go. I don't get a choice.'

'Then we'll just *have* to get married. I've been working hard and saving up.'

'You're sweet, Alan, and I think I do love you. But we can't. My parents will say I'm too young.' She sighed. 'It would be nice though. If only we were both twenty-one.'

'Don't say that. I'm not ready to get old. I like things as they are.' He tugged at the lapels of his jacket. 'I want to wear what I like and do as I please.'

'You've got a shock coming then. Next year you'll be called up to do your National Service. They'll cut your hair and make you wear a uniform.'

'You must be joking. I'm not having any of that rubbish. I'd rather join the Merchant Navy.'

'And what about me? If you join the navy, I still won't see you. You'll be off around the world. Probably have a girl in every port from what I've heard about sailors.'

'No, I wouldn't. But on second thoughts, it's not such a good idea anyway.' Alan shook his head. 'I was sick once when Mum took me on the Woolwich Ferry. But I'm still not going in the army. I've got time to think of something. All I want is to marry you so we can be together.'

'It would be nice. I can just see us in our little home. We'll have a boy for you and a girl for me. And a puppy. I've always wanted a puppy. It could –'

'Hold on. We're not even engaged yet. Kids and puppies? I thought it would be just you and me.'

She fluttered her eyelashes and smiled. 'Of course, it will.'

'I could try flat feet.'

'Flat feet? What have they got to do with getting married?'

'Nothing,' he grinned. 'But I've heard they can fail you for the army medical if you've got them.'

'And have you?'

'Not that I know of, but perhaps there's a way to flatten them. It's worth a try.'

'And if you did, would you still be able to wear those shoes?' She pointed.

'Bugger! Never mind, I've got a year to come up with something.'

Chapter 19

Numbers can't hurt us. Or can they? Surely they are just an aid to help us understand the complex mathematical matrix which glues our existence together? But print them on sheets of paper, call it a calendar and certain numbers will have the power to tear at your emotions. They can induce euphoria. Or send you into the depths of depression. Give you a reason to celebrate. Or wish the date had never existed.

Today is one of those dark anniversaries best forgotten.
But how *do* you forget the loss of a child?
You don't.
Ever.
Dates come around as regular as clockwork and some of them can bring despair beyond other people's comprehension.

September the 15th.

To most people this would be just another date. But this is a date that has changed lives forever. It is a reminder of the day her heart had been broken. The day that would eventually lead to a child's parents deciding life was no longer worth living. Elizabeth often wished she'd shared their courage, stepped into the black abyss, welcomed death as a friend.

Instead, she is paying a heavy price for choosing to live. Her days are punctuated with grief.

But today is different.

Today is a triple anniversary. In addition to her wedding, it is the anniversary of the death of her daughter. And the day her granddaughter disappeared.

Today, grief will be replaced by abject misery.

*

Elizabeth set the tray down and sighed. 'Just look at all this dust.' She took out a handkerchief and wiped the parts of the table between the tea-service laid out in front of the teddy bears. One of the bears slid sideways. Elizabeth pulled him back onto his chair. 'Whoops, you nearly fell, Barney. That wouldn't do, would it.' She held him firmly and used her makeshift duster to clean his amber eyes. 'That's better.' Glancing around the table she added, 'It looks like you all need a clean.' Putting the handkerchief to her lips she moistened it. 'Come here, Rufus, you're next. No…don't struggle. It's for your own good.' One by one the bears were attended to. Glass eyes gleamed. Black stitched noses shed their dust. Golden fur reflected light from the window.

Elizabeth managed a fleeting smile. 'You're all looking very smart. Mary will be pleased.'

Her audience remained silent.

The door opened. Carl hesitated, transfixed by the sight of his wife crouched on the floor, talking to the bears. He crossed to her side. 'She loved those teddies, didn't she?' he said, kissing her hair. 'But you're spending too much time in here today, my dear, why don't you go back to bed? I'll have a meal sent up to you.'

'It's so peaceful in this room, it brings me comfort. I'm sure I can still feel them both in here.'

'Of course, you do, dear. Now come on, let's get you back to your bed.'

'Why don't you miss Mary as much as I do?' She brushed away a tear. 'She was your grand-daughter too.' Elizabeth rested her head on hands spread out on the solitary empty chair. The box containing links to Mary and her daughter lay by her side. Teardrops glistened on the lid.

*

Holding the tray pushed against her ribs with one hand, Margaret checked the meal as she tapped on the door. Freshly-cut slices of bread, buttered just as Elizabeth liked it. Poached eggs topped with slices of salmon. The silver cruet. A sprig of parsley for decoration.

Margaret's nostrils twitched as the smoky aroma from Lapsang tea teased them. She smiled as she thought about the sandwiches she had made for her husband's lunch. Mouse-trap cheese, with spots of mould scraped off, wedged between slices from a loaf destined for the bin. Tea, so weak it would probably have to be helped from the mug. Her contempt for him the very opposite of the concern she felt for her employer.

'Come in,' the invitation was barely audible.

Turning the handle, Margaret nudged the door with her knee and entered the room.

Green velvet drapes, tied back at the sides of the window, allowed sunlight filtering through lace curtains to add a little warmth to the room. Elizabeth was propped up against a surfeit of pillows; she closed a Morocco leather-bound book and slid it beneath the bed covers.

Crossing to the bed, Margaret placed the tray onto the counterpane. 'Here's something nice for your lunch,' she said, smiling.

Elizabeth waved her away. 'I don't want anything. I told Carl. Why doesn't he listen?' She touched her eyes with an embroidered handkerchief.

'It's salmon,' Margaret said, 'and cook's poached your eggs just as you like them, nice runny yolks.'

'You're most kind, all of you, but no, thank you.'

'Aren't you feeling well?' Margaret frowned. 'Your husband is very concerned.'

'I don't know why. I'm fine. Really, I am. He shouldn't fuss so.'

'I think you worried him this morning, saying you have the feeling Susan and Mary are still here.'

Elizabeth put her hands over her face and shuddered. 'Why is it only me who senses their presence? Am I going mad?'

'No, of course you're not.' Margaret moved closer. 'You're still grieving for them, it's understandable. Why don't you try to eat something, I'm sure you'll feel better.'

'I can't. I really can't. Please take it away, it's making me feel quite nauseous.'

As Margaret picked up the unwanted lunch her hand bumped against the hidden book. 'Sorry,' she said. 'I didn't realize I'd disturbed you reading. Is it good?'

Elizabeth reached beneath the covers. 'Yes, it's very interesting. Carl ordered it for me from London.'

Margaret smiled. 'Is it a love story? Or a mystery? I do love a good read.'

'It's neither.' Elizabeth feigned a yawn. 'It's not a story really. Anyway, I'm feeling rather tired. Would you mind taking the food away and leaving me please.'

'Of course.' Margaret turned and walked towards the door. 'Perhaps you'll have found your appetite when I bring your afternoon tea.'

As the door closed, Elizabeth pulled out the book and flicked through the pages. 'Well, Sir Oliver Lodge,' she sighed. 'It's nice to know I'm not alone.'

Half-an-hour later she placed a bookmark between the pages and lay back on her pillows. The conclusion of *"Raymond, or Life and Death"* would have to wait.

*

Margaret sat at the refectory table and absentmindedly stirred a cup of hot cocoa. The swirls of milk mesmerised her. She picked up the fine bone china cup, and sipped. *I know she keeps the room just as it was, but if she thinks Mary's spirit is still in there…No wonder her husband is concerned.*

'Did she not eat anything?' cook asked.

'No. I'm sorry. I tried to encourage her but she hasn't touched a thing.'

'Not to worry. I'll have salmon and eggs for my tea. It would be a wicked shame to waste beautiful fish.'

Margaret smiled.

Chapter 20

The village dozed in the afternoon sun. In the tea-room, Edward Stanton spooned clotted cream onto a scone while surreptitiously listening to a conversation between two women.

'Yes, that's what I said. Tried to kill him, they did.' The plump one of the pair wiped a crumb from the corner of her mouth. 'Bert the butcher told me.'

'Well, I never. Who would do such a thing?' the other woman asked.

Edward leaned imperceptibly towards the women.

'If I knew that I'd be wiser than they are, wouldn't I. All I'm saying is the police are treating it as –'

'Murder?'

Edward closed his eyes, straining to isolate this tantalising conversation from the others around him.

'No. Attempted murder.' The plump woman's bosom swelled as she inhaled deeply. 'He's still alive, but only just, Bert said.'

Her companion gasped. 'Poor man. As if he hasn't suffered enough.'

Edward turned his head and glared at the women. Gripping the edge of the gingham tablecloth, he scrunched it beneath the table. *Poor man? What about my son?*

'Yes,' the rotund woman agreed. 'All that time in hospital. They say he suffers from amnesty, brought on by the war.'

'Amnesia, dear.'

'Yes, that's what I said.' She put a hand in front of her mouth. 'It means he's gone a bit doolally. Says he's lost his memory. Such a shame.'

'Oh. So that's what the matter with him is. I've tried speaking to him but you may as well talk to a brick wall. I just thought he was being a bit rude.'

The plump woman beckoned for more scones.

'Bert says he doesn't even remember his parents.' She shook her head. 'The Miller's lad that is…not Bert. Can you imagine? Fancy having a son who doesn't know you.'

Edward frowned. *Better than not having your son at all. But my time will come.* At the counter, he presented his bill. As he waited for his change he muttered, 'If at first you don't succeed, try, try–'

The woman rummaging through the coins in the cash register glanced up. 'Sorry, sir, I didn't catch that.'

'Take no notice.' He shifted his weight from one foot to the other. 'It's just a saying I picked up somewhere.'

*

'Are you sure you don't need help with it?' Patricia Miller encouraged the second sausage to leave her frying pan. 'Alan's always looking for the chance to earn extra money and I'm sure your father would pay him.'

Brian looked through her. 'No. No thank you. I don't want anyone else digging there.'

She appeared puzzled. 'As you wish, dear. It was just a thought. I mean, you worked so hard on your shelter I thought you'd be in a hurry now the police have finished.' As she moved to put the pan back on the cooking range her hand brushed against the hot metal. She dropped the frying pan. Hot lard splashed up the cooking range. Rex rushed to retrieve rashers of bacon. Brian jumped to his feet. One foot inadvertently prevented the collie dog from adding another bacon rasher to his score. Losing the battle to retain his balance he crashed down. Patricia gasped at the sickening sound his head made as it hit the floor. Slapping a hand to her forehead, she yelled, 'Oh my God! Brian, are you okay?'

The whiteness of Brian's skin answered her question. She rushed to the stairs. 'Douglas, get up to the Big House and hurry, Brian's hurt himself!'

Mr Miller clattered down the stairs, a hand towel tucked into his shirt front, shaving soap only partially removed by a cut-throat razor. 'What's happened?' Seeing the prostrate body on the kitchen floor he rushed over and fell to his knees. Gently lifting his son's head, he looked up at Patricia. 'He's knocked himself out. And his hair's sticky. Give me something to put under his head, quickly.'

Patricia threw him a tea-towel before rushing upstairs for a pillow. Clutching it to her bosom she hurried back down. 'Out of my way. You go for help. I'll look after him.' She pushed Douglas aside. 'Wait. Lift his head for me again…gently…that's it. Now go, hurry.' Brian lay as limp as washing hung out on an autumn day.

Rex sidled up and licked Brian's face. Patricia pushed the dog away. Getting to her feet, she ran from the kitchen into the hall. Picking up her handbag she searched inside. Returning, she bent down and held the phial of smelling salts under Brian's nose. There was no response. Patricia left his side and went back upstairs. Taking a blanket from the bed, she muttered. 'Keep the patient warm. Yes, keep the patient warm. That's what they always say.' Carefully looking over the top of the bundle she descended the stairs.

*

The ambulance crew clutched mugs of tea as Patricia swirled a wet mop around the kitchen floor. 'I can only apologise again,' the taller of the two men said. 'We got here as quick as we could. But it *is* forty miles you know.'

'Never mind.' Patricia rammed the mop into her bucket and squeezed the head against the in-built strainer. 'Luckily Mr Lyonaisse has a car. As I said, his chauffeur and my husband took him to hospital themselves. We couldn't wait for you any longer.'

'Sorry, but that's life I'm afraid. We'll be off now, thanks for the tea.'

*

In a darkened room, Douglas sat beside the bed and held his son's hand through the bedside rail. Bandages wrapped around Brian's head merged with white starched pillowcases.

The nurse grasped the patient's other wrist and stared at her watch. Turning towards Douglas, she smiled. 'Don't worry, he'll be fine.' Brian's eyes flickered briefly and Douglas felt his son's grip tighten.

'See?' the nurse said. Taking a thermometer from a glass on the bedside table she tried to place it beneath Brian's tongue. She put a hand on his forehead. 'Don't upset yourself, I'll leave it for a while and try again later. I'm sure there's nothing to be concerned about.'

Douglas looked concerned. 'Is it all right for me to stay? I'd like to be here for him when he –'

'Of course. Would you like another cup of tea?'

Brian blinked then opened his eyes. His hands appeared from beneath the bedclothes and gripped the side-rails. Douglas was taken by surprise at this sudden action. Quickly putting his drink down, he reached out and grasped Brian's arm. 'How are you feeling, son? Just lay back while I call the nurse.'

'Where am I?' Brian licked his lips. 'Can I have a drink, please?'

Douglas walked around the bed and poured water from a jug. 'There you are. Let me hold the glass, you'll spill it with your hand shaking like that.'

Brian peered around the room. 'Am I in hospital? What happened?'

'Don't you remember? You banged your head.'

'Oh. Are my men safe?'

'Men? What men, Brian? I don't know what you're talking about.'

Brian sank back into the pillows and stared up at the ceiling. He grasped the rails of the bed, knuckles whitening as his grip increased. 'Oh God,' he murmured, 'It wasn't my fault.'

Douglas leapt to his feet. 'I'll fetch the nurse. She'll give you something.'

*

'How is he?' Patricia walked toward the hospital bed. 'I brought some magazines, Lucozade…and these.' She held out a bag of mixed sweets. 'I got four ounces of both. I'm not sure which are his favourites.'

Tucking her headscarf into a pocket she looked for a place to hang her coat. 'Has he woken up at all? Have they said he's going to be all right? Did –'

'Slow down, love, you're making *me* feel dizzy. One thing at a time. Just wait while I find you a chair.'

'Now,' Douglas said. 'The nurse said it's just mild concussion. There's nothing to worry about, he'll be fine.'

'Why isn't he awake then? It is visiting hours. As the bus doesn't run late, Mr Lyonaisse asked his chauffeur to wait for me.'

'Has he? That's good of him.' Douglas glanced towards the bed. 'Brian's tired. And probably all the pills he's had to take have knocked him sideways.'

'Oh.'

'Plenty of rest. That's what he needs.'

Patricia laid a hand on her recumbent son and patted him through the bedclothes. 'And his mum's love.'

'He may be a bit delirious for a while. When he came round, he kept on about his men, were they safe? It didn't make any sense.'

'Perhaps that's why he has those nightmares.' She gazed at Brian. 'He said something to me about seeing faces the other night.'

'We could try asking him again I suppose. See if he remembers anything. It may help if we can get him to talk.'

Brian stirred. Patricia gently shook him. 'Wake up, darling. Mum's here.'

Her son's eyes opened at her touch. He blinked.

'It's me, sweetheart,' she said softly.

A hand emerged, found Patricia's and gripped it. She winced as her rings dug into the sides of her fingers. 'It's all right, dear. We're both here.'

The squeak from a wheel interrupted her as a woman with an infectious smile wheeled a trolley down the ward. Aluminium covers being removed from plates and stacked on top of each other added to the disturbance. The woman's white teeth jarred with dark skin as she joked with patients. Sounds of knives and forks scraping against plates marked her progress.

Brian drew his knees up toward his chest as the clamour increased. Patricia forced his hand free of hers and massaged her fingers.

Douglas leaned forward. 'It's dinner time, Brian. You'll need to sit up. It smells jolly good.'

Patricia's eyebrows met in the middle as she frowned. 'Yes, it does,' she lied. 'Come on, do as your father says. Sit up, please.'

Slowly Brian pushed back the covers and eased himself back onto the pillows as Patricia plumped them up. 'There. That's better.' She smiled. 'The shepherd's pie looks good.'

Douglas stared as the trolley arrived. 'Is that what it –'

'Yes, *dear*. And cabbage is full of iron, just what's needed to build up strength.'

'Oh.' He was far from convinced. 'As you say, my love, as you say.' Turning to his wide-eyed son he added. 'Try to eat, then we can get you back home with us. We're having spotted dick and custard tonight. Then –'

The look on Patricia's face silenced him.

'Don't worry, I'll save you some,' she said, glaring across the bed. 'Mind what you say, Douglas. Can't you see he's upset enough as it is?'

A plate of encrusted mashed potato, congealed gravy and dejected cabbage sat on top of the bedside locker beside the bottle Patricia had brought with her. Brian held a glass of the fizzy energy drink and stared straight ahead. Patricia used her handkerchief to dab at something stuck on his chin. He didn't react in any way.

'Drink up,' Douglas said. 'It'll do you the world of good.'

'I don't think anything will help me.' His voice sounded vacant.

'What a strange thing to say, dear. Why ever not?' Patricia rustled a brown paper bag. 'Have a sweet.'

Brian shook his head. 'No, thank you.'

Patricia forced a smile. 'Just as you please, dear. All we want is for you to come home as soon as possible. But why do you say nothing can help you? Your father and I will do whatever is needed.'

'You don't understand. My memory is starting to come back.' He held his hands up to his face and sobbed.

'But surely that's a good thing.' She placed her hand over his.

'Is it? I don't think so. I'm beginning to put names to the faces.'

Chapter 21

Tommy Green ran along the top of the low wall, arms
spread wide. Today he was a fearless pilot, hot on the tail of
the Red Baron. The gate of the village hall stopped his
imaginary flight, forcing him to jump down. As he
scrambled back up on the other side of the wall, he saw a
poster had been pinned to the notice-board.

"MYSTO"
World famous magician!
Back by popular demand!

Attached to this hand-painted advertisement was a smaller
piece of paper giving the times of the performances and
stating tea and cakes would be on sale by the Women's
Guild.

Tommy grinned. 'He's coming back tomorrow. Brilliant.
Now's my chance to get even with him.'

*

Back home, Tommy stealthily made his way upstairs. This
was a secret commando raid deep in enemy territory.
Entering one of the bedrooms he went to the place where his
elder brother had concealed a pack of playing cards. These
cards had been sniggered over by Tommy's friends when he
had smuggled them from the house and taken them to
school. Now he had other plans for them.

With his prize safely tucked into a trouser pocket, Tommy
crept along the landing to what was now his older sister's
room. She and Tommy had shared it until his mother
decided the age difference of five years made this

arrangement impossible. He now occupied what was referred to as the box room.

Cautiously opening and closing drawers he searched until he found one containing piles of neatly ironed underwear. Stories of what girls wore were a popular talking point behind the bicycle shed, but Tommy's sister it seemed had more conventional tastes. Just as he was about to abandon his search, he found what he was looking for. 'Wow. Bet Mum doesn't know you've got these.' He giggled. 'I wouldn't want to be you, especially if you had to go out on a frosty night.'

*

Next day, Tommy loitered around the village hall, waiting for a chance to enter without being challenged by enthusiastic helpers from the Women's Guild. Eventually, through an open window, he heard the sound of chairs scraping across the hall floor and female voices. He decided it was safe to carry out his plan.

Going around to the front door, he crept into the building and down the narrow corridor towards the main hall. As he passed the kitchen area, he glanced at women washing cups and plates. Others were covering sticky cakes with grease-proof paper, guarding them from the attention of flies.

Further down the hallway he saw a star pinned to a door. Despite valiant efforts by the women of the Guild, the pointed arms still managed to maintain the curl of the Christmas wrapping paper it had been cut from. Tommy guessed this was the room allocated to the magician.

As he approached the door, the handle turned. Startled, he took refuge behind a row of hats and coats hanging on the wall. He watched as the door opened slightly and a face peered out. Tommy held his breath as he heard Mysto say, 'Plenty of time for a swift pint.'

When he was sure Mysto had left the building, Tommy abandoned his hiding place and rushed to the temporary dressing-room. Inside, he was pleasantly surprised to see his intended victim had made things easy for him. The magician's props were laid out in readiness for his first performance. Tommy chuckled as he set to work.

*

Tommy's mother held out her hand as the volunteer tore two tickets from a roll. 'There you are, dear,' the woman gushed. 'Enjoy the show. It's all for a good cause.'

'Thank you.' His mother put the change back in her purse. Looking down at Tommy she said. 'As you saw him at your party, I'm surprised you wanted to come.'

He grinned. 'I wouldn't swop this for anything.'

The vicar and his wife had centre seats in the front row close to the stage, placing them in full view of the villagers. As the profits were going to the church fund, the vicar decided it was only right and proper he and his good lady be seen to attend both performances.

Mysto ploughed through his tired routine while the vicar dutifully clapped at the end of each trick. The less than enthusiastic audience followed his example by applauding politely. A shake of a coloured handkerchief produced a budgerigar. Wrapped back in the silk square and tapped with a magic wand the bird duly disappeared. The vicar raised a hand to his mouth, stifling a yawn. His wife nudged him with her elbow and glared.

Next, a box, shown to the audience as empty, now contained a glass globe complete with water and what appeared to be a comatose goldfish. Feet scuffled on the hall floor. Crisp packets opened noisily. Cigarette smoke drifted lazily towards the open skylights near the ceiling. A woman stood up, apologised to the person next to her and made her escape.

'Are you enjoying it?' Tommy's mother asked. She bent towards him and whispered. 'His tricks aren't very good, are they. Do you want to go home?'

Tommy smiled. 'No, Mum. It's going to be a laugh, wait and see.'

'Is it? Why did you say that? You haven't been up to mischief again I hope?'

His freshly washed face combined an angelic look with one of shocked denial. 'Who? Me? I've been sitting here next to you.'

Unsure what to believe, Mrs Green turned her attention back to the stage.

Mysto produced a battered metal tube which had once been painted green. With a flourish he held it up to the audience, inviting them to confirm it was empty. After covering it with the ubiquitous handkerchief and rapping it with his wand he held it up. Inserting two fingers, he pulled out a length of string joining the flags of the world.

At first sight the vicar assumed the black flag to be the notorious pirate emblem. But black lace soon dispelled this thought. What hung between the Union Jack and the Stars and Stripes was not the symbol of a buccaneer.

People leaned forward in their seats.

'That's a pair of knickers,' a startled woman yelled. 'Disgusting!'

The vicar's wife blushed.

Tommy almost choked as he fought to suppress his laughter.

His mother turned to glare at him. 'If I didn't know better…'

On stage, Mysto reacted quickly and gathered up the flags from the stage floor. Regaining his composure, he carried on with his act. From inside his coat pocket, he produced a pack of cards and asked for a volunteer. Nobody moved. The vicar lowered his voice and spoke to his wife. She stood up and nervously mounted the stage.

Tommy stepped into the aisle.

'Get back here,' his mother said sharply. 'Sit down.'

'In a minute, Mum. I want to see this.'

Mysto fanned the playing cards and held them out, face down, toward the vicar's wife.

'Take a card, any card. Show it to the audience. Look at it, then put it back in the pack wherever you like.' He tilted his head and gazed up at the ceiling.

She stared at the backs of the cards and saw there were three or four of a different shade. Thinking this was to help the magician perform his trick, she picked one of them.

'Have you chosen?' Mysto asked.

'Yes.'

'Please show it to the audience, then replace it.'

She held up the card as requested. A man sitting beside the vicar struggled to control a coughing fit. The woman next to him went red in the face and pointed accusingly at the card. The vicar's wife turned the card over to see what the fuss was about. As she did, a voice in the second row yelled, 'Bet you don't get many of those to the pound.'

The sound as Mysto's cheek was slapped echoed around the hall. The vicar bounded onto the stage and caught his wife's arm just in time to prevent her adding a second red mark onto the magician's face.

'How dare you,' she screamed at Mysto. 'You horrid rude man. I've never been so insulted in all my life.' She threw the offending object to the floor.

The vicar's eyes opened wide as he saw the photo on the card. 'Good heavens.' He ran a finger around his clerical collar. 'Phew. I say.'

His wife trod on the card and ground it with the sole of her shoe. Catching hold of her husband's arm, she swept him from the stage.

Mysto glared at the young boy standing in the space between the seating. The boy put his fingers in his mouth and pulled a face.

The magician pointed an accusing finger. 'I remember you,' he yelled. 'You little so...so and so, I'll get you for this.'

The audience realized who was responsible for breaking the monotony of the show.

They began to clap.

Tommy took a bow.

His mother grasped one ear and dragged him, still protesting his innocence, up the aisle and out of the hall.

'It *was* you. I might have known. How could you show me up like that?'

He pulled himself free from her grip. 'He shouldn't have made me look stupid on my birthday.'

Mrs Green shook her head.

She waited outside the hall until she saw the vicar and his wife leaving and hurried over to them.

'Vicar. I'm so sorry. And your wife. Poor Agnes. I can't apologise enough. Just wait until I tell Tommy's father, he'll take his belt to him.'

'Please don't, Mrs Green, it's fine, really it is. No real harm done. Just a little childish exuberance.'

'But the show was ruined.'

'That's a matter of opinion.' Turning away from his wife, he winked. 'I wonder what he'll do for an encore tonight.'

'One thing's for sure,' Mrs Green said firmly. 'Whatever it is, it won't be anything to do with my Tommy. He's going straight to bed without any tea.'

*

As the vicar watched, a blackbird tipped its head to one side. Swiftly the bird's beak thrust down into the vicarage lawn and a life-or-death tug-of-war commenced. The worm, thick as a pencil, was determined not to allow itself to be pulled from the ground. But the battle was short lived.

'*The Lord gave, and the Lord hath taken away.* Job 1, verse 21,' he said, gazing up at the sky.

'What did you say, dear? Were you talking to me?' Agnes sounded slightly agitated.

He turned in time to see her sweep out through the French doors, clutching a tray piled high with sandwiches. 'No, my dearest, I wasn't. But can I help you? You seem so busy today.'

She made a shushing noise; one he had grown accustomed to hearing over the years. 'Nonsense. It's just a little something for our guests. You know –'

The sound of a Pekingese dog barking inside the house interrupted her.

'That must be them. Answer the door for me, please, Robert. I've still got a pot of tea to make.'

Elizabeth Lyonaisse screwed her eyes up as she tugged at the brim of her straw hat.

Agnes smiled. 'I think it would be better to move your chair, the sun is really strong today, but it makes a nice change don't you think. I did ask Robert to put the parasol up but he's probably been side-tracked with his Sunday sermon.' She smiled. 'With all the bad weather we've been having lately, I quite expect it to be about Noah and the floods.'

Elizabeth stood and moved around the table.

'Milk or lemon?'

'Lemon, please,' Elizabeth replied, smiling politely.

'And for you, Mrs Harrington?'

'Milk, please. My husband, Bert, drinks his black with four sugars.' She shuddered. 'I think it's standing on sawdust all day makes his throat dry.'

'Possibly, but sawdust must make it easier to clean his butcher's shop floor.'

Mrs Harrington smiled as she bit into a cucumber sandwich. 'Mmm! These are nice.'

'How would you like yours, Mrs Green?' Agnes asked. There was no reply.

Agnes tapped a teaspoon against her saucer.

'Pardon?' Mrs Green sat bolt upright. 'Did you say something? Sorry, I must have dropped off. This weather makes me so drowsy.' Her blush went unnoticed. A slight touch of sunburn covered her embarrassment.

'That's quite all right, I understand. I just asked if you would like milk or lemon.'

'Neither, thank you. I'd prefer barley water if you don't mind.'

'Not at all. Please help yourself. I expect this fuss about the Suez Canal is helping your husband to sell more papers, isn't it?'

'I suppose so. Lot of nonsense if you ask me. Grown men arguing over a bit of water in the desert.'

Agnes kept her thoughts to herself.

'So…any more ideas for this year's fete?' Agnes held her fountain pen poised over a writing pad. 'I like the idea of throwing wet sponges, but do you think we can get the cut-out made in time? We've only got about four weeks.'

'I could ask our gardener, he's good at making things.' Elizabeth sipped her tea.

'That would be nice. I'm going to ask the Guild for contributions, buckets, sponges, prizes, anything useful. They've never let us down before.'

Mrs Harrington beamed. 'And why don't I ask at the croquet club? Perhaps they could bring a few mallets and things. We could set up an area and charge threepence…or maybe sixpence for a game. There'll be plenty of room this year, now Mr Lyonaisse has said we can use his grounds.'

'What an excellent idea. Well done.'

'And the magician? We could ask him back. I know we've only just had him, but –'

'It's a perfectly good idea, but I'm not totally sure,' Agnes interrupted. 'Do you think he's got over his embarrassment?'

'Ha, ha, ha.' Mrs Harrington rocked back in her chair. 'Oh dear, it was so funny.' She put a hand to her mouth. 'Sorry.'

Mrs Green raised her cup. 'I vote we should ask him. The Guild said they had no trouble arranging a date. Seems bookings for his type of act aren't thick on the ground. He'll probably jump at the chance.'

'Lovely. All these splendid ideas.' Looking towards the church, Agnes smiled. 'If we can raise enough money, we'll be able to have the organ and the clock, serviced. They are both long overdue… More tea, ladies?'

The vicar closed his bible and shuffled the notes he had made. 'How did it go, my dearest? Plenty of good ideas, I'm sure.'

'It all went very well. The ladies always manage to come up trumps and this year will be no exception.'

'I have an idea for you to consider. Why don't we have a Beetle Drive? We could make room at one end of the refreshment tent.'

'Splendid. It's always very popular in the village hall.'

'And it may be prudent to have a few games under cover, in case we get more rain.'

'Rain?' Tilting her head back, she stared at the clear sky. 'It's never rained on our fete. But I suppose it could... Perhaps we should move the knocking-down-tins game inside. The wind played havoc with it last year.'

Turning his attention back to his sermon her husband ran a pencil through a sentence and added some new thoughts.

She waited for him to finish. 'Oh, and Mrs Harrington suggested having the magician back. He would *definitely* be better off under cover. Don't you agree?'

'Yes. I don't see any problem. But who's going to keep their eye on Tommy Green?'

'That's unkind. Nobody's really sure it was him.'

'Apart from his mother you mean? She apologised to me right after the show. You were there too, remember?'

'Hmm, yes, I do. But surely he wouldn't—'

'The Devil finds work for idle hands, so who knows? May I suggest you have a word with her.'

Chapter 22

Shirt off, trouser braces dangling from his waist, John Reardon turned his face from side to side in the mirror. Gone was the pallor brought on by toiling in a factory under constant artificial light. The benefit of working outdoors, even in inclement weather, was apparent. He ran his fingers over the stubble on his face, like the remnants of wheat in the fields after harvesting, but grey, not golden. The mirror danced on the wall. He reached out to steady it.

'For the last time, turn that bloody row off,' he yelled, plunging his shaving brush into the sink. 'If I hear it again at this time in the morning, I'll toss that bloody machine out the window.' With a dramatic flourish he covered part of his face with shaving soap and attacked it with a razor. 'Damn! Now look what you've made me do.' The soap decorating his chin turned pink. It formed miniature stalactites to drop into the foam-flecked water. Dabbing the cut with a flannel, he tore a tiny piece from a sheet of Jeyes toilet paper and stuck it over the wound.

Alan came out of his bedroom and raised two fingers towards the bathroom. Going back into his room he turned the record player off. 'It's like living with bleedin' Hitler. Do this. Don't do that. On and on he goes.' Weaving his way across the small room he stood facing black and white photos cut from newspapers and magazines. 'It's all right for you lot,' he said accusingly. 'You've all got proper lives. Yes, and pots of money.' Elvis, James Dean and Brigitte Bardot remained silent. Alan punched the wall. 'He's driving me nuts. I've *got* to get out of this place.'

Tipping the contents from a jam jar onto his bed, he separated coins from banknotes and counted. 'Fifteen pounds, eighteen and sixpence…not bad…about what I could earn in a fortnight when I had a *real* job instead of grubbing around these bloody gardens.'

He kissed the cold jar. Wrapping it in the detested Fair Isle jumper an aunt gave him last Christmas, he pushed it back under his bed.

'Stop shouting at him,' Mrs Reardon yelled from the kitchen. 'I like his music. Bit more lively than this rubbish.' She turned up the volume on the wireless. The closing bars of *The Teddy Bears Picnic* blared out and Uncle Mac introduced the next record. 'I know it's just for children, but I ask you,' she said, stirring the omelette with increased vigour. Glancing over her shoulder she shouted up the stairs. 'I remember the days when you took me dancing at the Palais.' Her wooden spoon darted around the frying-pan. The white and yellow egg mix spluttered in hot margarine. Brown frills formed around the edge. 'Mind you, only because I've got a good memory.' She gave the omelette another fierce stir as she muttered, 'I tell you what, that man on the wireless who calls himself *The Memory Man*...what's his name, oh yes, I remember, Leslie Welch. I bet he could learn a thing or two from me.'

Blue smoke, her trade mark, hinted the toast was ready. Using her pinafore she gave a plate a cursory wipe, tossed the burnt offerings onto it and covered the evidence with her excuse for an omelette. 'It's on the table! Don't let it get cold.'

Alan clattered down the stairs. 'Is this mine, Mum? I'm starving.'

'No, love, I'll cook yours now.' She smiled. 'What would you like? Bacon and eggs? Porridge? Cornflakes with cream off the top of the milk?' Taking a mug off its hook on the wall she ran it under the tap, dried it with a tea-towel and poured Alan some tea.

'Bacon and eggs, please. And two slices of bread with
some of your homemade marmalade.' He pointed at the
plate on the table and pulled a face. 'What on earth's that?'

Carefully placing rashers of bacon into the pan she said,
'It's your dad's breakfast.'

Alan leaned forward for a closer look. '*Is* it?' Putting his
mug down, he said, 'It looks horrible.'

'Cheeky. Anyway, it's all he's going to get.' She plonked
a bottle of brown sauce onto the table. 'Why I married him I
don't know.' Cracking two eggs into the circle formed by
bacon rashers she slid the frying pan back and forth.

'You must have loved each another once,' Alan ventured.
'Surely you haven't always been having a go at each other.'

Gently shaking her head, she sighed. 'You're old enough
to know the truth I suppose.' Emptying the contents of the
frying-pan onto a clean plate, she wiped her hands down her
pinafore. 'You're right. We did love each other. Probably
more than was good for us.'

'What's that mean?' Alan mumbled.

'It means…it means we –'

'Had to get married?'

His mother gasped. 'How did you know?'

Wiping egg from his chin, he smiled. 'Come on, Mum, it
didn't take a genius to work it out. I know my own birthday
and when Aunt Pat was talking about the old days she
mentioned being at your wedding. Put the dates together and
bingo.'

'Proper little Sherlock Holmes aren't you.' She sniffed
and dragged the back of a hand across her nose.

'Don't upset yourself, Mum. At least you didn't give me
up for adoption.'

'That's true. Lots of people said I should. But I was stupid
enough to think everything would work out if I married your
father. Huh!' She slammed the hot frying-pan into the sink.

Water seethed and spat at her in protest. 'How daft could I have been?'

'If I wanted to get married, would you and *him*…give your permission?'

'Married? At your age?' She turned to face him. 'Don't tell me you've got some poor girl in the family way. I don't believe it. Not after –'

'Keep your hair on, Mum. No, I *haven't*. I just wanted to know.'

'Thank God. But the answer's no, at least it is from me. He might say yes though. He'd love to drive you and me apart.'

The door to the bathroom opened. John stormed down the stairs into the kitchen.

Margaret turned away, trying not to smile.

'Go on,' he shouted. 'Have a good laugh, why don't you.' He put a hand to his chin, checking pieces of paper staunching the results from his shave.

'Blimey.' Alan grinned. 'Did the Deptford razor boys give you a going over?'

John raised his hand as if to strike his son. 'It was that bloody row of yours. Anymore, and one of us is going to have to go.'

'Promises,' Margaret said softly behind the hand held over her mouth.

'What did you say?' He moved towards her.

Alan jumped up and stood between his parents. 'You just dare,' he snarled. 'Lay a hand on her and I'll –'

'You'll do what? Hit me?'

'Yes.'

'Go on then.' He put a finger on his jaw. 'Go on, *little* boy. Hit me.'

Alan looked at his mother.

'No, don't,' she pleaded. 'Please. He didn't mean it.'

Punching a fist into an open hand Alan glared at his father. 'You better just leave her alone. I've had enough of you throwing your weight around.'

'Have you now? That's interesting. Now, you just listen to me. I run this house. If you've got a problem with that, sling your bloody hook.'

'I will, and the sooner the better as far as I'm concerned.'

John pushed past him and opened the door. 'Good. I'm off. There's work to be done.'

Margaret picked up the plate and held it out. 'What about your breakfast?'

'Call that a breakfast? Give it to the Miller's dog. No, on second thoughts, don't, we'll have the bloody RSPCA after us.'

Chapter 23

The early morning peace in the household was assaulted by the strident ringing of a telephone.

'Answer that, please,' Elizabeth Lyonaisse called down the stairs, clutching a silk dressing gown to her body.

In the spacious hall below, the butler cleared his throat and picked up the instrument. 'Yes, sir, this is the Lyonaisse residence. Who do you wish to speak with?' As he listened, he checked his uniform in the gilt-framed mirror hanging on the wall opposite. Brushing a gloved hand over his jacket he nodded imperceptibly. 'And who shall I say is calling, sir? Nicholas Steed...yes, sir. One moment, please, I shall see if Mr Lyonaisse is at home.' Taking a pristine handkerchief from a trouser pocket he wiped the handset, placed it on its side, and walked regally up the staircase.

Knocking on the door he waited.

'Yes. Come in.' Carl put down his newspaper.

'Sorry for the intrusion, sir, but you are wanted on the telephone by a Mr Steed. He said you would know him.'

'Thank you. I'll be down right away.'

'Yes, sir.'

'Hello Nicholas, nice to hear from you. How are you?' Carl pressed the phone against his head. 'That's good...Your friend, you say? Yes, of course. Brian would be thrilled I'm sure...Wednesday, around lunch time? Perfect. I'll inform the Miller's and look forward to seeing you and Victor.'

Carl glared at the phone and tapped it sharply on the table. Putting it back to his ear he said, 'Sorry, I didn't catch the last bit. Bit of a crackle on the line...A new car? Sorry, would you mind speaking up? Hello? Can you hear me? Oh, never mind, I'll phone you back. Goodbye.'

*

Douglas Miller stopped turning the soil over as he heard someone approach. He pushed a trowel into the garden and straightened his back. 'Good morning, sir.'

'Morning, Douglas. How are you? The garden is looking splendid.'

Douglas dragged the back of one hand across his forehead. 'Fine, thank you. Having our daughter and her family help out has made it easier for me.'

'Good, I'm pleased. Now, I've some news which I realize may be a bit of a shock. A business acquaintance of mine phoned to say a friend of his thinks he may know your son. They would like to visit.'

Douglas frowned. 'Where does he know Brian from? Were they at school together? Did they –'

'Hold on. One question at a time.'

'Sorry, sir. But you took me by surprise.'

'Quite so. It seems the chap fought in Italy, the battle for Monte Cassino to be precise. And his officer was a Brian Miller. Be a strange coincidence if it wasn't your son, eh?' Carl watched Douglas mentally wrestling with this bombshell.

'I don't know what to say, sir.' Douglas scratched the back of his neck. 'Even if he does know Brian, I'm not certain Brian would be able to recognise him. His memory is getting better but…'

'Good point. But I'm afraid I've already said yes. They'll be down on Wednesday.'

'Oh.'

Seeing Douglas was perturbed, Carl placed a hand on his shoulder. 'I tell you what. Why not bring your son up to the house? Then he can leave if he feels uncomfortable about the situation.'

Douglas pursed his lips and breathed out. 'That's very kind. I'm sure he *would* like to meet this man.'

'Consider it settled. Of course, you and your good wife are invited too.' He patted his stomach. 'We can rely on cook to put on a decent spread.'

*

The group outside the columned entrance to Oakwood House stopped talking as a magnificent car swept through the gates. As it drew nearer, Nicholas Steed took one hand off of the steering wheel and waved from the open window.

With a sound like waves retreating over pebbles the vehicle coasted to a stop, scrunching against the shingle drive.

'Good afternoon.' Nicholas stepped from the car and held out his hand to Carl. 'How are you?' Without waiting for a reply, he continued. 'What a glorious day. It's been a pleasure to drive down.'

'Good afternoon, Nicholas, nice to see you again.' Carl stepped towards the car. 'So, this is the Mk VII? It's a beauty. Makes my Daimler look a trifle shabby.'

'Do you think so? I *am* rather proud of her, I must say.' Nicholas patted the top of the car's roof. 'Fairly flew along and the road holding is fantastic. The Jaguar boys have come up trumps with this model in my opinion.'

'I can't argue with that. The business *must* be doing well. Perhaps I'll cash in some shares and treat myself.'

Nicholas smiled. Opening the rear door of the Jaguar he stood back. 'Mustn't forget what all this is about. I'd like to introduce you to my good friend, Victor.'

Carl shook hands with him. 'Pleased to meet you, Victor, nice of you to come all this way.'

'Nice of you to invite me. Splendid place you have here.'
Victor suddenly gasped as he stared over Carl's shoulder.
'My God, it *is* you, sir. I'd recognise you anywhere.'
Ignoring the others, he held out his hand. 'How long has it
been? How *are* you?'

Brian moved a foot, drawing an arc in the gravel. 'I am
very sorry. Who are you? Do you know me?'

'Know you? Of course, I do. I'm Victor, Victor
Whitehead. You must remember me, surely.'

'Sorry, no.'

Carl turned towards Douglas. 'It's not looking good, is it?'

'I did think this might happen.' Douglas sighed.

Patricia gripped her husband's elbow. 'Give them a
chance. You never know, maybe Victor can jog Brian's
memory.' Turning to the visitor she said, 'Pleased to meet
you. I'm Brian's mother and this is my husband.'

'The pleasure's all mine. Brian was a fine officer. I'm
proud to be able to say I served under him in Italy.'

Carl stepped forward. 'Let's adjourn, shall we? Cook has
prepared afternoon cakes and tea.' He licked his top lip. 'I
really shouldn't have the cream but…'

'That was lovely,' Patricia said, pushing her plate away.
'Thank you.'

'Yes,' Douglas agreed. 'Homemade strawberry jam and
clotted cream. You can't beat it.'

'I can see *you* enjoyed them. I don't know where you
found room for them all.' She glared at her husband. 'It's a
shame Victor didn't –'

Victor gave a short laugh and waved dismissively. 'It's
okay, I'm fine. Cream scones aren't really my thing
anyway.'

Nicholas dabbed his mouth with a serviette and stood up.
'I would love to see the grounds, Carl, what do you think?
Shall we leave Brian and Victor to talk about old times?'

'Good idea. I think the rain will hold off for an hour or two yet. How about it, Douglas?'

'Yes, sir, I'd be pleased to show off my flowers and vegetables. Sorry, I mean *your* flowers and vegetables.'

Carl laughed. 'Nonsense. The gardens would be nothing without your sterling efforts. Let's enjoy a spot of fresh air.'

Patricia brushed crumbs from the front of her blouse. 'I think I'll pass, thanks. I've still got a lot to do. Cook wants to speak to me about the last lot of groceries that were delivered, and I need to get home to prepare tonight's meal.' She looked towards Victor and Nicholas. 'It's been nice to meet you. I hope you enjoy your chat with Brian.'

Victor smiled, put the strainer on top of his cup and poured more tea.

Opening the French doors, Carl ushered his guests out onto the paved area leading to the more formal part of the gardens.

Amongst the well-trimmed bushes, stood Douglas's first foray into topiary. He had intended to prune the privet hedge into an elephant, but an accident with shears while shaping its trunk had reduced his aspirations to that of a large pig.

Hidden from view the tinkling of a fountain suggested other hidden treasures. Nicholas pointed. 'What splendid gardens. I had no idea.'

Carl's chest puffed with pride. 'Thank you. But I do apologise, I should have shown you around last time.'

Douglas bent down, plucked a white rose and offered it to Nicholas. 'For your button hole, perhaps? It's one of my favourites. The scent is out of this world.'

'Thank you.' Nicholas held the bloom close to his face and inhaled. 'You should try bottling this, you'd make a fortune.'

Douglas smiled. 'That sounds like a good idea. I could certainly use more money.'

Carl ignored the hint. 'I suggest we take the long walk around the gardens, then return to the house,' he said. 'By then I'm sure Victor and Brian will have said all they have to say to each other.'

*

'Do you not remember *anything* about the war, sir?' Victor's eyebrows met in the middle as he frowned.

Brian stared at his interrogator. 'Why do you keep calling me, sir?'

'Because you were my officer, and a damned good one.'

'Oh, but please call me Brian.'

'As you wish, sir. A few more like you would have saved a lot of wasted lives. I wouldn't give tuppence for most of the officers I've served under.' Victor's cup rattled against the saucer as memories flooded back. 'But you were different.'

'I don't remember much,' Brian replied. 'But I do have nightmares. I see faces.'

'Just faces?'

'Yes, most of the time. Sometimes they hold out their arms towards me' He hesitated. 'They really scare me.'

'Who are they? These people you see?'

'Some wear army caps. Another is a girl.'

Victor put his cup down. 'And you don't know who they are?'

'I wish I did. Perhaps they'd leave me in peace.' Brian screwed up his face. Tilting his head back, he gazed at the ceiling. The nervous twitch returned. 'You said you served under me.' He tapped the side of his head. 'If you did, can't you help me get things sorted out up here?'

Taking a deep breath, Victor replied, 'I don't know. But I can try to jog your memory if it would help.'

'Thank you. I'd like that. If it's not too much trouble.'

'Nonsense, I'll be glad to. Try and relax. I'll tell you about the last day I saw you and the Italian girl. I'll begin with her…it was the same day as the disaster.'

Brian crossed both hands on his lap and sat back in the upholstered leather chair. 'Disaster?'

'Yes, sir. But it wasn't your fault, despite what was said at the time. I should know, I was one of the only two survivors.'

Brian groaned. 'I don't think I want to hear this.'

'I think you should. It may help explain things.'

'If I ask, would you stop please?'

'Yes, of course.' He cleared his throat. 'You were leading us down the main street when the shelling started. But it was our lot, not the Germans.' His face showed the anger burning inside. 'It was another bloody cock-up. Nobody told us about the bombardment. They were supposed to have warned the civilians, but…'

Brian's breathing rate increased; the colour in his cheeks increased. 'Go on.'

'A girl ran out of one of the houses, screaming. You ordered us to keep moving to the position we had orders to occupy. Then you left us and ran down the street towards her.'

'Did I? What happened?'

'Shells were falling thick and fast. Someone shouted, and we ran. Walls collapsed. Clouds of dust filled the air. The noise was terrible. We took cover in a cellar to wait for you.'

Brian licked his lips. 'I don't remember. Please, carry on.'

'It must have been half-an-hour or more. The shelling eased off and we heard you shouting. You looked a mess. Covered in white dust, your uniform shredded and soaked in blood. We all thought you'd bought it, but when the medical officer checked you weren't wounded.'

Gripping the arms of the chair, Brian sat up. 'The girl? What happened to the girl?'

'Nobody knows. The German guns opened up again. Both of my eardrums were bleeding, two of our men had been wounded and–'

'But was she saved?'

Victor spread his hands wide. 'It's anyone's guess. As far as we know you were the last person to see her.'

Brian's fingers resembled the mating rituals of adders, interweaving, raising up, and falling back. He unlocked his hands and wiped sweaty palms down his trousers. 'Oh – my – God.'

'Are you okay? You've gone as white as a sheet.'

Brian stared down at the carpet. 'Yes, thank you for asking.'

'Should I fetch someone? Or maybe a drink would help?'

Brian shook his head. Taking a deep breath, he held it and closed his eyes.

'Are you sure?' Victor asked

'Yes. Tell me more about…what did you call it? Oh, yes, *the disaster*.'

Victor hesitated. 'Hmm…I'm not sure you're up to it. You don't look at all well, if you don't mind me saying so.'

'Please. Please go on. I get these flashbacks, faces. It's horrible. I need to know what happened.'

Lifting the tea-pot Victor filled a cup for Brian, added three teaspoons of sugar and stirred vigorously. 'Here, drink this. It's probably stewed by now, but it will do you good.'

Brian took the cup and sipped.

Victor smiled. 'Perhaps I should have given you more sugar, you look as if you're sucking a lemon.' He paused to light a cigarette. 'As I said, our orders were to mount a frontal attack on the monastery. Everyone knew it was hopeless. We had about as much chance as a snowball in Hell.' He leaned back and blew a smoke ring towards the ceiling. 'The Germans were dug-in. We were in the open. Do you remember?'

'No.'

'As you led us forward, they let us have it with bloody machine guns and mortars. We lost three men in as many minutes. Young Jimmy was next. A bullet caught him in the neck. He bled to death next to me.' Victor tapped his cigarette on the onyx ashtray.

Brian held out a hand. 'Could I have one? I don't think I've ever smoked, but I fancy one now.'

Offering the pink packet of *Passing Clouds* to Brian, Victor waited for him to take one. Leaning across, he flicked his lighter.

Brian coughed, put a finger to his lips and wiped away a strand of tobacco. 'Thanks. Please go on.'

'You sent a runner back. I remember you saying, "Ask the stupid buggers what we're supposed to do, chuck stones at them? Give us artillery support or pull us back." You might not have said *buggers*, sir, you were very angry.' Victor ground out his cigarette and lit another. 'While we waited for an answer, the mortar shells were falling closer and closer. There was nowhere to hide, just piles of stones. The ground was rock-hard, our folding shovels were useless, and all the time the machine gunners sought us out.'

Brian gave up trying to smoke. He sipped his tea. 'Did the runner get back? I mean, it sounds as though he didn't stand a chance.'

'He made it back all right, but when you read the message, your face turned purple. You snapped your cane over your knee and stormed off. I picked up the paper and read it. "Advance as ordered. Have no artillery to spare." Those generals must live in a world of their own. I mean, how were we supposed to attack dug in crack German troops?'

'Where did I go? Why did I leave you?'

'We didn't know at the time, you didn't say. But while you were away, things got worse. Some of us hid behind the dead. I can still hear the thud of bullets hitting those men. It was straight from Dante's Inferno.'

Brian's eyes became moist as he stared at Victor. He swallowed loudly. 'I wish I could remember.'

'Don't. Think yourself lucky. I wish I could *forget*.' Victor picked up the cigarette packet and stared at it. 'I think this picture is called, "The Laughing Cavalier." There was nothing to laugh about where we were.'

'Please, tell me more. Things are coming back to me.'

Victor stared out through the large window at the far side of the room. 'How peaceful it is here. You're a lucky man.'

'Yes. They tell me I grew up here, but I don't remember. Now, please finish your story.'

'Where had I got to?'

'You said you were hiding–'

'We didn't know what to do. We couldn't advance and we couldn't retreat. The Germans had us at their mercy.'

'Where was I?'

'I'll get to that in a minute. I called it a disaster, and a disaster it was. The mortars homed in on us. Rocks and stones rained down. Hot steel fragments sliced through us.' He winced. 'I remember trying to dig with my bare hands. I can still see blood from my fingernails mixing with the dust.'

'How did you get out of there? Did they send reinforcements?'

Victor laughed. 'Did they hell. No, we were hung out to dry and no mistake. Anyway, I've almost finished. As if things weren't bad enough, the German big guns opened up.' His hands shook as he fumbled with his cigarette packet. 'A shell landed not far from our position. I saw the ground erupt in front of us. And the noise. My God, I thought that was it. I could hear voices, but it was as if I was under water. There were bodies on either side of me. The only other person I could see alive was Morgan.' Victor waited to see if this name would register with Brian. 'He had lost his rifle but was clutching his diary as if it would shield him from the bullets. He loved that book. Mind you, I don't blame him. All those wonderful drawings and sketches of his mates. He always said he was going to get a job at *Punch* magazine when the war was over.'

'Did he?'

Victor shrugged. 'Maybe. As I said, I just wanted to make a fresh start, and not in England. What we came home to was…well, you know.'

'No, I don't know. Was it bad?'

'Let's just say it wasn't pleasant. But let me finish my story. As Morgan and I shared my last cigarette, you appeared. I don't know how to put this…please don't feel embarrassed…you were almost naked.'

Brian gasped. 'Naked? Really?'

'Yes, sir. And you gave a good impersonation of a ghost. Covered in dust, eyes like piddle holes in the snow. Bits of shredded uniform. Blood everywhere. Awful. I took the liberty of pulling you to the ground. Bullets were buzzing like wasps at a Sunday school picnic.'

Victor lit another cigarette and coughed. 'You were in a bit of a state, if you don't mind me saying so. Eventually you told us you'd made it back to Head Quarters to query our orders. When they confirmed we had to hold our position, you told them to… well I leave that to your imagination.'

'My God… so only you and this Morgan fellow were left alive? What happened after I got back? How did we survive?'

'Believe me, Brian, I have no idea. Just as you were telling us the bad news, another shell landed close by. I saw Morgan run for his life. I scrambled to my feet and looked all around, but I couldn't see you. Presuming you'd been killed, I reported you lost with all the others when I finally made it back to our lines.'

'I wish I could remember.'

'It was a great shock when Nicholas told me you may still be alive. Morgan and I came close to being charged with desertion, it would have helped if you had been there to confirm what really happened.'

'Sorry. I should have been. I wonder what became of me.'

'Perhaps you were shipped back home. Like I said, you were in a bad state even before that last shell found us.'

'Maybe. All I can tell you is I had army papers when I was admitted to hospital a few years ago. The thing I don't understand is you say I was an officer, but the papers belonged to a private. And if my *parents* are right, they weren't issued to me.'

Victor watched as another smoke ring drifted up towards the ceiling. 'Beats me. But at least you made it back safe. It sounds as though your injuries may have affected your mind. And no wonder.'

Brian slumped forward. 'I *am* beginning to remember things. The trouble is, I wish I wasn't.'

Chapter 24

Brian hummed a tune as he walked along a path parallel to the railway line. Remembering some of the words, he sang to himself. *I'll never forget, the moment we met…* 'Strange,' he muttered. 'How can you never forget? I can.' He frowned. 'My troubles start when things I *thought* I'd forgotten come back to me.' Despite the warmth of the day, he shuddered.

Trainspotting was something Douglas had enjoyed as a boy and thought it may provide a source of stimulation for his son. So, equipped with an exercise book and pencil, Brian was strolling through the fields, heading for the bridge over the railway track. Douglas had recommended it as it offered the opportunity to see the trains head on. Although Brian doubted the value of jotting down train numbers, he hadn't raised any serious objections.

An approaching train announced its presence with a shrill whistle. Brian turned and gazed down the track.

The noise as it thundered past caught him entirely by surprise. Clapping both hands to his ears he crumpled to the ground. He was back on the hillside in Italy. The overwhelming sound of the engine was enemy shells homing in on him. Screams and cries for help reverberated in his skull. With his eyes closed tightly he could still see bodies pirouetting in a macabre dance, choreographed by the Devil, machine guns providing the tune.

With a final clatter, the guard's van at the rear of the train passed by, leaving an eerie silence in its wake. Brian watched through splayed fingers until it was lost from his view. Clambering to his feet he dusted the knees of his trousers and undid the top button of his shirt. Sweaty hands, coated with dirt, marked the collar as he loosened his tie. He swallowed and licked dry lips. Checking his pockets for the exercise book and pencil he looked around to see if anyone had witnessed his panic attack. The path was deserted in both directions.

When the Victorians had driven the railway line through this farm, the bridge had been built to allow the movement of livestock. Now it was suitably surfaced for farm tractors and the odd motor car to use. What had once been a country lane was now shown as a B road on maps. The idyllic countryside had been desecrated by man's inane desire to get from one place to another as quickly as possible.

Reaching the bridge, Brian rested his weight on both elbows and peered down at the shiny steel rails. Climbing up onto the double row of bricks forming the arch he got to his feet and steadied himself. Concentrating, he walked slowly up the incline until he reached the centre of the arch.

He waited for the next train. His head swam. He began to sway. Recovering his balance, he sat with both legs dangling over the track, hands knotted, sweat running down his back.

It was almost an hour before the train steamed towards him. Hypnotically staring at the rapidly reducing distance he gripped the brickwork and braced himself.

When the smoke dispersed, he realized he had forgotten why he was here. His hands were clamped around the brick ledge, fingers drained of blood. He could feel his heart pounding. Squeezing his eyes shut he tried to block out the image of his body being ripped apart. He thought about telling his father what had happened, and then wondered if it would be better just make up some numbers to enter in his book. The realization he didn't have any idea how many numerals there should be made his decision easy.

*

'Never mind.' Douglas placed a hand on Brian's shoulder. 'Better luck next time, eh? At least the walk did you good.'

Brian wasn't so sure, his knees still felt tender. He hadn't confided in his father about the effect the first train had on him, contenting himself with an edited version of events. 'I did enjoy it…but next time I'll get some numbers to start my collection.'

Patricia looked around from the sink. 'That's nice. Let me know and I'll make you some sandwiches to take.'

Chapter 25

Leaning his bike against the gate post, Frank bent to pick up a smouldering cigarette tossed from a car. 'It must be my lucky day.'

It wasn't.

*

Mothers, on their way to school, crossed the road and led their children past the scene of the incident. An ambulance and a solitary police car partially blocked their view while police officers made sure pedestrians could not approach attempts being made to save Frank.

One of the women, Mrs Grayson, pulled her daughter aside. 'Don't look, Pearl,' she said. 'Something's happened to that poor man.'

The small girl slipped from her grasp as she recognised the ancient bicycle. 'Mum, it's the Captain.'

Mrs Grayson caught hold of her arm. 'Come away. You *naughty* girl.'

'But Mum, the Captain's been hurt.'

'Who? That's Frank. He's not a captain.'

'He *is*. He's our captain. He lets us visit him on his ship in the woods. We–' Pearl suddenly remembered her pirate oath made to Captain Black Bart.

'Are you making all this up?'

'No. Cross my heart and hope to die.'

'Don't say things like that. I think we'll pay a visit to the police station. You can tell them what you've just said.'

Mrs Grayson opened the door for Pearl. Inside, an inescapable smell of furniture polish leached from the oak counter. The gleaming black Bakelite telephone appeared to have received its share of beeswax polish too. High on the wall an octagonal oak-cased clock ticked loudly. She dragged the reluctant child across the tiled floor.

'Good morning,' she said, then looked down at Pearl. 'Pearl's been telling me about Frank, the tramp. She says he's got a camp in the woods where *girls* come to see him.'

'Are you sure?' The sergeant behind the front desk screwed up his face. 'The woods on Mr Lyonaisse's land?'

'That's what she says. She said he calls himself Black Bart, or some such nonsense.' Mrs Grayson shook Pearl. 'We never knew. If we had she'd have got a good hiding from her dad, make no mistake.'

'It's obvious he must have slept somewhere I suppose. He never gave us any real trouble so we left him alone. The place won't seem the same without him.' Stepping back to block Pearl's view, he mouthed, 'We think it was a heart attack.' Lifting the flap of the desk he stepped through and bent down. 'Now, little lady, tell me where this camp is.' He smiled. 'You're not in any trouble, it's just we need to see if it's true.'

Pearl fidgeted, tugging at one of her plaits. 'His name is Captain Black Bart. And it's not a camp, it's a pirate ship,' she mumbled.

'Don't be silly. Just tell the man what you told me,' Mrs Grayson demanded. 'Go on, tell him.'

The sergeant reached beneath the counter and produced a paper bag. 'Would you like one?' He held out the bag towards the small girl. 'They're winter mixtures, my favourites. Try a red one, you'll like those.'

Mrs Grayson held Pearl back. 'No, thank you. She's in my bad books. She's certainly not having any treats.'

The sergeant popped a sweet into his mouth. 'Lovely. I missed these during the rationing.' He pushed the sweet into the side of one cheek, making it bulge out. Pearl smiled. 'Now, tell me about Captain Black Bart and his pirate ship. What did you do there?'

'Nothing. Just played.'

'What did you play? Did Black Bart make up the games?'

'No. It's a secret. The Captain said we mustn't tell anyone.'

Mrs Grayson shook her head. 'She's been like this all the way here.'

'In that case we will have to get your daughter to accompany one of my constables to the woods. Then we'll see if there's anything to all this.'

'I agree.' She sniffed. 'But it's getting late and I've still got to get my husband's tea. Can we leave it until tomorrow?'

Glancing up at the clock on the wall the sergeant nodded. 'Yes, that would be fine. George is going off duty in half-an-hour and I'd rather send him. Come back in the morning as early as you can, then we'll ask your daughter to show us the way to this camp, *if* it exists.'

Pearl stuck her tongue out.

'Don't do that,' her mother said sharply. 'It's very rude.'

While Mrs Grayson bent to admonish Pearl, the sergeant put a thumb to his nose and wiggled his fingers. Pearl's mouth opened as she pointed. 'Look, Mum, he's being rude to me.'

Butter wouldn't have melted in his mouth as the sergeant returned the mother's icy stare.

Grabbing Pearl by the hand she dragged her towards the door. 'What have I told you about telling fibs? This camp of yours better be there, or you'll be for it, my girl.'

'It's not mine, it's the Captain's.'

*

Pearl and her mother waited as George removed his helmet and wiped his brow. He looked at a path, worn through tall grass, leading to where a breach in the wall broke the symmetry of the architect's design. 'It's a wonder Mr

Lyonaisse hasn't had this repaired,' he said. 'I can only guess he didn't want this tree felled.'

'Are you sure this isn't all a load of nonsense?' Mrs Grayson said sternly to Pearl. 'If you're telling fibs and I ladder my stockings…' she gripped her daughter's shoulder. 'You won't be getting a doll for your birthday.'

Pearl pursed her lips and stamped her foot. 'That's not fair. You promised. I'm not telling fibs, I'll show you.' Wriggling free from her mother's grasp she darted into the gap in the wall. 'Come on, you slow coaches.'

George put a hand on Mrs Grayson's arm. 'I think I should go first,' he said.

Easing their way past the tree trunk, stepping over fallen stones from the wall, the trio entered the woods. Patches of sunlight flirted with ferns hiding in the shade. George turned on his flashlight and probed the gloom. A squirrel ran across the fallen leaves and scampered up the side of a tree.

'You don't need that.' Pearl pointed at the torch. 'It's not dark in here.'

Glancing sheepishly at Mrs Grayson, George turned it off.

Pearl took hold of her mother's hand. 'It's not far, Mum. You'll see.' She skipped through the woods, leading the way with George close on her heels. Mrs Grayson made frequent stops to peer back over her shoulder. She sensed the trees were somehow closing ranks behind these interlopers. And it was eerily silent. She had expected woodland to be filled with the sounds of birds.

'Pearl,' she called out. 'This isn't funny. Tell the nice policeman you were telling fibs.'

The girl turned and grinned. 'But I didn't. You'll see.'

George stumbled as he came close to colliding with her. 'Watch out, you nearly had me over.'

Mrs Grayson gasped. 'If you're doing this just to get off school you'll be in trouble, my girl.'

Pearl pointed ahead. 'There it is. There's the Captain's ship.'

George shone his torch around the camp. 'Where *on* earth did he get all this stuff from?'

A builder's tarpaulin, stretched between four trees, defended much of the area from the weather. Leaves and twigs gathered in its folds. Two battered umbrellas hung from branches alongside a pair of dead rabbits. Large stones circled a fire pit. Half-consumed logs and charred bones littered the area.

George stared around the camp. 'Just take a look at all this junk.' He picked up a small suitcase and sprung the locks. 'What's this? Kids comics? It's full of them.'

Using the toe of his shoe he moved empty bottles and piles of clothing. Numerous insects scuttled from the intrusion. Leaf litter gave off a damp smell.

Pearl shook free from her mother's grasp and pointed. 'Those comics belong to the Captain. We gave them to him. They're his favourites.'

Her mother scowled at her. 'Why would a grown man be interested in those?'

'Because he needs them,' Pearl said. 'Put them back, he'll be very cross if you don't.'

George placed the suitcase back and continued his search. 'There's nothing here of any importance. I'll inform Mr Lyonaisse about this place. I'm sure he'll be keen to clear it away.'

'No!' Pearl ran at him and beat her fists against his legs. 'You can't. The Captain *lives* here.'

He frowned. 'I take it you haven't told her?'

'No.'

Putting his hand on Pearl's shoulder he bent down. 'The Captain won't be coming here anymore. He had to go away.'

'But he never said. Besides he *can't*. We haven't finished his lessons.'

Her mother frowned. 'What lessons?'

'We're showing him how to read. That's what his comics are for.'

George looked puzzled. 'Who's showing…I mean teaching him? You?'

'Yes. We all take turns. He pretends the comics are treasure maps and takes one of us into the woods so he can learn.'

He raised his eyebrows. 'Into the woods? Just one of you?'

'Yes. He's very shy.'

'And you teach him how to read? Is that all you do?'

Her mother gasped. 'Oh, Lord Jesus, surely you're not suggesting –'

'No, not at this point. But we have to be certain a crime hasn't been committed.' He stared into Pearl's eyes. 'You must tell me if he said or did anything bad.'

Pearl bit her lip. 'I told you. We help him with his words. And how to write. He says all pirates have to read and write or they won't be able to make treasure maps.'

Her mother took hold of her arm and shook her. 'Is this the *truth?* Who else came here? Tell the policeman.'

Pearl gave the constable the names of her friends. He dutifully made notes. 'I have to get back to the station and make my report,' George said. 'We'll be speaking to your daughter's friends of course, but I'm fairly sure there's nothing for you to be concerned about. I don't think he was up to anything.'

Mrs Grayson bent down and put her arms around Pearl. Try as she might to erase them from her mind, images of what *may* have happened in these dark woods caused her to sweat. It was cool under the trees, but her forehead and armpits acted in contradiction.

'But you never found the missing girl, did you.' She swallowed and licked her lips. 'Perhaps you should search this place. Who knows what's buried here?'

'As I said, Mr Lyonaisse will want this place cleared up.' He took a deep breath. 'Naturally we will liaise with his workers. Anything suspicious will be investigated.'

Pearl's mother shivered involuntarily. 'This place is giving me the creeps.' Turning Pearl to face back the way they had come; she pushed her forward. 'Take us back, quickly. You've already missed Assembly but you should be in time for your first lesson if we hurry.'

Chapter 26

The sky lightened as the sun approached the horizon. Cigarette ends and packets competed for space with wild flowers trying to grow on the roadside verge. Rabbits abandoned grass, speckled with dew, as the two lovers trudged towards them. If Hollywood were to judge solely by appearance, it would not cast them in romantic roles. The lack of sleep and hours of walking was taking a toll.

Sheila clutched Alan's arm as they walked beside the arterial road. A few cars and motorcycles separated the commercial vehicles heading north. She was trying to thumb a lift. On her own she would not have had to walk far. But as a couple, drivers chose not to see them.

Alan struggled with two suitcases. One was his. The heavier case was hers. Stopping frequently, he changed them from one hand to the other.

The top three buttons of his shirt were undone despite the chill in the air. Beneath his jacket, sweat patches grew larger. His tie had been removed and consigned to a trouser pocket.

'We'll have to stop for a while.' Alan lowered the cases onto the grass. Straightening his back, he took a deep breath and sighed. 'That's better. God, I feel like I did when I first started gardening for old Mr Lyonaisse.'

Sheila stumbled, held out a hand and steadied herself against him. She kissed his cheek. 'Sorry. I'm just so tired.'

'Sit down, my love.' He waved a hand at her case. 'Get the weight off your feet, take your shoes off. You look all in.'

Dropping the coat she'd been carrying, Sheila opened her handbag, took out a compact and flipped it open. Staring in the mirror her fears were confirmed. 'I look as though I've been dragged through a hedge backwards.' A quick search produced a comb. Removing the Alice band, she attacked the tangled mess on the head of the apparition staring back at her.

Lipstick came to the rescue and she nodded her satisfaction. She brushed a hand down her legs. 'Oh, no, just look at all the ladders in my stockings. I can't wear these. And I've got blisters.'

'Me too. Blisters I mean. But we've come a hell of a way.' He stared down the ribbon of road stretching back as far as he could see. 'It's the bloody hills that get me. The rest of it's not too bad. I did think we'd be able to scrounge more lifts though.' He lit a cigarette. Scratching the side of his head he looked at her. 'Perhaps this wasn't such a good idea after all. Sorry.'

She tried to appear enthusiastic. 'I'm not. Getting married is what I've always wanted to do ever since I played with dolls.'

'I know one thing.' He shuffled his feet on the grass. 'When we do get married, I don't want to be like my parents, always having a dig at each other. I want us to be happy together.'

'We will. I know we will.'

Alan moved his suitcase and sat next to her. Putting his arm around her he gently pulled her towards him. She laid her head on his shoulder and despite the passing traffic the pair were soon asleep.

'You two. Romeo and Juliet. Want a lift?'

The car had two wheels up on the grass. Its driver was leaning across the front passenger seat and calling to them through the open window.

Alan opened his eyes and blinked. He shook Sheila gently. 'What?' she murmured. 'Are we there yet?'

'Wake up. I think we've got a ride.' He looked at the vehicle. Moisture glistened on black paint. Wiper blades cut twin arcs through water droplets on the windscreen.

The man leaned across, opened the door, and beckoned. 'Do you, or don't you? I haven't got all day. Make up your mind.'

Alan jumped to his feet. 'Come on, love. Get in, quick.'

She was still rubbing her eyes as she got in the back of the car. Alan bundled their cases onto the seat beside her and got in beside the driver. 'Thanks. How far are you going?' he gasped.

'Whitby. Where are you two off to?'

'Gretna Green. We're going to get married.' Alan turned and smiled at Sheila. 'Aren't we, love.'

'Yes.' She turned her head towards the driver and added, 'We haven't got to. I'm not expecting if that's what you're thinking. I'm not that sort of girl.'

'Good for you.' The driver said. 'Too many girls end up in trouble these days, if you ask me.'

'We didn't want to have to do it like this.' Alan sighed. 'But our parents said we had to wait, said we're too young.'

'So you decided to go to Gretna. I don't blame you. I should have married *my* first girlfriend. I know I'm only twenty-four but I wish I'd done things differently.'

The car pulled off the verge and bumped back onto the road.

'My name's Bob,' the driver said. 'You don't have to tell me who you are if you don't want to.'

'Not a problem. I'm Alan.' He turned in the seat. 'And she's…out for the count! Her name's Sheila.'

'You both look all in. Try and get some sleep if you can. I'll wake you up when I stop for petrol or a cup of tea.'

'Thanks. We've been asleep, I think, but I can still hardly keep my eyes open.' Resting his head against the window, Alan tried to make himself comfortable.

*

The change in sound as tyres moved from concrete to loose stones jerked Alan back from his dreams. He rubbed his eyes. 'Where are we?' Turning around he saw Sheila was awake. 'Hello, my love. Are you okay?'

'Yes, thanks. Not much room though, with these cases I mean.'

Bob grimaced. 'I can't make space in the boot, it's full, sorry. Never mind, let's go in for a bit of breakfast, shall we?' He waved toward the eating place. 'Come on, let's see what this place has to offer. Mind you, it can't be any worse than the last place I stopped at. Talk about indigestion.'

Sheila took hold of Alan's hand. 'I need the Ladies first,' she said. 'And I bet you need the Mens.'

He winced. 'You're right, I do.'

*

'Not bad. Not bad at all.' Bob dabbed his mouth with his handkerchief. 'What was yours like?'

'Good. Really good. I didn't realize I was hungry. Must be all the walking we did last night.' Alan grinned as he ran a finger around his plate.

'Mine was nice,' Sheila said slowly. 'But I reckon I could have made a better job of cooking it.'

'Yes,' Alan agreed. 'I bet your mum's going to miss you.'

'I know she will. I expect she's found my note by now. Hope she understands.'

'Note? I never thought of that. I just packed what I could and left.'

Sheila's eyes opened wide. 'So…your parents don't know where you are?'

'No. Do yours?'

'Not exactly,' she said, looking around the roadside café. 'I told them I was going to stay with you for a while. It's not really a lie is it, just not the whole truth. I can write to my Aunt Lil when we're settled, she always knows how far the fair is round the circuit. She'll let mum know I'm okay.'

'I bet my mum's worried sick. Why didn't I think about letting her know where we're going?'

'Don't worry, I'll remind you later.'

Pushing his plate aside Bob said, 'I think you two will do well together. In fact, I may be able to set you on the right path.' He turned towards Alan. 'That's *if* you're serious about getting a job. From what you've said your track record's not that great.'

'It's all got to change, I've got to knuckle down now,' Alan protested. 'Once we're married it's up to the man to bring in a decent wage.'

'Fair enough. Like I said, this could work out right for both of you. I'll have a word with my brother-in-law. He's started up a holiday camp just outside Whitby. There's bound to be a couple of jobs going. Anyway, that's enough for now, if you're ready, we should push on.'

*

Bob swore as his car hit a rut in the ground.

Alan woke with a start. 'What was that?'

Sheila sat up and rubbed her eyes. 'Where are we?'

'Sorry about the bump.' Bob drove over and stopped beside the petrol pumps. 'Bloody lorries. They churn the mud up when it rains, the sun comes out and it sets like cement.'

'I didn't know I was asleep,' Alan said, drowsily. 'Can we get another cuppa? I couldn't spit a sixpence.'

'Nor me,' Sheila agreed.

'You're in luck. Look, there's a woman selling tea in that shed thing. Can you see her?' Bob jabbed a finger against the windscreen. 'Get me one will you. Two sugars and plenty of milk.' He got out and spoke to the pump attendant. Putting his head back inside the car he said, 'I should have asked. Have you got the money for teas?'

Alan grinned. 'Yes, thanks. I've been saving up for weeks. I'll get them.'

'Okay. My turn next time we stop.'

Sheila nuzzled up against Alan as they waited to be served. 'Have you got enough to buy one of those buns? The ones with icing on and a cherry?'

'Of course. You can have anything you like, love.'

The woman batted a persistent wasp away as she handed Alan the sticky bun. Licking her fingers, she poured tea from a large enamel tea-pot. 'Help yourself to sugar,' she said, pushing a jam-jar across the counter. 'The spoon's on a string.'

Bob walked over and picked up a mug. 'Cheers.' He grinned. 'I filled up so we don't have to worry for a while. Now…about what I was saying before we pulled in here. The job would –'

Alan turned away from Sheila and apologised. 'Sorry, Bob, I didn't catch what you said.'

'Not a problem. My mother used to say I could put a wooden leg to sleep the way I go on. Bloody cheek.' He used the spoon to stir his drink. 'You sure you put two in?' Before Alan could answer Bob added some more and sipped. 'Right, drink up, there's still miles to go.'

*

'So, what do you think? I'm sure my brother-in-law will be up for it.' Bob glanced into the rear-view mirror.

'Sounds brilliant. And you reckon he'll be interested in giving Sheila a job as well?'

'I don't see why not. Especially if she can cook. He'll probably take you both on for a trial period, and then it'll be up to you to prove yourselves. But first I expect you want to get married. That was the plan wasn't it.'

'You bet. Our only problem is we've got to find somewhere to stay for a couple of weeks, to qualify for residency.'

'Not a problem. My sister lives in Rigg, she'll put you up. It's close to Gretna so it should work out. And if you get the jobs, he gives married couples accommodation.'

'Great. I can't believe it. At last something's going right for a change.' He turned and brushed his lips against Sheila's. 'We'll soon be man and wife.'

'There is one fly in the ointment,' Bob said. 'You'll need to pay for your digs and I'll have to ask you for petrol money to take you there. I haven't taken anything off you yet, because I'm not going out of my way.'

'It all sounds fair to me, and I always pay what I owe. We'll manage somehow.'

Chapter 27

'Alan!' Margaret Reardon yelled as she poured tea for the second time. 'Breakfast. Hurry up. It's getting cold.'

John Reardon stepped from the bathroom. 'What's all the bloody noise for?' he shouted down the stairs.

Removing the greaseproof paper cover from a jar of homemade marmalade, she ignored him.

'Oi, answer me! Is he *still* in bed, the lazy little sod?' John slipped both arms through his braces. 'I might as well save my breath. I'll get him up.'

Margaret closed her eyes and sighed. 'Here we go again.' She listened as a door banged.

'The bugger's not up here.' John descended the stairs, looking puzzled. 'It doesn't look as though his bed has been slept in. Did you know he was going to stay out all night?'

Standing with an open jar in one hand, she put the other over her mouth. 'What do you mean he's not there? Of course he is.'

'Do you think I'm stupid? He's *not* in his room. Go and see for yourself.'

Margaret rushed past him, still clutching the marmalade.

John helped himself to the toast and tea. Upstairs he could hear her scurrying around. Rubbing his hands together he smiled. *Please tell me he's out of my life at last.*

Margaret stood at the top of the stairs. 'He's gone! You were right, he hasn't been home.'

*

Margaret Reardon sat at the kitchen table. Dirty crockery threatened to spill out of the sink. The kettle on the range was empty, it's task of obscuring the windows with condensation complete.

John came clattering down the stairs. 'Breakfast ready?'

'Breakfast? How can you think of your stomach at a time like this?' Her face registered the distress she was feeling inside. 'He's been gone for two nights now.'

'And bloody good riddance I say. At least I'll get a bit of peace and quiet now without all that bloody jungle music of his.'

Crossing to the cupboard he sawed at a loaf on the drop-down flap. 'It's time I had a bonfire.'

'What for?'

'To clear his room of all his junk of course.'

'You wouldn't.'

'Wouldn't I? You just watch me.' He scraped dripping onto both slices and shook the salt-pot vigorously. 'Any tea?'

'The kettle's boiled.' She pointed across the kitchen. 'Help yourself.'

John picked the kettle up, dropped it and swore. Rushing to the sink he ran his fingers under the cold tap. Water hit the plates and saucepans splashing his shirt with the residue of previous meals. 'Now look, this is my last clean shirt!'

Despite her sadness, she managed to smile.

He scowled at her. 'That's it. Grin like a bloody Cheshire cat. The sodding thing's red hot. It's a wonder there's any bottom left.' Going back to the range, he used a cloth to retrieve the kettle.

She watched disinterestedly as he held it under the tap. 'They've asked me for a recent photo of Alan,' she said quietly. 'So I'm going back down to the police station.'

'What for? It's obvious he's left home. Why waste their time?'

'Because I think something must have happened to him, that's why. All of his records and most of his clothes are still in his room. If he's run away, why did he leave them?'

'So I can burn them at last.'

Margaret tied her headscarf beneath her chin, picked up her handbag and umbrella then opened the front door. Turning around she tip-toed back into the kitchen and picked up the tin she had just remembered. As she walked towards the gates guarding the estate, she saw Douglas pushing a lawnmower between the raised flower beds. Rex was lying in the shadows cast by tall flowers, watching his master at work.

She stopped to pat the dog. 'Hello Rex. Good boy.' Glancing up she called out, 'Good morning, Dad. The grass is looking nice.'

Douglas paused in his task. 'Hello, love. I'm trying to get this lot cut before the Heavens open again.' He stared up at the sky. 'Is there any news of Alan? Mr Lyonaisse was as concerned as me when he heard he'd gone missing. He's given strict instructions to MacIntyre to watch for intruders in the grounds.'

'No, there's no news I'm afraid. As a matter of fact, I'm just off to take his photo to the police station.' Glancing down at the brown paper carrier bag she was holding a blush came to her cheeks. 'He said they'd circulate it, now he's been missing so long.'

'Oh…I see. Anything I can do?'

'I don't think so. Thanks anyway.' She hesitated. 'Would you do me a big favour?'

'If I can. What is it?'

'I need to clear Alan's room. All his clothes and records. Everything. His father's threatening to light a bonfire and burn them.'

Douglas frowned. 'Why would he want to do that?'

'Try jealousy for a start.'

'Hmmm. So where do I come in to all this?'

'Perhaps you could make sure John's busy in the grounds then go in our house and take Alan's belongings out. It would be a great help.'

'Are you sure? And what am I supposed to do with it all?'

'Hide them in your shed? *Please,* Alan will be heartbroken if his records and things aren't here if….I mean *when* he comes back.'

'Fair enough. I've always got on well with Alan. I'm sorry I can't say the same about your husband. If he catches me…'

'He won't. Not if you find him something to do, as far away as possible.'

'Leave it to me. I'll sort something out. Alan is my grandson after all.'

*

Margaret approached the desk inside the police station. 'I was just passing and thought I'd pop in to ask George if there was any news. And I've brought the photo of Alan.'

The desk sergeant took the photograph from her and shook his head. 'George is not on duty at the moment. But I can tell you there's nothing new. Don't get too worried, it's early days yet. I'm sure Alan will turn up.' *Just passing?* The sergeant frowned. *On the way to where?* 'These things take time, you know,' he said. 'He'll be fine, you mark my words.'

Patricia pulled a round tin from her bag. 'Would you give this to George, please? It's a seed cake. I baked it myself. And can you ask him to let me have the tin back when he's finished with it.'

She wrung her hands together. Her wedding ring dug into her fingers. The ring was the result of letting her emotions get out of hand, something she constantly regretted. She loved her son; had done from the moment he was presented to her in the hospital bed. But love, or lust, and marriage had not gone hand in hand. Her husband's resentment grew in direct proportion to the love she showed for Alan.

Chapter 28

The man deftly swung the metal arm supporting a hose across the pavement. Removing the filler cap of the Hillman Husky he started the transfer of petrol. 'Three gallons did you say?'

'Eh? Oh…no, better make it four please.' Edward Stanton appeared distracted as he watched the man. 'And do you have a can I could buy? I'd like another gallon for my journey. Better safe than sorry as they say.'

'I think we've got one to spare.' The pump attendant turned towards the garage. 'Give me a minute and I'll take a look for you.'

*

In the kitchen, Douglas tested the seal of the Thermos flask by tipping it on its side and shaking. Picking up the sandwiches wrapped in brown paper he called up the stairs. 'Bye, dear, enjoy your bath. I won't be long. Just going to see how Brian's getting on and take him some lunch.'

Her muffled reply wasn't made any clearer by the echo of the small room. 'Bye, love. Brian's are the ones with tomato.'

The walk through the meadow was too pleasant to warrant anything other than a slow pace. Grasshoppers sprang up as he disturbed the grass, butterflies danced amongst wild flowers and grasses. High up in the sky a skylark sang of its joy to be alive on such a day.

Douglas set the flask and parcel down while he relit his pipe. Puffing contentedly, he resumed his walk with Rex beside him.

*

Edward Stanton also stopped and put his burden down. His obvious fatigue was entirely due to lugging an ex-army fuel can along the footpath leading from the village.

Douglas's flask and sandwiches were testament to the love he felt for his son.

The contents of Stanton's Jerry-can were the very antithesis. Revenge slopped back and forth as he walked towards the meadow.

*

Inside the refurbished dugout, Douglas watched Brian use a darning needle to ease the burning wick up through the lid of the ink bottle made into a lamp. The light level in the dugout changed from dim to bearable.

'What a clever idea,' Douglas said. 'I wouldn't have thought of that. And I'm surprised you got this shelter sorted out so quickly.'

'It wasn't as bad as I thought,' Brian replied, biting into a corned-beef sandwich. 'Thanks for these. Did you make them?'

'No. Your mum did. Speaking of which, we really would like you to start calling us Mum and Dad. I know you're still not sure, but it would mean so much to her.' Douglas swallowed. 'And to me.'

'I can try.'

'Well, I think the local Rabbi would show more enthusiasm if Bert the butcher put his pork sausages on special offer. But I'll have to be thankful for small mercies I suppose.' Douglas wiped his mouth with the back of his hand. 'More tea?'

'Yes please, *Dad.*'

Douglas smiled. 'That's better, *Son*.' He ran a finger around his shirt collar. 'Gets warm down here, doesn't it. Must be the lamp. Do you mind if I go out for a while? It's very stuffy.' Without waiting for a reply, he ducked his head and mounted the steps cut into the ground. 'You've made a good job of these,' he said, looking down at the lengths of wood wedged into position.

'Thank you. I seem to remember buildings like this during the war. Sometimes I wish I didn't.'

Douglas paused. 'Why? Surely anything that can help you recall your life must help?'

'You'd think so, wouldn't you? But let me tell you, some things really should be forgotten.'

'Your dreams, do you…What was that? Rex heard it too, look at his hackles.'

The dog growled deep in his throat and moved towards the entrance. Douglas followed. 'Won't be a minute, you stay where you are.'

Douglas stepped out of the shelter and stared at the man a few yards away. 'Good afternoon. Can I help you? Are you lost?'

Rex bared his teeth and growled.

Edward Stanton appeared surprised. 'Who are you? Is the dog dangerous?'

'Sometimes, he's a good guard dog.' Douglas placed a hand on the dog's head. 'I work here, but you're trespassing on private land. You're lucky the gamekeeper hasn't caught sight of you, he tends to fire his shotgun first and ask questions afterwards.'

'Does he. He sounds like someone best to avoid.'

Douglas caught sight of the can Stanton was holding. 'What on earth are you doing with that?'

Stanton looked back across the meadow. 'This? Oh, my car broke down. Out of petrol I think.'

'On Mr Lyonaisse's estate? There's only the front drive and that's way over there.' He turned and pointed with an outstretched arm.

'I got lost. I thought the main road was this way. Sorry if I'm intruding.'

'The village is back that way,' Douglas replied. 'About a mile and a half. The road you're looking for must be the High Street. And if I were you, I'd stick to the paths on your way back. Keep out of the woods.'

Brian appeared from his shelter. Stanton dropped his can and stepped forward aggressively. 'You,' he hissed. 'At last!'

Rex rushed towards him. Douglas grabbed the dog's collar. 'Hold it. What's going on? Brian, do you know this man?'

'No. I've never seen him before. Who is he?'

Douglas frowned. 'That's a good question.' He edged closer to Stanton. 'Just *who* are you and what do you want?'

Stanton forced himself to recover his composure.

'I told you, I ran out of petrol.'

'I don't believe a word. And why did you say, "You, at last." It seems a strange thing to come out with, unless of course you know my son. Do you? If not, what's your game?'

'I thought I recognised him. My mistake. I'll go now, sounds like I've got a bit of a hike ahead of me.' He turned and headed towards the village.

Father and son watched until the stranger was out of sight. Douglas put an arm around Brian's shoulder. 'Are you certain you didn't recognise him? It's obvious he thought he knew you, even if he did deny it.'

'No. I've no idea who he is. He seemed very angry though.'

'I suppose if he was telling the truth, about breaking down I mean, then he probably had good reason to be annoyed. He must have walked miles.' Douglas stared in the direction of the village. 'I wonder if he's the person who tried to kill you. Bit strange turning up with a can of petrol. I think you'd better not use this shelter of yours for a while. He could try again.'

'But I've never seen him before. Why would he do these things?'

'Who knows? But I'm going to report this to the police.'

*

Stanton looked back. Satisfied he was out of view of his intended target he hid the Jerry-can in crops lining the footpath. 'That's the second time you've been lucky,' he muttered. 'But I'll settle accounts with you yet.'

Chapter 29

Victor Whitehead held the envelope with one hand and slipped an ivory paper knife beneath the flap. The motif of the International Red Cross singled this letter out from the pile of invoices and cheques awaiting his attention.

It was the second such letter to arrive on his desk in as many weeks, but this time he was anticipating information, not more questions. He hoped the results of his diligent searches at the local library, added to a visit to the Public Record office, had been sufficient to fill the missing gaps in his original enquiry.

Smoothing the folded page, he read it again. 'That's right. I remember now…hmm, I didn't know….' He reached for his coffee. 'Now that's promising…the age is about right. I guessed she'd be in her twenties by now. That's *if* she survived.' The empty cup caught the rim of the saucer as he put it back without paying attention. He rattled his Parker pen between his upper and lower teeth, a habit acquired over the years whenever he became agitated. 'It *is* her. It's got to be. Most of this confirms…'

The office door opened and his secretary entered. 'More coffee?'

'Yes. Thanks, Carol.' He leant back in his chair and smiled.

'I saw you'd received another reply from the Red Cross. Good news this time?' She picked up his cup.

'It's certainly looking good. I've still got another page to read, but I'm certain I'm on the right track.' Opening a drawer, he pulled out a Michelin map and spread it out. Checking the letter, he traced a small area with his index finger. 'This makes sense…if it is her, she hasn't moved very far….it's where we were when we took a pounding from those German bastards.'

'Oh, very nice,' Carol said reprovingly as she returned with his drink. 'I thought you said it was good news.'

'Sorry. Mind you, anyone who was there would have had to have been a saint not to swear.'

She placed his coffee down. 'In Italy you mean? From what little you've told me –'

'Sorry to interrupt, do you speak any Italian?'

'Afraid not. Why?'

'I need to write to someone. But she probably doesn't understand English.'

'I had the same problem on the bus today.' Carol laughed. 'Where do they find these conductors?'

'The Commonwealth usually!'

'I asked for that, I suppose.'

'Right, now let's get back to my problem. Take an extra hour for lunch today and buy an English to Italian dictionary. Then I'll leave it to you to translate my letter.'

'Probably not a good idea. Why don't I contact the schools around here? One of them may teach Italian. I could get someone to do it for you.'

'Excellent. I'll pay for their time of course, and remind me to take you for a meal sometime.'

'Can I bring my husband?'

*

'How did it go?' Victor frowned. 'I tried to keep it simple.'

'It's fine. He was very knowledgeable about Italy. His speciality was ancient Rome and he made it sound interesting. Even to me.' She passed him the handwritten page. 'Would you like me to type it?' she asked. 'Or will you send this?'

'I think I'd prefer you to type it. Then we can hold onto this in case I have to re-send it for any reason. Who knows what the postal system is like in Italy.'

'That makes sense. I'll get started right away.'

'Thank you. As soon as you finish, I'll sign it. Then you can walk to the Post Office and get it sent by air-mail.'

Chapter 30

The teddy bears remained silent as Elizabeth Lyonaisse refreshed their food and drink. As a child she had left mince pies and a glass of water on the hearth of the inglenook fireplace for Father Christmas. Her parents had perpetuated this belief by removing the pies and emptying the glass while she slept. Nobody played this game with biscuits and orange juice. Mythical figures are one thing. Missing children are another.

She sat on the carpet, staring at the empty chair and sobbed. After a while she imagined the bears were mocking her. She glared at their cold eyes and hand-stitched smiles. *What are you all smiling about?* Getting to her feet she grabbed the nearest bear and shook it. Then she held it to her face and kissed its nose. 'Sorry, bear. It's not your fault. I know you were one of Susan's favourites. And Mary loved you too.' Putting him back in his chair she wiped away her tears and tip-toed from the room.

*

Turning the page, Elizabeth placed a hand on her book and gazed out of her bedroom window. Douglas was clipping a hedge. Rex lay on the path, watching his master at work. Everything seemed so normal. But how could it be? The relationship she had enjoyed with her daughter, Susan, and the magic of Mary's infectious laughter were missing.

She took a small glass bottle from the pocket of her skirt and unscrewed the lid. Picking up the glass from Mary's room she drank orange juice to wash down the tablets.

Each time she reached the bottom of a page she swallowed some more pills. She felt drowsy and had to concentrate to co-ordinate her hand movements.

The glass tumbler was empty. So was the bottle. Elizabeth sat slumped in her chair. Sunlight streamed through the window, gently warming her.

Downstairs, Carl took the tea-tray from Margaret. 'Here, let me,' he said, 'I was just going up to see Elizabeth.'

'I thought I'd take her some tea, and a piece of Madeira cake,' she replied. 'Patricia said a sparrow would have eaten more lunch than she did today.'

'Thank you. It looks very tempting.' He rubbed a hand up and down his stomach and smiled. 'And thanks again for all your help. Patricia has been a very good housekeeper over the years but I'm sure she appreciates all you do to help. We're all getting older aren't we, and she has that son of hers to care for now.'

Carl nudged the door to Elizabeth's room open with his foot and stepped in. Elizabeth sat with an open book on her knees. Seeing she was sleeping he turned to leave, but as he did a small bottle dropped from her hand. Puzzled, he put the tray down and moved towards her. Her chin rested on her breast as she slouched in the high-back wicker chair. Stooping down he retrieved the bottle. *Aspirin? Having one of your days again?*

Reaching out, he placed a hand on her shoulder. The sleeve of her summer dress was warm to his touch. Light, penetrating through lace curtains, dappled her face. 'Wake up, my dear. I've brought you some tea.' He stroked her hair. There was no response.

Carl looked at the bottle in his hand. Suddenly the realization of what she may have done hit him. He shook her, violently. The book fell from her lap. 'Elizabeth, how

many of these have you taken?' His heart raced, sweat formed on his brow. 'Oh my God!'
Stumbling down the stairs he yelled. 'Somebody call the doctor, Elizabeth's not well!' Carl slumped over the bannister as he reached the bottom of the staircase. 'Help me.'

Margaret was the first to reach him. Undoing the collar stud of his shirt she called out to Patricia and the butler.

The doctor removed his stethoscope. 'Your heart's a little irregular. But it's nothing to worry about. Now, as soon as we get your wife to my car, I'll drive her to the hospital.'

Carl shifted in the chair. 'Thank you. Will she be all right?'

'Too early for me to pass an opinion. If I knew how many tablets she'd ingested, I *might* be tempted to hazard a guess. As it is, we'll just have to wait.'

*

Two days later Carl was pleased to announce his wife had been moved to a private Convalescent Home following a brief stay in hospital. He didn't disclose the nature of her illness, but assured everyone she was making good progress and would soon be home.

Patricia was surprised at his instructions regarding the medicine cabinet, but dutifully added yet another key to her chatelaine after a lock had been added to its door.

Chapter 31

Carl assured the telephone caller Elizabeth was home again and doing well. He didn't go into the details of the orders he had issued regarding the close watch over his wife. 'I should have been more vigilant. I would never have forgiven myself if she…anyway, let's get back to your news.' He retrieved a cigar from an ashtray on the hall table. 'Are you sure, Victor?' His eyes widened as he held the phone closer to his ear. 'Yes? Well…in that case, go right ahead. I'll willingly share the cost.' Smoke lingered in the air around him. 'Let's hope there's been no mistake. After all these years, who would believe it? But I agree, if it *is* her then she could be a great help to Brian. Speak up…Anna? Her name's Anna. Yes, I got it, thanks.'

The cigar became a shadow of its former self before the conversation ended. Victor enthused about his search and the letters exchanged with Anna through an employee. For his part, Carl listened intently. He decided against passing the information to Douglas, reasoning it would do no good to raise his hopes then have them dashed to the ground if Victor were proved wrong.

*

Weeks later, Victor phoned again. The excitement in his voice was contagious. Carl was delighted to hear his news. 'Splendid. Well done. How is she?'

Elizabeth stepped into the hall. 'Who is it, dear?' she asked.

He put a finger to his lips. 'Later, my love, later. Sorry, Victor, that was my wife. Yes, she's fine now, thank you. Please carry on. When will you be able to bring this girl down?'

Elizabeth frowned.

Carl turned away from her gaze. 'Yes, fine by me. I look forward to it. See you both then…Goodbye.'

Crossing the hall, he took hold of Elizabeth's hand. 'Sorry, my love, I didn't mean to be rude. The line is playing up again, bit difficult to hear at times. How are you feeling today?'

'Much better thanks, and it's all right,' she said. 'You don't have to tell me who it was if you don't want to.'

'Nonsense. It's *not* a secret. Well, actually it *is*, but not from you. Let's go into my den and I'll tell you all about it.'

*

'So there you have it. You're as wise as I am now. Let's just hope Victor is right. He's arranged for her to stay with Nicholas's secretary for the next couple of weeks.' Carl shifted position in his chair and smiled.

Elizabeth sat with her mouth open. 'I can understand why you want to keep this quiet. How amazing. And you really think she's the one? What a shock it will be for Brian.'

Carl leaned towards her. 'My only concern is to make sure you are feeling well enough to have visitors. The last thing I want is to have you upset again. I really thought I'd lost you.'

'I am so sorry. Losing Susan so soon after Mary, things get on top of me at times. It was silly of me I know. It won't happen again.'

He kissed her gently on the cheek. 'That's a comfort to know, my love. I couldn't go on without you.'

'There's something, I –'

'Name it. I'll willingly do anything for you.'

She smiled. 'I was only going to say, I think you *should* tell the Millers. I understand your reasons for keeping it as a surprise, but it's not a good idea.' Her bosom rose and fell as she breathed deeply. 'Poor Brian will probably need time to recover when he's been told. You can't just produce someone from his past without warning him.'

'I did when I invited Victor to visit the first time.'

Elizabeth's smile returned. 'No, you didn't. You told Douglas.'

'I meant his son, Brian. It was a surprise to him.'

'Perhaps. But I expect his parents told him. Not that it seemed to have made any difference. He didn't recognise Victor, did he.'

'You're right as usual. I'll have a word with Douglas. He can decide whether to tell Brian or not.' He gazed up towards the ceiling. 'Better mention it to cook. She'll have to start swotting up on Italian food. I expect –'

Elizabeth laughed. 'Why would she need to? You surely haven't forgotten she's originally from Tuscany? I think she may have *some* idea of Italian cuisine, don't you?'

Carl closed his eyes and gently shook his head. 'Of course. It's such a shame her husband died so soon after they were re-united. All those years in a POW camp. It was probably our British weather finished him off.'

'Maybe. But they enjoyed the brief time they had together.' Her voice faltered. A tear trickled down her face. 'I can only guess how she must have felt when she lost him.'

'Please don't upset yourself, my love. Let's make this visit a wonderful day for everyone.' He fiddled with his wedding ring. 'Think how the poor girl must feel, coming to a strange country to meet people she doesn't know. Victor has put a lot of work into bringing her to see Brian, so we owe it to him to help her feel at home.'

*

Carl arranged for chairs to be put on the lawn. He sat next to Elizabeth. Douglas and Patricia were seated on either side of their son. Victor Whitehead and the household cook sat next to Anna. Folding tables, draped with white tablecloths and topped with jugs of iced cordial and sandwiches, formed informal divisions among the seating arrangements.

Carl lit another cigar. 'Cook, please ask Anna to tell us her story.'

The young woman's voice faltered at first, but with encouragement from the cook she gradually gained confidence. Cook intervened at suitable points to translate any words Anna had difficulty with, although her command of English was very good. Patricia and Douglas exchanged glances as the story unfolded. Brian sat bemused. Anna's hands became more animated as her excitement mounted.

Douglas eventually took his pipe from his mouth and tapped it in the palm of one hand. He glanced across the table. 'Are you certain Anna recognises Brian?'

'Yes.' Cook sighed in exasperation. 'As she just said, she owes her life to him.'

Brian reached out and grasped Patricia's hand.

'It's all a bit confusing,' Douglas replied. Facing Anna he said, 'Could you repeat it, please?'

They listened in silence as Anna repeated her story of how an English soldier had found her wandering in the rubble of her town. She told them once again how she had been wounded by the shelling and this soldier had carried her to safety. She had lost a lot of blood. Her neighbours had helped him attend to her wounds. He had not been able to stay with her, as he had to return to his men, she said. Fierce shelling forced her and her neighbours to stay in a cellar for days and she believed the soldier had probably been killed.

'And now you say Brian was that soldier? Are you sure?' Douglas looked at his son.

Anna looked surprised. 'Would *you* forget someone who save your life?'

'No. I suppose not. Please, carry on. Sorry I interrupted, but you must admit, it is all a bit unusual.'

Victor scratched his chin. 'I spent a lot of time checking the details. For my part I'm sure Anna's story is true. Don't forget, it was *me* who found *her*, not the other way round. If I hadn't tracked her down, she wouldn't be here to tell you her story.'

Carl smiled. 'And we're all very grateful you did.' He turned to Brian. 'Do you remember any of this?'

Brian stared at Anna. 'Yes…she's the girl who haunts me at night.'

Patricia gasped. 'Why? She said you saved her.'

He stared down at his feet. 'I was afraid it was Mary.'

Carl got out of his chair. 'Mary? Why would you –'

'Because the police took me away. I was outside.' He pointed across the lawn towards the gates. 'It was about the time Mary went missing. But I realize now I was having nightmares before that happened.' A rare smile replaced his worried look. 'And Anna's very much like the girl I always see.' He moved close to the shy girl and held out both hands. 'Thank you for telling me.' He turned to the cook. 'Please…make *sure* Anna understands how grateful I am to her.' Looking back towards Carl he said, 'The girl in my nightmares is covered in blood. She always runs towards me with her arms stretched out. I was beginning to think–'

'Nonsense, Brian.' Carl rose to his feet. 'No one *ever* connected you with what happened to Mary. After all, at the time we still believed you'd been killed in the war.' He took a deep breath. 'If George hadn't been off sick that day, a lot of what has happened to you may have been prevented.'

Victor gathered his thoughts. 'I must just say this. When Anna answered my letter, I was relieved to hear from her. Don't get this wrong, I've always had the utmost respect for

Brian, but the little Italian girl always troubled me.' He moved his attention to Brian. 'Awful things happened out there. If only you had told us what happened to her.'

Brian shook his head. 'I didn't tell you because I couldn't remember. But I do now, thanks to Anna.'

Victor smiled. 'Perhaps your other nightmares will leave you in peace too. As far as I'm concerned you gave your utmost for all of us. None of the lads who were killed would have blamed you, I'm sure.'

Patricia threw her arms around Brian. 'My poor, poor, boy. Now I can see why you have all those dreadful nights.'

'Victor,' Douglas said, 'I can't thank you enough. Perhaps Brian will cope better now he knows the truth.' He turned to Anna. 'And thank you, my dear, for making the journey to see us. I hope you will stay for a while. I'm sure Brian has a lot to talk to you about.'

Carl smiled. 'All taken care of, Victor and Anna are my guests for the weekend. I'm sure there'll be plenty of time for you all to talk.'

Chapter 32

Anna and Brian spent the rest of the day walking through the gardens of Oakwood House, talking and laughing as she struggled to find the right words. He showed her the shoals of golden fish in the ornamental pond. She told him about the fish market in the village where she now lived.

They lingered in the Italian garden, admiring marble statues brought back at great expense by Carl's father. She asked if they were ever to be returned.

After wandering through the delights of the rose gardens they sat on a wrought iron bench and basked in the late evening sun. She expressed her opinion on the weather in England, contrasting it with the Mediterranean climate. Brian laughed, but was inclined to agree with her.

*

As Victor and Carl sat in the comfort of his den, Carl sighed. 'It's nice to see Anna and Douglas enjoying each other's company, especially when you know what they've both been through. Pity it's such a short visit. Perhaps she could stay on here for a while?'

'Well, as you know, I have to go back, but I can see no reason why she can't extend her visit if she wishes to. I could come down and take her back when she's ready.' Victor tweaked his nose between thumb and finger. 'I can't really see any problem.'

Carl smiled. 'So, can I leave it with you? I'm perfectly happy to have her stay for as long as she wishes. She and Brian seem to be getting on like a house on fire. Douglas and his wife will be delighted.'

'Fine. I'll have a word with Anna and if it's what she wants I'll sort things out with Nicholas. I imagine your gardener and his wife must be happy to see their son act normally.'

'Yes, Douglas has already said how pleased they are to see Brian like this. Be a pity to split them up, you never know how things may work out.'

*

Next day Brian and Anna were up early. They met by the summerhouse as arranged and resumed their leisurely walks around the estate. They stood at the edge of the pond watching dragonflies hover above the surface as Brian explained how the pond had been the result of a flying bomb.

He spread out his jacket for her to sit on when they reached the meadow. She sat with her hands grasping her drawn up knees, gazing out across the expanse of grass and flowers. Brian lowered himself down beside her.

'So beautiful,' she murmured. 'This make a painting I think.'

'Yes. I love it here. We'll rest for a while then I will take you to my shelter.'

'For rain?' Anna looked up.

Brian laughed. 'No. It was something I felt I had to do when I came back home. It's hard to explain. Maybe the war –'

'War? I not want to see.'

'Oh…that's a shame. I put a lot of work into my shelter. Twice in fact, because I had to virtually rebuild it.'

Brian and Anna held hands at the kitchen table while Patricia fussed around them. The plate of sandwiches Anna had brought down from the Big House sat alongside Patricia's home-cooked fairy cakes.

'I think you're brave coming all this way to see Brian,' Patricia said. 'Fancy travelling all that way on your own.'

Anna looked at Brian. 'I am happy. I never see Brian since the Germans are coming.' She shuddered. 'We have a bad time. Better I forget.'

'Me too,' Brian agreed. 'Some things should be forgotten. It's a pity there's not a switch in your brain you can turn off every time you remember something you'd rather not.'

'I know not what you mean?' Anna frowned.

'He's just being silly,' Patricia said. 'Do have another cake. And are you sure you wouldn't like tea? It seems strange to see you drinking water while we have a hot drink.'

Brian got to his feet. 'I could go to the house and ask cook for some coffee.' He smiled at Anna. 'Dad only drinks *Camp* coffee. I'm not sure you'd like it. I certainly don't, but then I prefer tea anyway.'

'Thank you. Water is good.' Anna smiled. 'Also the…how you say? Cakes?'

'Why don't I wrap some sandwiches for you? You two could take them into the grounds.'

Brian stared out of the window. 'No, Mum. I'm going to the railway line. I still haven't got any train numbers for Dad.'

'Can't you do it another day?'

He thrust both hands into his trouser pockets. 'But I told Dad I would do it this afternoon.'

Patricia looked across at Anna. 'Would you like to go and see the trains with Brian? It's a nice walk.'

Anna smiled at Brian. 'Yes. I go with you.'

Outside the house, Brian slipped the strap of a khaki knapsack over his head. Once it had held a gas mask. Today: sandwiches, cakes and a bottle of Tizer. 'Come on,' he said pointing into the distance. 'It's not far and there are plenty of places for us to eat lunch. I went the other day to do some train-spotting.'

'I go with you. I am happy.' She squeezed his hand.

'Me too. I'll take my notebook for the train numbers.' He patted his jacket pocket. 'I must see if I can get at least one for Dad this time.'

*

'There it is. We can sit on the embankment.' Brian gently grasped Anna's arm as he pointed. 'There's a good view of the line and it'll give us plenty of time to get onto the bridge before any trains come along.'

Brian had tried explaining train-spotting to her as they walked and talked but she remained mystified. She asked why his father's hobby as a young boy was important to his own son who was a man. Brian was bemused too, lists of train numbers meant nothing to him. They both wondered why anyone would want to do such a thing. But Douglas had been enthusiastic and Brian was eager to comply with his wishes.

A mile down the road, on the other side of the bridge, Edward Stanton ran his hands through what was left of his hair. He kicked the flat tyre. 'I can't drive far on that,' he muttered. 'And I haven't seen an AA box round here, so I'll have to try and change it myself. Damn!' Wrenching open the rear door, he searched for his car jack and tools.

Reaching a patch of grass between gorse bushes, Brian spread out his jacket and invited Anna to join him. They sat holding hands, each waiting for the other to break the silence.

Eventually Anna spoke. 'This is a nice place. Thank you for carrying me here.'

'Bringing you,' he corrected. 'Yes, it is nice. Listen to the birds singing. It's so peaceful here.'

'How different it was when we meet. No birds, just bombs.' She released his hand and brushed her hair back out of her eyes. 'I never think I live. Bad things still come to me.'

He shuddered. 'I know. I still have nasty dreams too.' Looking straight ahead he said, 'Maybe you will forget.'

'And you? Will you forget?'

'Who knows?'

'You have family. In Italy family is important.' She gave a deep sigh. 'I miss my family much.'

'I lost mine too for a while.' He tapped the side of his head. 'In here. My mind was, well still is I suppose, messed up. The war you know. But Victor says I'm one of the lucky ones. Me, lucky? I'm not so sure. There are worse things than dying.'

Anna tipped her head back and gazed up at the sky. 'If not for you I would die. The people in my town tell me this. I must have many luck.'

'Much luck. Not many.' His forehead creased as he concentrated. 'I still don't remember rescuing you. Or much else either. But I'm glad Victor brought you to this country.' He pulled the sleeve of his shirt back and looked at his watch. 'I think there'll be a train coming soon. There was one about this time the other day. Let's get to the bridge. I don't want to miss it.' He stood up, held out both hands and gently pulled Anna to her feet.

As Edward Stanton tightened the final nut, a high pitch whistle sounded in the distance. He put the hubcap back in place and encouraged it to fit with the heel of his shoe. After wiping his hands on a rag, he wrapped it around the car jack and foot-pump. Placing them back in his car with his tool kit he slammed the rear door shut. Minutes later he continued his interrupted journey towards the railway bridge.

*

'Listen. Did you hear that? It's a train. Quick, let's get to the middle, I should be able to see the number from there.'

Anna gazed towards the sound of the whistle. Small clouds of smoke advancing across the countryside marked the train's journey. 'Yes. I can see.'

Brian leant the knapsack against the bridge and pulled a notebook from his pocket. Anna moved closer as the train came into view. She put an arm around him and edged him closer to the parapet as a car approached. Brian automatically turned as the vehicle passed. Stanton gasped as the two men recognised each other. He struggled to keep the vehicle under control.

'It's him again,' Brian shouted.

Anna clutched his jacket.

The tyres on the Hillman Husky smoked as the car ground to a halt. Stanton leapt from the car and ran back towards the bridge. Brian clenched his fists and pushed Anna away as the enraged man approached.

'You're the man with the petrol can.' Brian stepped forward to shield Anna. 'What do you want? Why do you think you know me?'

'I know *about* you,' Stanton snarled. 'Thanks to your cowardice, I lost my only son.'

Anna hid behind Brian, gripping his jacket, her face contorted with fear.

'How? I don't know who your son was.'

Stanton drew back his fist and lashed out. Anna quickly moved aside as Brian fell against the wall of the bridge. His arm took the full impact and was trapped against the brickwork by his body. Dazed by the unexpected blow,

Brian blinked, trying to clear his mind. He brought his knee up, but missed, succeeding only in making contact with Stanton's upper leg.

Stanton was possessed of a strength he had not thought possible as he forced Brian backwards over the wall. The train was closing the distance rapidly. Brian's shoes lost their grip on the road. Grabbing the brickwork, he held on. 'Get help,' he yelled. 'Quickly, Anna, go for help!'

'Too late.' Stanton's eyes bulged as his face grew redder. 'You jumped up little Caesar. Ordering men to defend a bit of ground. What the hell for. It was a complete waste of lives.' Taking full advantage, Stanton seized his victim by the throat. He smiled at the sight of the engine steaming towards the bridge. Arms outstretched, he pushed Brian further off the bridge.

The driver sounded a warning as the train thundered towards the drama being acted out ahead.

Spots of light danced in front of Brian's eyes; his heart raced as he fought to breathe. He was jolted back to his senses by a loud crack as something solid struck bone. Clouds of smoke billowed up, enveloping the two antagonists.

Anna swung the knapsack and struck Stanton a second time. He released his hold.

'Help me,' Anna cried. 'Brian!'

Brian coughed and winced as he tried to pull himself upright.

Stanton was on his knees with Anna standing beside him, the knapsack raised above her head.

'Don't,' Brian gasped. 'Don't hit him again.'

'But he try to kill you,' she protested. 'Why not I hurt him?'

'Because it's my turn,' he answered. Gripping the lapels of Stanton's jacket, he thrust his face to within inches of the other man's. 'Get this into your thick head. I *don't* know your son.' Releasing his hold, Brian stepped back and swung a fist. The punch caught Stanton squarely on the chin, jerking his head back. Brian spat on the road. 'You asked for that.'

Anna dropped her weapon and ran towards him.

Brian took the knapsack, grasped her arm and led her away. 'Thanks, you saved my life,' he panted. 'If you hadn't hit him, he would have killed me.'

She nestled closer and smiled up at him.

He held out the bag. 'I thought you had gone for help. What made you think of using this?' He laughed. 'I bet he's the first person to get a headache from Tizer.' He bent and kissed her. 'Well done. If I really did save you during the war, we are quits now.'

She frowned. 'What is quits?'

He smiled. 'I will explain later, let's just go home.'

'Not to polizia?'

'Good thinking.' Brian searched his pockets. 'I'll make a note of his car's number plate. It's not what I brought this pad for, but it'll come in handy just the same.'

She took hold of his hand. 'You are a brave man. I am happy I come to see you.'

Brian pulled her close. 'Not as happy as me. You have made me feel so much better. I don't want you to ever leave me.'

'But I have to go back. Victor has make the ticket for me.'

'Then he'll just have to tear it up. I need you to stay. In fact, I want to marry you. I know I am older than you, but not by much.'

*

The sergeant took down the details and the car's registration number. Bria told the officer the man who had attacked him was the same one his father had described in his statement concerning a can of petrol.

'I see.' The sergeant looked up from his notes. 'And you say you have no idea who this man is, or why he would try to kill you?'

'No. None at all. He said I was responsible for his son's death.' Brian shook his head. 'But I have never seen him before, apart from the day in the meadow when he turned up with a can of petrol. I now think he was the same man who tried to bury me.'

'Very possibly. We should be able to confirm it if we ever catch up with him,' the sergeant said. 'We took casts of the footprints. If they match this man's shoes, it will prove he was at the scene.'

The sergeant made notes of all Brian and Anna could remember about the struggle on the bridge. 'Seems to me it's time we had a word with this gentleman.' He sniffed. 'To start with I'll put out an alert for the car. Shouldn't be too hard to find from what you say. My guess is it's a Hillman of some sort, judging by your description. Not many of them around here.'

'But he could be miles away by now. Perhaps he's given up trying to kill me and gone back to wherever he came from.'

'Possibly. But we'll find him, don't you worry.'

Brian opened the police station door for Anna. His hand closed around hers as they walked away. 'Thank you for coming here. It means a lot to have you with me.'

She took her hand from his and put her arm around his waist. 'I feel the same,' she said, looking up at him. 'I tell Victor I am not ready to leave.'

'Did you? When? What did he say?'

'He say not a problem. He say when I tell him, he comes for me.'

Brian smiled. 'Good. I get the feeling he may be waiting a long time.' Putting his hands on her waist he picked her up and twirled her around. 'In fact, I think it will be a very long time.'

Chapter 33

Kit Carson, Indian agent, or to be more accurate, Tommy Green, crawled on his stomach through the long grass. Tommy used his elbows and knees to inch forward. He was tracking the renegade trading guns and fire-water to his friends, the Sioux.

Edward Stanton, who had unwittingly become Tommy's adversary, had no idea he was the target of a child's imagination, but the pair shared something in common.

Tommy was tracking a man in order to prevent imaginary dastardly deeds. Comic books, and Saturday mornings spent in the cinema, fuelled the drive to imitate his hero.

Stanton had just been prevented from exacting retribution for the death of his son.

One of these two was playing a game. The other was deadly serious.

A bell rang and Tommy turned his head towards the road. A tricycle was being pedalled by a man selling ice cream. He was wearing a light-weight white coat and an RAF side-cap. Tommy knew him well. Many times he had listened to stories of bomber raids over Germany and life in a POW camp. In return for his interest and patience as the tales were repeated over and over, he was usually rewarded with a free ice lolly.

Children emerged from nowhere and rushed towards this modern day Pied Piper. Seeing the crowd gathering around the trike Tommy realized the futility of trying his patronising subterfuge today. When he looked back the gun-runner had disappeared into the trees opposite the woods of the Lyonaisse estate.

Scrambling to his feet he jumped onto his imaginary horse and galloped after the man. One hand held out in front, clutching the reins, the other hand slapping his backside, he urged his mount on. Reaching the woods, he caught sight of his foe. He dismounted and tied his horse to the trunk of a silver birch tree. Keeping a careful eye on the man, he made his way from one hiding place to the next.

Edward Stanton sank onto a bench under the shade of a tree, used a handkerchief to mop his brow then checked the back of his head for the medical dressing nestling in his hair.

Tommy lay amongst bracken and peered at him from a safe distance.

Edward leant back, thrust his legs out and closed his eyes.

Suspecting it may be a while before his tracking skills would be needed, Tommy turned his attention to the insects living amongst the detritus on the woodland floor.

A millipede crossed the fallen leaves, legs rippling along the length of its body. Tommy held a twig in front of it and smiled as the creature sought to climb over. Suddenly his concentration was broken by the emergence of two stag beetles approaching each other on a piece of rotting wood. Fascinated, he watched them fight, antlers locked, much the same as their namesakes at rutting time.

Glancing up from this territorial battle, Tommy swore. The bench was empty. 'Bugger! He's got away. I bet he's gone to where he stashes his whiskey and guns.'

Running to the bench, Tommy looked up and down the woodland path. He was disappointed. Edward Stanton had moved on. But then his keen eyes spotted a silver object on the ground. As he picked up the sixpence, he was delighted to see other coins scattered around. 'Wow. This is better than the goldmine I found last week. Look at it all. There must be at least five bob.'

Kicking at the leaves he circled the bench. In the shadows, a black leather wallet was almost invisible.

But not to the eagle eyes of Kit Carson.

Tommy picked it up and opened the stud fastener. His smile threatened to stretch from ear to ear as he fingered its contents. 'Pound notes. I'm *rich*.' He sat on the bench and studied his find. Slowly the realization of what he was holding sank in. 'I can't keep all this. It's too much. I better take it to the cop shop and hand it in.'

*

The police station adjoined a pair of semi-detached houses providing homes for serving policemen and their families. A low brick wall divided the front gardens. Neatly trimmed rose bushes lined the edges of the lawns.

In stark contrast, grey cobblestones fronted the approach to the station.

Outside the main building, a glass-fronted notice board displayed a colourful warning, describing Colorado beetles and what to do if they were found.

Tommy placed a hand on the gate and vaulted over, caught the toe of his shoe and crashed to the ground. He sat picking tiny pieces of stone from his knees. Spitting on his hands he winced as he rubbed the injuries.

'Hello, Tommy.' The desk sergeant smiled. 'What have you been up to now?'

'Nothing, sir, I found something.' Tommy emptied the pockets of his short trousers. A grubby handkerchief joined a length of string on the counter. A sticky boiled sweet, attached to a fair amount of pocket-fluff, sat amongst a group of marbles.

'Watch it.' The officer pushed Tommy's treasures back. 'What are you doing? The cleaner will have your guts for garters.'

Tommy finally produced the wallet. 'Here it is. Is there a reward? There should be.'

Carefully picking it up between thumb and finger the sergeant swallowed. 'Was it in this state when you found it?'

'Sort of,' Tommy mumbled. 'It's got loads of money in it.'

Reaching beneath the counter the sergeant produced a yellow duster and proceeded to wipe the leather. 'That's better. Now, let's see what you've found.'

Tommy's mouth hung open as he watched the money being counted. 'You're right, Tommy. There's a lot of money in here. Well done, lad.'

'I hope the man's grateful when he gets it back,' Tommy said. 'It's more than a whole year's pocket money all at once. Especially when it gets stopped for things that get broken even when you're nowhere near them when it happens. There ought to be a law –'

'I dare say the owner will give you something.' As he spoke, the sergeant examined the contents. 'A lot of people would have been tempted to keep this. Did you see anyone near where you found it?'

'I might have done. I was tracking a man but he got away while I was watching some Stag beetles. It was great.' Tommy put his belongings back into his pocket. As coins jingled his cheeks flushed. He shifted his weight from one foot to the other.

'But you didn't recognise this man?' The sergeant shook his fountain pen, used a piece of blotting paper to soak up an ink blot, and filled in a small form.

'No. He's not from around here.'

'I see. And where exactly did you find this wallet?'

'It was in the leaves, behind the bench. The one in the woods, by the pond.'

'By…the…pond,' the sergeant said as he wrote. Satisfied with his work he signed it with a flourish. 'And did you find anything else?'

Tommy swallowed. 'No, sir. Just that.'

'Thank you. Now, sign your name here. We keep things for six weeks, then, if they've not been claimed, the finder gets to keep them.'

'Wow. I get *all* the money?'

'Yes, Tommy. Remember what they teach you in Sunday school. Honesty is the best policy.'

Tommy took the coins from his pocket. 'I found these too.'

The sergeant frowned. 'But I've filled in the report now...oh, you keep it. Buy yourself an ice cream.'

'Thanks.' Tommy scooped up the coins and ran before the man changed his mind.

'And don't go putting your head through any railings,' the sergeant shouted. 'Not with ears like yours.' Shaking with laughter he picked up the wallet and checked its contents once more. Taking out a newspaper cutting, he scratched the side of his head. 'Must be somebody local,' he muttered. 'Who else would be interested in the coach crash?'

*

Edward Stanton searched his pockets. The woman serving him leaned forwards and rested her ample bosom on her arms. The glass counter top creaked. She smiled as she waited patiently. 'Can't find it, dearie? You must have left it at home. Happened to me once. Was my face red.'

Edward tapped his jacket. 'I thought perhaps my wallet had slipped through into the lining. But it hasn't, it's gone. How embarrassing.'

'Oh, well, never mind, dear. Worse things happen at sea.' She undid the twirled corners of one bag, removed the crusty rolls and put them back in a wicker tray. Undoing the second bag she took out a doughnut and shook her head. 'Can't put this back,' she said. 'Half the jam's stuck to the bag.' Edward watched in dismay as scarlet lips parted and what should have been part of his late lunch was bitten into with relish. 'Mmmm, lovely,' the woman mumbled, wiping sugar off her chin.

Edward opened the shop door.

'Bye, love, I hope you find it,' the woman called after him. 'I close at five.'

He stepped into the street without acknowledging her parting words. Outside the baker's shop, Edward checked all his pockets again. With a deep sigh he turned and headed back towards the woods.

*

Striding through the woods he scrutinised every inch of the tree-lined path. Pausing now and then he used a stick to poke dead leaves. Each search brought the same response. 'Damn!'

He sat on the same bench, emptied his pockets and groaned. 'Apart from what I left in the holiday cottage, all my money is in my wallet. Where *could* I have lost it? Damn!' Gathering up what was left of his loose change, along with his keys and handkerchief, he slapped his forehead. *I know. I'll try the police station. Perhaps it's been found and handed in.*

Chapter 34

Agnes looked around the circle of women in the village hall.
'Good morning, ladies. I'm afraid I have some grave news.'
She paused, waiting until she was sure she had everyone's
attention. 'As you can see, Mrs Reardon is not here today.
She came to the vicarage to tell me her son has run away
from home.' Her audience stared at each other in disbelief.
'At least that's what she's pinning her hopes on, poor dear.
The alternative is too terrible to contemplate.'

Mrs Harrington was the first to break the stunned silence.
'Oh dear. How distressing. My heart goes out to her. Just
wait until I tell my Bert.'

'It's lucky Mrs Lyonaisse couldn't make this meeting.'
Agnes sighed. 'This will bring back the loss of her
granddaughter, I'm sure.'

'But little Mary, god bless her, didn't run away,' Mrs
Harrington replied. 'She was taken and probably –'

'Yes, yes.' Agnes scowled. 'And now we have a second
child on their estate who's gone missing. Let's hope there's
no connection.'

Tommy's mother stopped knitting. 'What are the police
doing about it?'

'They've been very prompt, Mrs Green. Mrs Reardon
gave them a photo and they've sent it to the police station
where the Reardons lived before moving here. The chances
are Alan misses his friends and has returned to the area of
his old home.'

A general discussion ensued about the validity of this
assumption. Opinions were divided.

Agnes coughed politely and called the meeting to order. 'I
am sure we will all make an effort to support Mrs Reardon,
and, I know I needn't say this, but please…if you do see or

hear anything out of the ordinary, please let the police know straight away.'

'You said you hoped there was nothing to link Alan with Mary. Why was that?'

Agnes peered over the top of the notes she was holding. 'I didn't mean to imply there *was* a connection. But there could be. Two missing children in two years?'

'Pure coincidence if you ask me.' Mrs Harrington stared at her watch. 'I don't wish to be rude, but isn't it time to get down to business. There aren't many weeks left before the garden fete.'

Mrs Green stood up. 'I can't stay. Sorry, Agnes, but my Tommy's out playing somewhere. I need to find him and warn him –'

'I quite understand.' Agnes wagged a finger towards her audience. 'If I had children, I would feel the same way. But I'm sure there's nothing to worry about. After all, Alan Reardon is not a vulnerable young child. He's almost a grown man.'

'I know, but I can't help worrying.' Tommy's mother looked flustered. 'And you all know what my Tommy's like. If there's any trouble it's sure to seek him out.'

'More likely the other way round,' one of the other women muttered under her breath. The woman sitting next to her smiled.

Mrs Green waved a hand as she headed for the door. 'Bye everyone.' As she passed Agnes she said, 'Sorry about this. I'm sure somebody will tell me later what's been decided for the fete.'

*

Tommy looked guilty. His hand-knitted jumper bulged, giving a glimpse of the shape his body would probably assume later in life. 'They're windfalls, Mum. Honest.'

'I never said anything about apples, I'll get to that in a minute.'

Tommy screwed up his eyes. *Now what am I supposed to have done? Was it...no, she can't have found out about that. Perhaps it's the milkman's horse...*

'I want you to keep an eye out for strangers and don't talk to them,' she continued. 'Alan Reardon hasn't come home and his mum's worried sick. There may be someone –'

Tommy breathed a sigh of relief. 'Don't worry, Mum. I never talk to strangers. You've told me before.'

'I know. You're a good boy. It's just...well... do you remember Mary and what happened to her?'

'What did happen? You never told me.'

'Because I don't know, nobody does. That's why I want you to be extra careful when you're out playing. If you see any strangers you're to come home straight away. It's no good me telling you to stay indoors, I know I'd just be wasting my breath.'

Tommy grinned. *I don't think the drainpipe would take my weight again.* Then his expression changed. 'There was a man the other day. I was tracking him and I think he lost his wallet. At least, I'm pretty sure it must have been his.'

'Lost his wallet? Does he live around here?'

'Don't think so. I've never seen him before. But he's going to give me a reward.'

She grabbed his shoulder. 'What for? Don't you dare take money from strange men.'

'Of course, I won't,' Tommy protested. 'You know the man in the cop shop, the one who came round about the greenhouse window that smashed when I was helping an old lady to cross the road. Well, he said I'd get a reward for handing in the wallet I found. There was loads of money in it.'

'Oh.' She ran her fingers through his hair. 'Well, you *do* deserve a reward for being so honest. Well done.'

'Can I go now?'

'Yes, just be careful. And put those apples in the kitchen. I'll make an apple pie if I find time. But if you've stretched your jumper –'

'Bye, Mum, see you later.'

'And don't speak to anyone you don't know. Do you hear me?'

'Yes, Mum.'

*

Margaret Reardon stood talking to George outside the police station. 'I met Mrs Green earlier, on her way home from Agnes's meeting about the garden fete. She's very worried about Tommy, frightened to let him out of her sight.'

George frowned. 'Why?'

'People are beginning to say perhaps my Alan and Mary Bridlington could be…could be…you know what I mean. They're saying perhaps the same person's responsible for both of them going missing.'

'Are they? Mary's disappearance has never been solved, I grant you that. But Alan's a teenager. They do these things.'

'What upsets me most, is he never even left me a note.'

'Perhaps he did. Have you considered you just haven't found it yet?'

Margaret smiled for the first time since Alan had left. 'Do you really think so? I'll go home right now and have a thorough search. Thank you, George.'

He watched as she hurried away. *So, people are linking things together, are they? I suppose it's possible, but…* The whistle from the boiling kettle in the tea-room broke his chain of thought.

Chapter 35

The High Street, as it had been so grandly named, was busy with housewives going about their daily shopping for fresh vegetables, bread and meat.

The fishmonger was struggling with a pole, trying to extend a blue and white striped blind.

Outside the toy-shop, children had chalked squares with numbers inside them on the paving stones and were engrossed in their game.

Brian bought a newspaper and sat on a bench, reading. His jaw moved rhythmically as he chewed. The shopkeeper had broken the bar of Palm toffee with a hammer and given him the pieces in a paper bag. Brian slid along to make room for two older women clearly intent on sharing the seat with him. They were already deep in conversation as they sat down.

'Yes, that's right. Fancy stealing from his own mother,' one of the pair exclaimed.

'But who said so?' the second woman demanded.

'I don't know. It's just what I was told. They said he emptied her purse and ran off.'

'I don't believe it.'

'Please yourself. But don't forget Alan Reardon's one of those Teddy Boys you read about in the papers.'

'Oh…I didn't know they –'

Brian folded his paper and stood up. 'Don't believe all you read, ladies,' he said. 'I know Alan and I owe him my life. Remember what they say, you can't judge a book by its cover.' Thrusting his newspaper under his arm he walked away before either of them could reply.

Passing the barbershop, he paused to straighten his tie. A vehicle mounted the kerb behind him. The two women on the bench jumped to their feet and screamed. Mothers pushing prams grabbed other children and ran. There was a noise like a clap of thunder. It reverberated back from the buildings as a cast-iron lamp post brought the Hillman Husky to an abrupt halt.

Stanton's head hit the windscreen, cracking the glass with the force of the impact. Broken headlights and pieces of chromed metal lay in a spreading pool of hot oil. Brian stared at the wreck. Through the wall of steam escaping from the car's radiator, he recognised the driver.

Racing to the car, a young man wrenched open the driver's door and switched off the ignition. He leant in to assist the injured driver. Mr Green rushed out of his shop to lend a hand. Between them they managed to extricate Stanton and prop him up against the shop wall. Mr Green loosened Stanton's tie. The other man used a handkerchief to dab at blood trickling from cuts above his eyes.

'What happened?' a pale faced woman asked, gripping the arm of her friend. 'I was looking the other way when I heard the crash. Did it skid?'

'It may have done, but I'd say it was deliberate,' her companion replied. 'That young man,' she added, pointing at Brian, 'was lucky, another couple of feet and he'd have been run over. Somebody should call the police.'

'I already have,' Mr Green shouted. 'And there's an ambulance coming too.'

Stepping proudly from the police car, George replaced his helmet and waited for the driver to join him. 'I enjoyed that,' he said, smiling. 'Makes my poor old bike seem a bit dull. And the bell of yours puts mine to shame.'

'I put in for a faster car months ago, but they said we had to wait until this thing gives up the ghost. I can't wait,' the sergeant said, a touch of despondency in his voice.

'One at a time, please. Can you form a queue?' The sergeant nodded towards George. 'If you could just tell my colleague what you saw, it would be most helpful. Thank you.'

George tugged at the hem of his jacket, checked his whistle and produced a notebook.

The sergeant moved to where Stanton was receiving first aid. 'Good morning, gents. How is he?'

The man bending over Stanton stepped aside. 'He's okay. And there's an ambulance –'

Pointing at Stanton the sergeant said loudly, 'You're the man who came into the station to claim a lost wallet less than an hour ago. What happened?'

'I lost control,' Stanton muttered, 'I must have hit something on the road.'

'I see. I'll go and check for my report. You seem to have got away with just cuts and bruises, it could have been a lot more serious.' Turning away he walked towards the vehicle embracing the ornate lamp post. Children peering through the windows of the car, reluctantly moved aside as he approached.

He stopped at the rear door and frowned. 'That's the same number Brian Miller gave when he reported the incident at the bridge. I'd bet my stripes on it.' Stepping off the kerb he walked up and down the road. Apart from obvious evidence the milkman's horse had recently passed through the village, the road surface was clear.

'I phoned to cancel the ambulance,' Mr Green said to the sergeant as he returned. 'He's going to be fine. There's nothing much wrong with him a nice strong cup of tea won't put right. My wife's got the kettle on.'

'Good thinking, thank you. It would be a shame for them to come out on a wild-goose chase.' He stared down at Stanton. 'If you're feeling up to it, I'd like to ask you some questions, sir.'

'My car. How bad is it?' Stanton groaned.

'Is it *yours*, sir?'

'Yes, of course it is. I need to get it to the garage.'

'All in good time, sir. As there is nothing on the road that could have caused this accident, I will have to ask you to accompany me to the station and answer some questions.'

'Why? What for? I can pay for any damage.' Stanton's face betrayed his concern.

'I would rather not say, sir, not in public. Please come with us.' He pointed towards the police vehicle.

'But my car?'

'It will be taken care of in the fullness of time. You're lucky the lamp post stopped you. If you'd hit the petrol pump at the garage, chances are you'd have gone up in flames. Grab an arm, constable, help me get Mr Stanton into the car.'

*

George put the tray of tea onto the table, then pulled a chair free and sat next to the sergeant. Opening a lined notepad, he licked the end of a pencil. After writing Stanton's name and address, the date and time, he raised his head. 'Ready when you are, sir.'

The sergeant waited for Stanton to help himself to one of the drinks. 'Right, sir. Now, let's see if we can clear a few things up. There has been a report of an assault by someone seen driving a car. The description and registration of the vehicle involved matches yours. The attack was reported to have taken place on a railway bridge not far from here. What can you tell me?'

Stanton glared at his accuser. 'There must be some mistake. Do I look like somebody who would attack anyone?'

The sergeant took a quick look at the man sitting opposite. 'No…I can't say you do. But the fact remains, a Mr Miller has accused you, so I have to investigate his claims.'

'Waste of time. The man is obviously confused or making up the story for some reason. I wasn't there and I don't know a Mr Miller.'

'I think you do, sir. The person with Mr Miller at the time of the incident confirmed his story.'

'So…it's their word against mine.'

'Yes, and the statement given by a train driver. He said he saw you struggling with Mr Miller and it appeared you were intent on pushing him off the bridge onto the line in front of the three o'clock train to London.'

'Rubbish. How could a train driver inside his cab see well enough to identify anyone up on the bridge?'

'So, you admit to being there?'

'No, I most certainly do not.'

'If you weren't there, why question the ability of one of the witnesses to see you?'

Stanton took out a handkerchief and wiped his brow. 'I was speaking hypothetically. I've already told you, I wasn't there.'

The sergeant drummed his fingers on the desk. 'Let me ask you this. How do you explain trespassing on the estate belonging to Mr Lyonaisse carrying a container of petrol?'

'I told the men I met. I ran out of fuel. I bought a gallon and a can. I was returning to my car and got lost.'

'Not true, sir. The petrol pump attendant said after you bought the fuel and the container, you drove off with it. How do you explain that?'

'I don't have to. Again, it's his word against mine. Anyone could have bought a can of petrol. It's not against the law.'

George emitted a sigh. 'He's right, sir. It isn't.'

Frowning, the sergeant said firmly, 'I know that.' Turning his attention back to Stanton he continued. 'Tell me what you were doing on the same estate on a previous occasion. An endeavour was made to take the life of the same Mr Miller who is now accusing you of assault.'

'This is getting monotonous. I haven't been there, apart from the day I ran out of petrol. Who said I was?'

'Nobody. We are waiting for witnesses to come forward. But we do have reason to believe someone matching your description was present.'

'At the risk of sounding repetitious, I wasn't. You've obviously got me mixed up with someone else.'

'Maybe.' The sergeant picked up his cup and drained it. 'One last thing, sir. I'd like you to remove your shoes.'

Stanton placed his hands flat on the table. 'Pardon? What on earth for?'

'We made plaster casts of footprints at the scene of the crime. If you would kindly let my colleague check your shoes, we can eliminate you from our enquiries.'

Stanton put a finger down his shirt collar and swallowed hard. 'What nonsense. I'll do no such thing.'

'Then I'm afraid I will have to insist.'

Stanton pushed his chair back, leant down and untied his shoelaces. Handing them to George, he snapped, 'Here you are. What a waste of time. I shall be speaking to a solicitor about this.'

Taking the proffered shoes, George turned them over and examined the soles as he left the room.

The door opened and George entered.

'Do they match?' the sergeant asked.

'Yes, sir. The positioning of the Blakey's Segs hammered onto the soles and heels are as good as a fingerprint. These shoes match our casts one-hundred-per-cent.'

Resting his elbows on the table, the sergeant placed the tips of his fingers and thumbs together and said in a measured tone, 'Edward Stanton, I am arresting you on two counts of attempted murder. You do not have to say anything. But it may harm your defence if you do not mention when questioned something which you later rely on in court. Anything you do say may be given in evidence.'

Stanton pushed at the table as he jumped up. 'Call this justice,' he shouted. 'What about the man who killed my son? Why isn't he being charged?'

George moved swiftly and grasped Stanton by the arm. 'Come along, sir. Please be careful, we wouldn't want you to hurt yourself, would we.'

Chapter 36

Bob took one hand off the wheel and knuckled his eyes. Leaning forward he stared into the gloom. Swollen rainclouds, disgorging themselves indiscriminately far and wide, ensured it was dark as night. Windscreen wipers valiantly ploughed through the rain pelting down. Oncoming lights turned raindrops running down the glass into bright points of colour. Water pulsed beneath the car, surging around the wheel arches, lashing against the underside. Behind him, on the back seat, Alan and Sheila slept blissfully, completely oblivious of the battle raging between man and the elements.

Bob was concentrating on the tail lights of a vehicle ahead. The two red dots, as hypnotic as a snake's eyes, gave him a point of reference in the gloom. As he watched, the lights became brighter and he realized the driver ahead was applying his brakes. Bob did the same, taking care not to react too fast and send the car aquaplaning. A gentle squeeze of the brake pedal followed by a firmer downward pressure caused the car to shudder.

The gap between the vehicles narrowed rapidly, the car in front moving to the left. Through the rain, Bob finally saw the glow from its indicator arm and at the same time became aware of pools of light swamping the forecourt of a café. He gave a huge sigh of relief. '*The Lucky Ace!* I thought there were miles to go before we got here.' He followed his pathfinder over the cracked tarmac and swung in beside it. Steam rose from the bonnets of both cars as cold rain battered hot metal.

'Bloody glad to find this place,' the other driver said, holding a folded newspaper over his head while he locked his car door. 'Bugger this for a game of soldiers.' Without waiting for Bob to reply the man hurried off towards the bright lights of the café. Through patches cleared in the condensation cloaking the windows, Bob could see people eating. Others were talking, but he couldn't hear them. It was as if he was watching an old-time silent movie to which somebody had added colour. He almost expected subtitles to appear along the bottom of the windows.

Opening a back door of his car he leaned in and shook Alan. 'Wake up, you sleeping beauties. Lunchtime.'

Sheila stirred. 'What?' She tried to sit up but Alan's body was resting heavily on hers. 'Alan. Wake up. You're squashing me.'

He blinked and raised his arms above his head until his fingers bent against the roof lining. 'Sorry. I was –' His next words were eaten by a large yawn.

'Here's the keys,' Bob said, tossing them onto Alan's lap. 'It's chucking it down out here. I'm going inside before I drown. Make sure you lock the car.'

'Thanks,' Sheila replied. 'We'll be right behind you.'

'I didn't know this was a pantomime.' Alan grinned.

*

Bob's stomach greeted the smell of cooking by emitting a low growl. He turned and closed the door against the weather. The Open/Closed sign rattled against the glass. Cigarette smoke mingled with blue haze from the hot grill at the rear of the kitchen area. Bob joined the queue and shuffled towards the counter.

He glanced at Sheila as she entered. She was holding Alan's jacket over her head. The rain turned Alan's shirt transparent as he held the door open for her. Sheila turned and fluttered her eyelashes as she handed him his coat. 'Thank you, Alan. You're a real gentleman.'

Putting it back on, he shivered as the garment forced his wet shirt against his skin. She kissed his cheek. Her action was greeted by wolf-whistles and ribald comments. Alan clenched his fists and stepped towards the nearest table. 'What's your problem, mate?' he demanded.

Sheila clutched his sleeve. 'Don't. He didn't mean anything. Besides, I'm used to it, working at the fairground. Come on, let's get something to eat. I'm starving.'

Alan glared at the two men tucking into their meal and shrugged his shoulders.

'I wouldn't advise starting anything in here,' Bob said, quietly. 'A lot of these drivers are regulars. I've seen them before. Any trouble and they'll stick together. I tell you, it's not worth it.'

Alan frowned. 'If I had my mates with me, we'd soon sort them out.'

The wall beside the counter was a working man's picture gallery. Colourful comic postcards which must have challenged self-righteous censors up and down the land. Alan's grin widened as he got closer and was able to read the punch lines. Sheila dug her fingers into his ribs. 'Don't go getting ideas. We're not married yet.'

Alan reached down and patted her backside. 'It's only a bit of fun. I wonder if the artist who did the drawings made up all the jokes?'

'Stop staring at them, we're next. Bob's just getting served.'

Bob wiped his plate clean with a slice of bread. Baked beans, egg yolk and brown sauce were mopped up, the bread folded in half and bitten into with enthusiasm. 'Don't know about you two, but I thought that was just what the doctor ordered.' Reaching over to an adjoining table he helped himself to a newspaper.

Sheila dabbed her lips with her handkerchief. 'Yes, it was.'

Alan put down his large mug of tea. 'I was going to –'

Bob pushed the folded paper across the table, one of his nicotine-stained fingers stabbed a small article at the bottom of a page. 'This could be you. Where did you say you two were from?'

Sheila grabbed the paper. 'Where? Oh, I see…You're right. Fancy them putting it in the papers.' She turned to Alan. 'I said you should have left a note. Now the police are looking for you.' Sliding the paper towards Alan, she looked at Bob. 'What should we do? Shall we call the police and tell them where we are?'

'You could do, Pet,' he replied, lighting a cigarette. 'Depends if you two want to get hitched. If the law get involved, they'll drag you both back home. Then what will you do?'

Alan thumped the table. Knives and forks clattered against plates. A sauce bottle toppled over. 'I bet that's my bleeding dad.' His forehead furrowed. 'No, I've changed my mind. It wouldn't be him, he'll be glad to see the back of me. It must be mum.'

'If you want my advice,' Bob said, blowing smoke from the corner of his mouth, 'You should contact your mother and put her mind at rest. I've got change if you want to use the phone.' He turned in his chair and pointed over his shoulder. 'It's on the wall, back there.'

Alan shook his head. 'No thanks. If I do, she'll call the coppers and get us hauled back home.'

Sheila placed a hand on his arm. 'You *should* tell her. Imagine what she's thinking, you going off without a word. She must be worried stiff.'

Bob tapped ash from his cigarette onto the floor. 'I agree with Sheila. Tell you what, why not write instead? That way you don't have to speak to her and it'll give you more time to get hitched.'

Alan jumped to his feet. 'Good idea. I'll be back in a minute. Do you want another tea either of you?'

Alan pointed at the saucy cards pinned to the wall. 'Excuse me, do you sell postcards?'

The woman behind the counter laughed. 'Sorry, my love, no we don't sell these. They're the ones our regulars send us. The cheeky monkeys, as Al Read always says.'

'Oh. Thanks anyway.'

'We do get a few others, scenic views and such, but customers prefer the saucy ones. I suppose they're what you're after.'

'No, not really. I need to write to my mother. I thought I could send her a card to let her know I'm all right.'

'Just wait a minute, love, I may be able to help you.' She disappeared through a door at the rear of the kitchen area. Minutes later she came back with a shoe box and rummaged through its contents. Eventually she found what she was looking for. Pulling it out, she held towards Alan. 'There it is. I knew it was in there somewhere. Perhaps you could use it for your mum.'

Alan took the card from her. 'But it's been used,' he said. 'I can't send her that.'

'I don't see why not,' the woman retorted. 'It's from old Josh. You can see he's as careful with ink as he is with money. If his writing was any smaller, you'd need a magnifying glass to read it.'

Alan smiled. 'I see what you mean.'

'So…just cross out the address and the message then use it again. Stick a new stamp over the old one and Bob's your uncle.'

'Actually,' Alan grinned. 'He's not. He's just giving us a lift.'

'Pardon?' The woman looked confused. 'Now you've lost me.'

'Never mind. It was meant to be a joke. How much for this card?'

'Nothing, love, you're welcome to it. But if you want a stamp, I'll take the money for that.'

'Thanks. Yes, please, I'd like a stamp if you've got one to spare.'

Alan offered the card to Sheila as he sat down. She pointed to the picture. 'This is Blackpool,' she said, 'Our fair's been near there a lot of times. I went on the pier once, it was great.' Turning the card over she exclaimed, 'Why did you get this? It's been written on. Haven't they got any new ones?'

'It's okay. Look, there's plenty of room left. I just need to scribble out those bits. I'm only going to tell my mum I'm safe, not write my blinking life story.'

'Don't have a go at me, I was only trying to help.'

'I know. I'm sorry. It's just I wish now I'd left her a message. You're right, I should have done.'

'Never mind.' She smiled. 'You write the card and we'll get it posted as soon as we can.'

Bob stubbed out his cigarette. 'Sounds like a plan, Pet. I'm sure we'll find a pillar box before too long.'

'Cheers, Bob. Have you got a pen?' Alan held out his hand.

Pulling a fountain pen from his breast pocket Bob passed it to him. 'Try not to cross the nib. It's gold plated.'

'Is it? That's a bit posh.' He crossed out the miniscule writing on the card. Looking up, he said, 'By the way, who is Al Read?'

'He's a comedian. He's got a radio show on the Light Programme. He's very popular, you must have heard of him, surely? Anyway, why do you ask?' Bob smiled. 'Going to write something funny to your mother?'

'No, of course not. It's just something she said.' He used the pen to point towards the counter. 'I listen to Radio Luxembourg but only when *he's* not around. My so-called dad, that is.'

'Sounds to me you're running away from home for more than one reason.'

'I suppose you could be right. He always said one of us had to go. Meeting Sheila meant I jumped before I was pushed. I always felt like a cuckoo in the nest. Perhaps I was. *It's a wise child who knows its own father,* as they say.'

Sheila frowned. 'Don't say things like that. It's not nice. Your father brought you up, don't forget. It can't have been easy for him, or your mother. All those bombs and doodely bug things every night. And rationing, my mum said –'

'Okay. Let's just leave it shall we. All I know is I'm not going to treat our kids the way he treated me.'

Sheila blushed. 'Don't get ahead of yourself. We're not even married yet. And stop snapping my head off every time I speak.'

Bob grinned. 'That's right, Pet, let him know who's boss.'

Chapter 37

Margaret entered the chemist's shop halfway down the High Street and handed her receipt to the man behind the counter. 'Good morning,' she said. 'If these are ready, I'd like to collect them, please.'

The man searched in a drawer beneath the counter. Straightening up he gave her an envelope. 'There you are,' He read the name on the envelope. 'Mrs Reardon. Three prints. He's a good-looking boy, you must be proud of him.' He paused. 'Sorry, I assume he's your son. I hope I haven't given offence.'

'No, no, you're right, Alan *is* mine.' She sighed. 'Well…he was. I don't know what's happened to him.' Taking out the photos she smiled. 'I took the original picture to the police station so I was lucky to find these negatives. They belong to Alan. We don't own a camera, waste of money my husband always says.' Placing them back she said, 'They're very good, thank you.

*

Margaret licked the stamp and positioned it carefully onto the envelope. Taking the photos from her handbag she put them inside along with a letter. The woman behind the grill leaned forward. 'That's your Alan, isn't it? Have you heard from him?'

'No. Nothing I'm afraid so I'm sending these pictures to a friend of mine in London. I've written to ask her to put them up in the local shops with a message. The police have already sent one to the police station where we used to live. They think he may have gone back there.'

'Do they? Why?'

'Alan doesn't like it here. No offence meant. I was brought up on the Lyonaisse estate. It still feels like home to me, but he misses his friends.'

'Yes, there's not much for youngsters to do here is there.'

'I suppose not. It was different back then. Now they want all sorts of things we never had.'

The woman nodded. 'I know what you mean.' She pointed to Margaret's envelope. 'I could put one in the window if you like. There's probably lots of people who don't know he's missing. It can't do any harm and you never can tell. It may just jog somebody's memory.'

'That's very nice of you. And it still leaves me three to send.'

Concern showed on the face of the woman serving. 'It will have to go in the front window though. We're not allowed to interfere with the Post Office area.'

Mrs Reardon pushed one of her handwritten messages and a photo under the grill. 'Thank you. You're so kind.'

'Think nothing of it. Is there anything else I can do?'

Mrs Reardon pushed her Post Office Savings book under the grill. 'Could I have five shillings, please? I've had a lot of expense this week and I don't want to trouble my husband for extra money.' She scowled. *Be a waste of time even if I did.* 'I just wish I knew Alan is safe and how he's coping without me. He's never been away from home before. How will he get his washing done?'

'Don't worry, the police will find him. I'm sure he'll be tickety-boo.' She held out the photo. 'There can't be many young lads dressed like this. He reminds me of the cowboy films they show at the Ritz. His jacket's almost long enough to be one of those gambler's coats.'

Mrs Green nodded. 'Did you know my Alan was in the paper?'

'No, I didn't. Which one? Did you cut it out?'

'The Gazette. If you like I'll bring it next time. Mind you, it's only a tiny piece. Just says he's missing from home and asking him to contact home. But it must mean they hope to find him.'

'Of course, it does. Cheer up. I expect you'll hear from him soon.'

'Good morning, Mrs Reardon.' The vicar held the door of the Post Office open. 'Have you any news about your Alan? I pray for his safe return every night.' He stepped aside to let her pass.

'No, Vicar, I'm afraid not.' She watched as her message, along with a photograph, was fixed inside the window and smiled. Pointing towards the shop front she said, 'I've sent more of those to my friend back where we came from. She'll put them in shop windows for me. I don't know what else I can do.' Turning back towards him, she said, 'But thank you for your prayers, I'm sure they'll help.'

'Put your trust in the Lord. Remember last week's sermon?' He coughed to clear his throat. *'Aren't two sparrows sold for a penny? Yet not one of them falls to the ground without your Father's consent.* Matthew 10, verses 29 to 31.' He hooked a finger under his dog-collar, as if it had suddenly become too tight for comfort. 'If he watches over every sparrow, then you can rest assured our Father is looking over Alan.'

Mrs Reardon felt embarrassed. Listening to the vicar in church on Sundays was one thing, but a private sermon outside the village post office was quite another. 'Thank you, Vicar. And yes, I do remember your sermon. Very moving it was too.'

He blushed at the compliment. 'You're too kind. We all serve the Lord, his works on –'

'How are the arrangements for Saturday's fete doing? I hear the weather forecast is good for a change.' She glanced down at her shoes. 'Just as well, any more rain and we'll all end up with webbed feet.'

'As far as I'm aware everything is fine. I know my wife heard from that Mysto chap the other day. I must say I'm surprised he accepted her invitation.' He smiled, conspiratorially. 'I wouldn't like you to repeat this...but I thought young Tommy Green livened up his show no end.'

Mrs Reardon smiled. 'Please tell Agnes I'm sorry I missed her last meeting but I've spoken to the others and I'll be there to lend a hand as usual.'

'That's very brave of you in the circumstances you find yourself in. I'm sure she will appreciate your help. I look forward to seeing you there.'

Chapter 38

Just as Agnes had predicted, Saturday, the day of the garden fete, dawned brightly.

MacIntyre was up before the birds had time to rouse themselves for another day. Despite Brian pointing out the area set aside for the day's festivities was clearly marked, the gamekeeper had insisted on fixing yards of rope along the tree line bordering the fete. Any large gaps between the trees now had wooden posts driven into the ground to ensure the rope remained taut. Small coloured pennants, left from the Coronation party, were tied onto the barrier to emphasise this was as far as visitors to the estate were allowed to roam.

Douglas and Brian had also been early risers. Trestle tables now decorated the area of lawn designated by Mr Lyonaisse. Stakes and garden twine marked out the area for the fete. Yesterday, they had set up as many canvas shelters as possible and with John Reardon's grudging help, erected the small marquee. John had complained about pain in his back last night and not appeared today.

Father and son opened the tall entrance gates to admit the baker and help unload trays of cakes and fresh baked loaves from his van. The pair tested the cream horns to ensure they were up to the standard Agnes would demand.

The milkman considerately made his delivery with as little noise as possible, knowing glass milk bottles chinking against metal crates were capable of waking members of any household. He also thought to judiciously place an empty sack behind his horse's tail to prevent any accidents. Douglas was disappointed, any source of rich manure was welcome as far as he was concerned.

With all the deliveries accounted for, it was time to prepare the stalls. Douglas puffed on his pipe as he stacked piles of tins on a table. On top of a row of four tins he placed three others, then two more and a final one to complete the target. Tied bundles of rags languished in buckets of water, ready to be hurled at his handy-work. Satisfied there was very little left to do, he told Brian he was going to fetch the plants he had chosen to offer for sale.

While he was away Brian unpacked boxes of cracked plates, odd cups and assorted saucers. He loaded them onto shelves backed by sacking, taking care a reasonable space separated the items. Jugs and teapots, minus handles or spouts, waited to be demolished by balls donated by the local cricket team.

An intermittent squeak, enough to put teeth on edge, announced the return of Douglas with his wheelbarrow full of carefully nurtured plants. Brian sauntered towards him and helped place them on and around one of the trestle tables. As the sun rose to bathe their accomplishments in its warmth, Douglas smiled in approval. 'Well done.' He looked all around the lawn. 'I don't think there's any more we can do at the moment so let's get some breakfast, shall we?'

*

Agnes stood beside the vicar as he prepared to cut the tape stretched between the lofty gates guarding the estate. As the scissors folded the material between its blades, Tommy Green and his friend grinned. The vicar's cheeks flushed as he sought to try again.

Stepping forward Agnes held out her hand for the scissors. As the ends of the tape dropped to the ground, spasmodic applause greeted her actions.

She smiled. 'Thank you, one and all. And thank you for supporting us today as we –'

Her impromptu speech was brought to an abrupt end by the melody issuing from the ice cream van inside the grounds. She was swept aside as youngsters dragged protesting parents through the gates towards this child-magnet.

'Never mind, dearest. Always remember. *The spirit is willing but the body is weak.* Matthew 26, verse 41.' The vicar sighed. 'And we really must have those scissors sharpened. I think pruning your roses has taken the edge off them.'

Douglas stood back to admire his work. Agnes smiled her approval. 'Thank you. That will be splendid.' She pushed a drawing pin through a corner of the poster into the cork board Douglas had fixed to one of the poles supporting the marquee. Using one hand to prevent the paper rolling back up she added three more pins. 'There. I do hope my idea for a treasure hunt is a success. The money denoted by Mr Lyonaisse for prizes was most generous.'

'Yes, it was.' Douglas scratched the back of his neck. 'Do you think sixpence is enough to enter? Maybe you should have made it nine-pence or even a shilling.'

'We'll see. If enough children participate this time. then perhaps next year we can raise it a little.'

'Good idea.' He studied the poster. 'I must say I do like the skull and crossed bones. Did you draw it?'

'No. *That* was my husband's contribution. I said I thought it may scare the younger children, but he didn't agree. What do you think?'

'Hmm…I see what you mean. But I wouldn't worry, I'm sure it will be fine.' He covered the leering skull with his hand, removed it, and then covered it again. 'I don't think it's going to put any of them off. Ten shillings is a lot of money.' Seeing the look on her face he reached out to the board. 'Why don't I put this up a bit higher so the smaller ones don't see it so easily?' Untying the twine, he raised the board and re-tied it. 'How's that?'

'Better I suppose. But if we do this again next year, I'll paint the poster without any help.'

'I can see it starts at three o'clock, but how exactly does this treasure hunt of yours work?'

Agnes drew herself up to her full height. 'I had ten corn dollies made, each with a number painted on it. They've been hidden in the grounds by MacIntyre. As gamekeeper he should know suitable places to hide things.' She unrolled a hand-drawn map of part of the estate. 'And this is so the children can mark down where they find each dolly and it's number.'

'How are they going to do that? They can't share the map surely?'

'Of course not.' She frowned. 'Do you think I haven't thought this through? I made copies using carbon paper. There are enough to go round, I'm sure. If not then some of the children will have to work in pairs or as a team.'

'And share the prizes?'

'I suppose so, yes. You said yourself, ten shillings is a lot of money.'

'Ah, but what if they have to share the second or third prize. Five shillings is fine…but half-a-crown? That won't go far if a *team* win it.'

Agnes turned to walk away. 'I will deal with that if, or when, it happens,' she said as a parting retort.

Mysto stared at the space set aside for his magic shows, the first of which was due to start at half-past-two. He had asked for ropes to be erected on three sides to distance him from his audience. His wishes had evidently been overlooked.

The woman arranging prizes on the Tombola stall was shocked by his language as he strode off to find Agnes and make his feelings felt.

'I hope he doesn't say things like that in front of the children. The vicar won't stand for it.' she said, staring after him. 'I wonder if Agnes would let me move. I don't feel comfortable being next to him.'

Mrs Green gave Tommy a shilling. 'That's all I can spare. Don't spend it all at once.'

'Thanks, Mum. Can I buy a lolly?' Tommy pointed to the ice cream van.

'If you want to. But we've only just got here, there's all day to go yet so don't come back asking for more.'

'How about next week's pocket money in advance.' He grinned.

'How about paying a bit more off what you owe for breaking –'

'Yes, Mum. Bye!'

*

Teddy bears stared out of an upstairs window. Elizabeth had tried to prop them up so they could see the fete. Three years earlier, Mary had taken her favourite bear to join in the fun. Weeks later she had disappeared.

This year, Mr Lyonaisse had wrestled with his feelings when Agnes asked if he would consider allowing part of his grounds to be used, as the fete had outgrown the village green. Eventually, he decided his civic duties must override his personal feelings and gave his consent.

Elizabeth had been persuaded to venture from the house and was seated outside the French windows overlooking the grounds. Alongside her high-back wicker chair a small table had been laid with a white cloth edged with broderie anglaise. A jug of water, with matching glass, sat next to a plate of watercress sandwiches. Through sunglasses, perched on the end of her nose, she was trying to concentrate on reading her leather-bound book.

Peals of laughter greeted the efforts of a stout woman, deprived of sight by a blindfold, trying to pin a tail onto a drawing of a donkey.

On a stall to one side of this spectacle, visitors were being invited to part with tuppence, study the large jar on loan from the sweetshop and guess how many dried peas it contained. Further along, rings made from coloured raffia by members of the Women's Guild were being tossed to try to circle prizes. Due to the lightness of the rings and the size of the objects to be won, winners were thin on the ground. But if a child managed to come close to succeeding, a slight nudge from the jovial woman running the stall, ensured the prize was won.

Mrs Miller watched with a sense of pride as wet sponges were hurled at the vicar whose face peered through one of the cut-outs in a hardboard sheet. Douglas had spent hours repairing the damage caused last year when a freak wind had sent it scuttling across the village green. She smiled when she saw Mrs Reardon's eyes were clamped shut while she occupied the other aperture, waiting for the next cold missile to find its target.

Mysto showed his audience the box was empty before tapping it with a short wand. Opening it, he produced a bunch of tired-looking paper flowers. One or two people clapped out of politeness.

'The moths have got at those, mister,' Tommy yelled.

Mrs Green clapped her hand over his mouth. 'Be quiet. I told you not to show me up this time.'

He shook himself free of her grasp. 'But it's true, Mum. Look.'

Mysto pointed his wand in Tommy's direction. His eyes narrowed. 'Not *you* again.'

Tommy snuggled up to his mother. 'Can't we go, Mum? He's scary.'

'I suppose so. I've seen it all before anyway. You'd think he could come up with something new.'

'I heard that,' Mysto said, loudly. 'Next time I'll try the "make a cheeky kid disappear" trick.'

Mrs Green stood up. 'Come on, I'll treat you to a candyfloss if they've managed to get the machine fixed.'

'Thanks, Mum.' Making sure she didn't see; he turned and stuck his tongue out. Mysto shook his fist.

Above the sound of people laughing and talking, a wind-up gramophone made itself heard. The volume grew as a red-faced woman wound the handle and the steel needle bounced around the shellac record.

Washing lines, knotted together, formed a crude boundary. Two teams of young girls, wearing either red or green sashes, stepped nervously into this circle.

Mrs Green dragged Tommy towards the crowd gathering around to watch the dance demonstration. He was picking pieces of mohair-wool off his candyfloss. 'Silly woman,' he muttered. 'How was I supposed to know she was going to turn round like that?'

'What did you say, dear? I didn't hear.'

'Nothing, Mum. Where are we going now?'

'To see the country-dancing. The girls have been practising for weeks. You'll like it.'

Tommy choked as he swallowed a piece of spun sugar. 'Girls! Urghhh! No thank you!'

'Don't be so silly,' she said. 'They're thinking of having boys in it next year. I could put your name down if you like.'

'Me? Dancing? With soppy girls? My mates would all laugh at me. I don't even want to watch. Can't we go and throw sponges at the vicar again?'

'No, I want to see the dancing. Come along.'

'But Mum…it'll be boring. Please, Mum, don't make me.'

She searched her purse. 'Oh, all right. Here's sixpence, it's all I can spare. Once you've spent it there's no more. You know where I'll be, so come back and find me. Promise?'

'Yes, Mum. I promise.'

Heading towards the sponge-throwing Tommy stopped to read a poster.

'Hello, Tommy. Are you going to enter? It's nearly three o'clock and the hunt starts in five minutes,' the woman behind the trestle table asked.

He switched his attention to the woman addressing him. 'Is that right, Mrs Harrington? The first prize is a whole ten shillings?'

'Yes, and five shillings for coming second. The runner-up will receive half a crown. It's sixpence to join in and you have to be back here when the final whistle is blown. Do want to try?'

'You bet, I mean, yes please.' Tommy held out his sixpence.

The woman gave him a drawing of the estate grounds. 'Take this. Wait for the starting whistle, then go off in any direction you fancy. The idea is to find these.' She held out a corn dolly. 'They've all got numbers and there are ten of them. All you have to do is find where they're hidden and write the numbers on your map. The winner will be the person who finds the most dolls and marks them on their map correctly.'

'Is it for boys too?'

'Of course, it is. It's for anyone up to the age of twelve.
Boys and girls.'

'Oh. I just wondered. I mean, looking for dolls?'

'Would you like your money back?' The woman held out
his sixpence.

'No. No thanks. I bet I can find silly dolls quicker than
anyone. Have you got a pencil I can borrow, please?'

As the whistle blew, excited young treasure hunters set off
in all directions.

Chapter 39

Tommy stared at the corn dolly nestled in the arms of a statue pouring water from a jug into the ornamental pond. 'This makes seven,' he panted, marking his map. 'The time must be running out, she said we've only got an hour. Where are those other blinking dolls hidden? I've been all round this stupid map. I think it's a fiddle. I bet there aren't ten after all.'

He stood with hands on hips and stared around the grounds. A girl skipped towards him, plaited pigtails flapping out behind her. 'How many have *you* found?' she demanded. 'More than five?'

'No. Only three so far. Show me your *five*, I don't believe you.'

'Show me yours first,' she countered. 'Then I'll let you see mine.'

'You must think I'm daft. I'm not showing you anything. I've found all the hard ones, the rest of them will be easy.'

He studied his map while he waited for the girl to move on. 'Where can they be?' Red, white and blue pennants fluttering in the breeze attracted his attention. 'I know. The woods. It's the only place I haven't looked.'

A round of applause greeted the girls as they curtsied at the end of their display. Mrs Green walked around the circle, looking for Tommy. 'Now where's the little scamp got to?' she muttered. 'I told him to come back and meet me here. Just wait until I get my hands on him.'

The villagers drifted away as the ropes were gathered up from the dance area. As the area of lawn was cleared, Mrs Green saw Tommy hadn't returned as promised. She hurried towards where she had taken him to throw sponges.

The vicar stood next to Mrs Reardon sitting on a garden chair. She had a towel wrapped around her shoulders and was using another to dry her hair.

Mrs Green stared at them. 'Have you finished? Aren't you doing it anymore?'

Mrs Reardon peered up at her and smiled. 'No, we've done our bit, Vicar, haven't we.'

'Yes, we certainly have. It's surprising how heavy some of those missiles are. Or maybe it is the level of enthusiasm that makes the difference.' He gazed at Mrs Reardon. 'I think I have been given an idea for my next sermon. *He that is without sin among you; let him first cast a stone at her.* John 8, verse 7.'

Mrs Green stepped towards the vicar. 'Have you seen my Tommy? I gave him sixpence to come here and –'

'Not for a while, Mrs Green. Not since he was here with you.' He rubbed the side of his face. 'He certainly has a strong arm for a boy of his age.'

'Oh, dear. I was certain I'd find him here. Where the devil…sorry Vicar, I mean where can he possibly have got to?'

Mrs Reardon stood up and dropped the towels onto the chair. 'Don't upset yourself. I'm sure he's not far. Why don't we look for him together? Two pairs of eyes are better than one, as they say. We can ask all the stall holders; someone's bound to have seen him.'

'Good idea, Mrs Reardon,' the vicar said. '*Ask, and it shall be given you; seek, and ye shall find.* Matthew 7, verse 7.'

Mrs Reardon scowled. 'Very *helpful*, Vicar, I'm sure.' She turned to Mrs Green. 'Come along, the sooner we get started the sooner we'll find him.'

'I'm getting very worried about Tommy. I know he's always into mischief, but it's not like him to break a promise. It's kind of you to offer to help me find him.'

Mrs Reardon waited until the vicar walked away. She lowered her voice. 'It's me should thank you. I think our vicar must have swallowed a bible. Every time he says anything he manages to find a quote.' Grasping Mrs Green's coat sleeve, she said, 'Poor Agnes. I wonder what he says to her in bed?'

'Mrs *Reardon*. How very rude. He is a man of god don't forget.'

'Yes, but he's still a *man*.'

Mrs Green shook her head. 'It's no use. He's not here. We've asked everyone apart from Mrs Harrington. Someone said she'd gone up to the Big House. I'll catch her later.'

'I don't think these boys of ours realize what they're doing when they go off like this. My Alan certainly –'

'I don't wish to seem unkind, but Alan is big enough to look out for himself. My Tommy's not.' She looked towards Oakwood House. 'I'm going to speak to Mr Lyonaisse, he'll know what to do. Thank you for helping, I'll see you later.'

*

Brian Miller put a megaphone to his mouth. 'Attention please! We have a missing child. Tommy Green hasn't been seen by his mother for nearly an hour. Would everyone who knows Tommy please begin looking for him.'

As Brian stepped down off the chair Douglas slapped him on the back. 'Well done. I knew you could do it.' Anna put her arm around his waist and gazed up at him. He handed the red cone back to Carl Lyonaisse. 'Thanks. Al Bowlly must have known what he was doing when he endorsed this. It works really well.' Turning to Douglas he took a deep breath. 'I couldn't have done it a while ago. But meeting Anna and Victor has helped set my mind at rest.' He held out a hand. 'And thanks, Dad. You, Mum and Anna have all helped give me my confidence back. I feel like a new man.'

'It's nice to have you back, now we're a real family again.' Douglas pulled his pipe from the top pocket of his jacket. 'Come on, let's find Tommy. His mother is going frantic. He'll be in for a good hiding when she finds him.'

Anna held Brian's hand and smiled up at him as they sauntered into the crowds. 'Let's see if we can be the ones to find him,' she said, giving his hand a gentle squeeze.

Carl Lyonaisse stood on the top of the steps and addressed the crowd. 'I am sure there's nothing to be worried about,' he said. 'Tommy's probably just forgotten his mother in all the excitement.' Mrs Green stood beside him; a handkerchief held to her mouth. Red-rimmed eyes did not agree with Carl's observation. 'The last thing we know for sure is he asked to go back and throw more sponges at the vicar. That was about three o'clock, he –'

'Excuse me,' a voice cried out. 'I spoke to him at three, he was at the treasure hunt.'

Everyone turned towards her.

'Can we have quiet, *please*,' Carl pleaded. 'Let's hear what Mrs Harrington has to say.' He waited. 'Thank you. Now…please come forward, Mrs Harrington. Tell all of us what you have to say.'

She threaded her way to the front and stared up at Carl and Mrs Green.

'Tommy was talking with me just a few minutes before three,' she said, loudly. 'I know I'm right about the time because he was the last person to enter the competition. He paid his sixpence and ran off with all the other boys and girls. I haven't seen him since.'

Carl drew in a deep breath. 'Thank you. Now we know where he is.' He smiled at Mrs Green. 'Looking for corn dollies.'

Mrs Harrington mounted the steps and stood next to Tommy's mother and shook her head. 'I don't think so, I'm sorry to say. The hunt finished over half-an-hour ago. He should be back by now.'

Carl repeated his call for silence before continuing. 'I suggest we all stay calm. Tommy may not have heard the final whistle. He's probably still racing around trying to win.' He turned to Mrs Green. 'Don't concern yourself, my dear. MacIntyre knows exactly where he placed all the dolls so I'll instruct him to walk the circuit. He'll find Tommy, rest assured.'

Mrs Harrington held onto Mrs Green as her legs sagged.

Elizabeth jumped up and rushed over to help. Together they helped the distraught mother to the wicker chair. Mrs Miller left the crowd, ran up the stairs and into the house. 'Water,' she called back over her shoulder. 'She needs a drink. I'll fetch some.'

Anna tugged at Brian's sleeve. 'Is she the mother?' She lifted her arm and pointed towards Mrs Green. 'I listen, but the man talk very fast.'

'Yes. She's very upset. Now I know what Mum and Dad must have felt like when they heard I was missing.'

'When I have children, I watch them. I be good wife and mother.'

Brian pulled her close and kissed her forehead.

MacIntyre briefly touched his flat cap as he approached Carl. 'There's no a sign of the wee boy,' he said. 'Sorry.'

'Thank, you. I'm sure you've done all you can. Please join the others, we're going to check the grounds one more time. Then, if we don't find him, I'm going to call the police.'

MacIntyre strode off to re-join the search.

Chapter 40

Carl organised the volunteers, asking them to spread out but not lose sight of their neighbours. The villagers did as he asked and the long line stretched from the house to the edge of the woods. Slowly and methodically, they covered the ground. Tommy's name reverberated back from the walls of the house as it was shouted by anxious voices.

Most of the villagers left the estate by ten o'clock, after promising to keep a lookout for Tommy in the village. Close friends of Mrs Green stayed on and together with the police they walked the grounds time and time again. Torch beams probed any recesses. Sticks prodded plants and were dipped into the ornamental pond. The water-filled crater received its share of prodding too.

Eventually the police sergeant called a halt. 'I don't think any more can be achieved tonight,' he said with a catch in his voice. 'We'll resume at first light.' Turning to Mr and Mrs Green he added, 'That's if Tommy hasn't returned by then of course. I'm sure he's just wandered off somewhere, playing one of those games of his.'

'If he doesn't, do you think there's any connection?' Mr Green asked. 'Between our Tommy and Mrs Reardon's boy, I mean?'

'And Mary. Don't forget her,' another woman ventured.

The sergeant thought for a moment. 'No, I'm sure there's not. You're talking about two boys and a girl, all of different ages. I can't see they have anything in common.'

'Apart from them all going missing from this estate, you mean?' a woman said. 'And the magician threatened Tommy. Lots of people heard him say he'd like to make him disappear. Now he has.'

'You're not being very helpful,' the sergeant snapped. 'My meaning is, that in the case of multiple abductions, they usually follow a pattern.'

'But you must admit,' the woman persisted, 'you've not found any of them yet.'

'I think that's enough speculation for now. I'm certain the disappearances of these three children are not connected. Especially as we are *almost* certain Alan Reardon left of his own volition.' He turned and crossed to Mr Green. 'Why don't you and your good wife go home and try to get some sleep? Leave it to us, I'm sure we'll find Tommy.'

'No, I'm going into the woods to join your men. MacIntyre offered to help. He's got a couple of torches. My wife will go back to our house and the vicar's wife offered to stay the night with her.' Mr Green looked around to see if his wife was within earshot. 'What do you really think, sergeant? Is there any hope of finding him alive?'

'There's always hope. As I said, I quite expect to find he's just gone off somewhere and lost track of the time. But tomorrow, if he's *not* back home, I'm going to get the fire brigade to drain both of the ponds.'

Mr Green's face turned pale. 'You think he may have drowned?'

'No, but I have to have it done or there'll always be questions asked. We did it when Mary disappeared. I'm certain we won't find anything this time either.'

'Thanks for your help, but I must go. MacIntyre will be wondering where I am. I've arranged to meet him by the fountain.'

*

Mr Green quietly let himself into his house.

'Did you find him?' Agnes asked.

'No. It was hopeless searching the woods in the dark. I'm sure we walked in circles a lot of the time.'

'Did you look everywhere?' Mrs Green pulled at her hair. 'What about the camp the tramp had? Did you look there?'

'Yes, dear. We checked. But there are miles and miles of woodland, you could hide an army in there. The police gave up before we did. You can't blame them. It was as dark as a moonless night in there.' He sank into a chair. 'MacIntyre said we would do better to wait for the morning. In the end I had to agree.'

'Shall I put the kettle on?' Agnes asked, heading for the kitchen.

'Yes, please, I could murder... sorry, I mean I could do with a nice cup of tea.'

'Are you going to search the woods again tomorrow?' Mrs Green asked. 'There must be places he could be.'

'I don't doubt it,' Agnes said from the doorway. 'But MacIntyre was right. You'll cover more ground once it's light. Now, I must get back home myself. It's way past midnight.'

'If you give me a minute to drink this, I'll walk you back.' Mr Green said wearily. 'It was very kind of you to stay. We do appreciate it.'

*

Early next morning, a fire engine drove slowly over the lawn, preceded by a police car. Reaching the pond, donated free of charge by the Germans during the war, it stopped and its crew rapidly deployed a length of hose into the water. People from the village who had returned to help watched with interest. Soon water gushed onto the lawn. A child jumped up and down. 'Look, fish, hundreds of them! And frogs. And newts.'

In the growing lake of water on the lawn, fish thrashed around in distress. Mr and Mrs Green retreated from the scene of watery chaos.

'Stop the pump,' Carl Lyonaisse shouted to the firemen. 'We need buckets. Quickly, someone.'

Douglas and Brian ran towards the house. The hose ceased its spasms as the last of the water trickled out.

Girls watched in horror as boys gathered up frogs and newts, storing them in their caps. Not knowing they were being saved many frogs leapt to freedom, to be pursued by their captors.

 Brian was the first to return carrying two buckets. Quickly he dipped them into the pond, then called the boys over. 'Empty them in…that's right, well done. Now, try and save as many sticklebacks as you can. Mind their barbs, use a hankie if you can. Quick now, they're gasping for air.'

Once most of the denizens of the pond were gathered up, Mr Lyonaisse signalled for the pumping to resume. The water flowed out at a tremendous rate, bringing with it more occupants of the once peaceful pond. Children, minus shoes and socks, splashed around rescuing more of the aquatic life as it floundered in the deluge. Soon it became a game. One child kicked water over another and a fully-fledged water fight broke out.

'Children,' Agnes shouted. 'Stop that at once. You're treading on the fish.'

A few dead sticklebacks floated amongst others still fighting for their lives. Boys returned to their rescue mission. Peace prevailed.

Accompanied by Tommy's parents, Mr Lyonaisse walked to the edge of the almost empty pond and gazed down. 'It's a lot deeper than I remember. Are you going to empty it completely?'

'No. There's no need, once we get it down low enough, we can send men in to search.' The chief fireman pointed. 'That way we'll leave enough for the wildlife to survive until the next lot of rain. Ground water will help, it won't take long to fill.'

'Have you found anything?' The police sergeant called to the two men up to their waists in water.

'No. Not unless you count tons of sticky mud trying to suck us down,' one of them replied.

'Make one more reconnoitre just to be sure, then call it a day. He's can't be there or you'd have found him by now.' He turned to his colleague. 'Right, constable, drive to the other pond. There's nothing we can do here and I need to get back to the station as soon as possible. I want to carry on talking to that Mysto fellow we took in for questioning last night. He may hold the key to all this.'

Ten minutes later, the fire engine trundled through the estate and parked beside the ornamental pond. The volunteers managed to arrive before them, using paths through the gardens.

'We've found the filter for the hose now it's too late,' the chief said. 'But we don't need to pump this one out, we'll just use waders again. The fish in this one shouldn't come to any harm. Sorry about the first pond, but I don't think much was lost.'

Carl frowned. 'I should warn you. This is deeper than it looks, and there are a lot of aquatic plants. Are you certain you wouldn't rather lower the level?'

'It's okay. We know what we're doing.' He motioned to the men, covered in mud. 'In you go, lads. The sooner we get started, the sooner we'll finish.'

Carl looked down at his feet. 'There's not much more we can do I'm afraid. The fire service has assured me both ponds are clear. Apart from the woods there's nowhere else Tommy can be on the estate. I'll instruct MacIntyre to join the police search of the woodlands.'

'Yes, I think it's the right thing to do,' Mr Green agreed. 'He must know them like the back of his hand. I'll go with him again.'

'You can if you wish, but I believe it would be better to let MacIntyre work alone. I know it's what *he* would prefer. Why don't you take your wife home and leave it to him? I'll send a message if there's any news.'

'Thank you. Perhaps you're right. We're both very tired, we didn't get any sleep last night.'

Chapter 41

As Bob closed the car door, he smiled. 'Are you sure you wouldn't like to ride up front? Let Alan take a turn in the back with those cases?'

Sheila kicked off her shoes and brushed at the pleats in her skirt. 'No, it's okay. He's got longer legs than me. I'll be all right.'

'I don't mind,' Alan protested. 'It's not fair for you to sit bunched up all the time. Come on, let me take a turn.'

She lent down and retrieved her shoes. 'Are you sure?'

'Yes. You'll be more comfortable next to Bob. Why don't we swap over next time we stop? You know, take turns in the back from now on.'

'Sounds good to me,' Bob said. 'But we're only going to stop once more. We're not far from the camp, just I always sleep at the next place, then finish the journey fresh the next day. Oh, and if you've written to your mother there's a post box there.'

'Have you written it?' Sheila asked, making herself comfortable next to Bob.

'Not yet, I'll do it as we travel.'

Sheila turned her head. 'Haven't you finished yet? It's only a postcard.'

Alan stretched his arms as far he could within the confines of the car and yawned. 'Of course, I've done it. I mean, there wasn't much room to write was there.'

'Can I read it?' She held a hand back over her shoulder.

'Yes, although it's a bit like a spider's fallen in the inkwell and crawled all over it. No offence, Bob, but this car of yours does rock 'n' roll.'

Sheila took the card and held it close to the window next to her. She began to read, very slowly, and in a monotonous tone. 'Hello Mum. Going to marry Sheila. Got a job and a place to live. Will write again soon. Alan.' She shook her head. 'Funny message. More like a telegram. And you didn't sign it "with love from," just Alan. What's she going to think?'

'I couldn't fit any more on. Give it back.' He studied his handiwork. 'Mmm, you're right. And the postman's going to have a job reading the address too. Still, at least I've told her I'm okay.'

'Don't worry. She'll understand. You can write again as soon as we get settled at Bob's sister's place or the holiday camp.'

'You're right.' Alan sighed. 'Then I can explain things better. And I can tell her I'll be back to collect my records and clothes.'

'If I was you, I'd send that one,' Bob said. 'By the time we get to the camp the last post will have been collected. And don't forget the next day will be Sunday.'

'I wouldn't worry about your things.' Sheila sniffed. 'We need things for *us* first. It'll be ages before we can afford the fare to go back to your house.'

For the first time the magnitude of his decision dawned on Alan. *All my records and my record player. And my suit. He'll chuck everything.* 'I hadn't thought of that.'

*

'This it. This is where we're going to rest our heads tonight.' Bob pulled up the handbrake and switched off the engine. 'Good job too, I'm shattered.'

'How are we going to sleep here?' Sheila's voice sounded incredulous. 'It only looks like a café. Where are the rooms?'

'Rooms?' Bob laughed. 'There aren't any. I sleep in the car, around the back.'

'But what about us?' Alan said. 'Where are we going to kip?'

'In the car. Why not?' He smiled. 'Don't worry, I sleep in it every time I do the London dock run for my brother-in-law. It works out fine. I grab an evening meal, use the facilities, and then crash out in the car. The chap who owns the café is okay about it. He shuts around eleven and opens up again at seven. I go back in, have a fry-up, splash my face and then I'm off.'

'Oh, well, I suppose we don't have much choice,' Sheila said to Alan. 'At least you can post your mum's card.'

Waking, Alan winced as his body protested about the unusual sleeping position. Rubbing his eyes, he struggled to sit up. In the front of the car Sheila's head was resting on Bob's shoulder. He was propped up against the driver's door with his arm draped around her.

'Oi! Get off her.' Alan reached forwards and tugged at Bob's sleeve.

'Keep your hair on. She fell asleep on me. I was just making sure she was comfortable.'

'But she was in the back with me. What is she sitting next to you?'

'I was getting cramp so I decided to move,' Sheila said. 'Don't I get a say in where I sit?' She moved the rear-view mirror and ran her fingers through her hair.

'I suppose so,' Alan replied, grudgingly. 'At least we'll have our own beds tonight.'

*

The smiling face of the sun on the sign welcoming visitors to the *Sunnyside Holiday Camp* looked out of place as rivulets of water dribbled down the painted board. Rain lashed the wooden huts. Huge puddles threatened to eliminate any dry space between the dwellings.

Bob pointed through the windscreen as the car swung into the entrance. 'Here we are. Home sweet home. At least it will be if you get taken on.'

'Is this it?' Alan glanced at Sheila then back through the space his sleeve had cleared on the steamed-up window. 'It looks like one of those army camps you see on Pathé newsreels. You know, rows and rows of wooden huts…listen.' He cupped a hand round his ear and leaned closer to the glass. 'Yes, I'm sure I can hear a cockerel crowing.'

She giggled. 'It does look a bit like that. Perhaps you'll be in the army sooner than you thought.'

The car lurched as Bob tried to avoid the larger of the puddles waiting to welcome excited families. 'If you two have quite finished taking the mickey. Those *aren't* huts, they're chalets.' He turned to face them. 'Do you want to work here or not? I can soon drop you off back up the road you know.'

Alan grinned. 'What and miss all the fun? This looks just the place for a holiday. Especially for ducks.'

Sheila dug him in the ribs. 'Sssh. Don't be so rude. I'm sure it's lovely when the sun shines.'

'Don't you mean *if?*' Alan grinned.

'Very funny, but I'm serious,' Bob said. 'Make your minds up. Do you want to work here, or not?'

'We do.' Sheila glared at Alan. 'Take no notice of him.'

'That's right,' Alan agreed. 'Can't you take a joke?'

'I can when I hear one,' Bob countered. 'Do you know any? I'll have a word with Entertainment for you if you like. I'm sure there's always room for a comedian.' Water surged over the kerbstones as the car pulled up. A man, carrying a child in his arms, quickly stepped aside to avoid the wave.

'Here you are, I got the keys from reception,' Bob said. 'I told them you're my guests. You can have this one, Pet.' He turned to Alan. 'Yours is at the end of the next line.'

Sheila stepped inside and fumbled for the light switch. 'It smells a bit,' she said, pinching her nose. 'Cigarettes, beer and –'

'Flush the toilet, Pet. It'll soon clear. And pull the curtain, let some light in.'

Alan caught hold of Bob's arm. 'Can't we share?'

'No. You can't. It's company policy. Married couples or single occupancy only. No hanky-panky allowed.'

'Alan, how dare you. You go off and find your own place. I'm going to clean this one.'

Bob frowned. 'Why? The cleaners will have done their rounds by now.'

'Tell them they missed a bit,' she said, closing the hut door.

'Get back in. I'll drive you to your place.' He looked up at the sullen sky. 'Thank God it's easing up a bit. Much more rain and we won't know where the boating pool starts or ends.' He laughed. 'See, I do like jokes.'

And this place certainly is one, Alan thought as he tugged at his coat collar. 'Is it far? I bet it's easy to get lost here, they all look the same.'

'The rows have all got names,' he pointed at a plank, nailed to a post. 'Look, this one's called "Sea View." And they're all numbered. You'll be in –'

'Who ever thought of calling this lot Sea View certainly had a sense of humour.' Alan smirked. 'We're miles from the beach. You could just about see it in the distance as we drove here.'

'People pay good money to stay here. You should be grateful.'

Yes, but they get to go home after a week. 'Oh, I am. Really. If you hadn't stopped and given us a lift, we'd never have seen all this luxury. I can't wait to start work here.'

Bob compressed his lips as he looked Alan up and down. 'If you're taking the piss, I can –'

'Me?' Alan held his hands up level with his head. 'I wouldn't do that. Come on, let's get to our hut, sorry, chalet. I could do with a wash.'

'Don't lose the key, they charge two pounds to replace it if you do.' Bob stepped back towards his car. 'Make yourself at home. I'll see you in the morning. We can talk to my brother-in-law about jobs for you both. Use the rest of the day to explore the camp, get to know your way around.'

'Cheers, Bob. And thanks for everything. I'm sure we'll love it here.'

Alan kept close to the huts as he headed towards Sea View. Head down into the wind, collar turned up, he splashed along the road.

Knocking on the door of Sheila's hut he stood shivering. *Hurry up. I'm freezing my nuts off out here.* A minute passed. He knocked again. 'Sheila. It's me. Open the door. It's raining cats and dogs out here.'

He heard her slide the bolt back. The door opened. She pulled the belt on her dressing gown tight and continued towelling her head. 'Sorry, I was washing my hair in the sink. Have you been out there long?'

'No. But can I come in, it's awful out here.'

She shook her head. 'You heard what Bob said, and we're not married yet, don't forget.'

'I only want to get out of this bloody rain,' he said, wiping a hand across his face. 'Let me in.'

'No. I don't want to get thrown out. I like having my own space. I'm not going to do anything to spoil it.'

'So, what am I supposed to do?'

'There are probably lots of indoor things and you'll catch your death if you walk around in the rain. I've got to dry my hair, see if you can find where we eat, then come back for me.'

Alan sniffed. 'Okay. If that's what you want. I'll be as quick as I can.'

*

'Line correct. Now eyes down for a full house.' The young lad reached up and dipped his hand into a sack suspended above his head. Producing the next table tennis ball with a number painted on it, he looked up and saw Alan lounging against the entrance. 'Come on in. The next game's just about to start. Only a few more numbers to finish this one.'

'No thanks. I'll give it a miss if it's all the same to you. Where's the staff's eating place?'

'You must mean the *communal dining area*.' The lad smiled and pointed. 'It's past the end of the entertainment suite, and then turn left. You can't miss it.'

'Cheers.'

'You sure you don't want to play? They're all top prizes, no rubbish.'

'Later, perhaps. I need to eat first.'

'Suit yourself.' He looked at the ball he was holding. 'Right, ladies, your next number. All the two's, *Two little ducks*.'

His eager audience shouted back. 'Quack, quack!'

'That's correct, twenty-two. Next, four and two, forty-two.'

Alan stepped back out into the drizzle and hurried past the slot machines, ten-pin bowls and the family quiz in full swing.

Entertainment suite. Alan smiled. *He's having a laugh.*

*

Alan knocked again. 'Sheila. It's me. Open the door.'
Frowning, he moved aside and put his face to the window.
One glance through a hole in the curtain was enough to
convince him she was not in. 'Now where are you? I told
you I wouldn't be long.' He knocked once more, then
kicked the door frame. 'Bollocks. I give up. Bloody women,
who needs them?'

  Patting her hair with one hand, Sheila stepped out of one
of the huts. Bob tapped her backside as he followed. He
turned and locked the door.
  '*Alan!*' She put two fingers to her lips. 'What are you
doing here?'
  'More to the point, what are you? Where were you when I
got back? You said you were just going to dry your hair.'
  Sheila gulped. 'I was. But…but the hair-dryer wouldn't
work. I…I saw Bob passing and he said I could use the one
in his chalet.' She blushed as she glanced at Bob. 'That's
right, isn't it.'
  'Of course, it is, Pet. I'll get maintenance to give your
chalet the once over.' He grinned at Alan. 'Having a good
time? Sheila is. Great place isn't it.'

*

The smell of fish frying, mixed with the pervasive odour of
wet clothes, gave the communal eating place a certain
ambience. Babies crying, toddlers having airs and graces,
older children sulking, all added to the overall charm. Lines
of benches meant diners sat in close proximity. Fluorescent
strip lights, hanging from rusty chains down the length of

the hut, did nothing to brighten up the lives of people who had paid to experience life at *Sunnyside*.

'You'd think being so close to the sea they could cook decent fish and chips.' Alan pushed his plate away. 'And if this ketchup is Heinz, then I'm a Dutchman.' Picking up a large mug, he sipped at its contents then spat. 'Jesus, I think they've given me the washing-up water. Call this tea? It's awful.'

Bob leaned closer. 'At least you're not paying for it.' He waved a fork. 'This lot are.'

Sheila cut a piece from her fish, held it up, frowned and put it back on her plate. 'Mine's not even cooked,' she said. 'It's disgusting.'

'I told you to have the stew, Pet.' Bob licked his lips. 'Nothing wrong with stew.'

'Only you don't know what the meat is,' Alan retorted. 'Sheila did ask you.'

'You southerners are too soft. Stew's stew, what does it matter what's in it?' He tried tearing the slice of bread he was holding, gave up the struggle and used the whole piece to mop his plate clean. 'Bread's a bit stale, I give you that.'

'What are we going to do now?' Alan asked. 'It's a bit early for bed.'

'Speak for yourself.' Sheila glanced at Bob. 'I think I'll have an early night.'

'Me too, Pet,' Bob agreed. 'It was a long drive today and no mistake. How about you, Alan? You ready for the Land of Nod?'

'No. I'll walk Sheila back to her chalet then go for a beer.'

'Good idea. Wish I was up to joining you.' He yawned and stretched. 'Try the *Blue Lagoon*, the beer's better there.'

'Okay, I passed there earlier, but it was closed.'

'That's because they don't allow children in. It only opens in the evenings.'

As he walked back towards the accommodation area Alan stopped and looked all around. 'What do you think of this place?'

'It's not *too* bad,' Sheila said. 'My chalet isn't as nice as our van back home, but I like it here. Tomorrow morning Bob's going to show me where I'll be working if his brother gives me a job.'

'Is he? He didn't ask me.'

'Well, you not going to be cooking are you.'

'No, but I should come with you. You are my girl after all.'

'Are you jealous? He's only taking me to the kitchens.'

'Okay, fair enough I suppose. I'll see you tomorrow. Give me a kiss.'

*

Next morning, Alan strolled towards the dining hall. As he approached, Sheila stepped away as Bob took his arm from around her waist.

'Morning. How's your chalet?' Bob grinned. 'Everything okay?'

'Where have you been?' Alan glared at Sheila. 'You were supposed to meet me.'

'Bob wanted to show me his office. He's got his own telephone.'

'We'll have our own phone when we get our house.'

'Will we? Bob says –'

'Shut up about Bob. He's not your boyfriend, I *am*.'

Bob moved between Alan and Sheila. 'Calm down. It's up to Sheila where she goes. What she sees in *you*, I can't imagine.'

'We were fine until you showed up. I wish we'd never got in that bloody car of yours.' He thrust a hand into his jacket pocket.

Bob quickly moved back. 'No, you don't. I've heard about you Teddy Boys and your knives.'

'Knives?' Alan pulled his hand from his pocket. 'It's the key to my so-called *chalet*. I'm going back.' Turning to Sheila he said, 'Are you coming?'

'Later. Bob's taking me out in his car. We…I mean I need some things from the village. The camp shop hasn't got what I want.'

'I see.'

'Don't be like that. We won't be long.'

*

The afternoon proved to be as boring as Alan had feared. By now he knew every inch of the holiday camp having walked around and around between showers of rain. He ventured out during a brief break in the drizzle, trudged down the road, hoping for some excitement. Having decided the spectacle of a hawk descending on its prey in an adjacent field was the highlight of his day, he turned and headed back.

The evening was no better.

He stood at the main gate, staring down the road. The rain had finally stopped. In the twilight, bats flitted, black shapes against the fading colours of the sky. 'Where's she got to? They've been gone for hours. How far *is* that bloody village?'

His stomach finally drew him away from his vigil.

The meal was advertised as fresh-caught fish. Alan chewed the rubber coating on the rock salmon and glared at the soggy chips. 'I reckon they're the ones I left at lunchtime. I remember those black bits.' He prodded a few. 'They've still got that rotten tomato sauce on them.' Picking up the plate he emptied its contents onto the floor between the bench stool and table. Using the sole of his shoe he smeared the food into the concrete floor. 'Now try serving them again,' he muttered as he stood up.

On the way back to the gate, he stopped and bought a hot dog with onions which he doused with mustard. 'Got to give it a bit of taste,' he said to the indignant stall holder.

*

Sheila had her key in the door when Alan put his hand on her arm. 'Where do you think you've been? I thought you said you were just going into the village for a few things. That was hours ago. It's dark now.'

'Bob treated me to fish and chips on the seafront. It was ever so nice.'

'Did he. Well, I've had it up to here with bloody Bob. What right's he got keeping you out like that? You're *my* girl.'

'Stop going on at me. Bob's really good company, more than I can say for you since we've been here.'

'I haven't had much chance to be anything else, have I. You're always off with him somewhere or other. I'm getting pissed off.'

'Don't be silly. He's just being pleasant. And remember, if you upset him, he won't take us to stay with his sister.'

'Has he said anymore about it? I get the impression he's in no hurry to help us get married.'

Sheila looked away. 'Perhaps he thinks we've changed our minds.'

'Do what? After all the trouble I've been through to get us this far? I'm going to tackle him in the morning, pin him down to a definite date. And I tell you something else, he can stick his job where the bloody sun don't shine.'

'You *have* got yourself in a bit of a state. Why don't you go for a beer, might calm you down.'

'Will you come?'

'No. I'm whacked. You go. I'll see you in the morning.'

'Why can't I come in for a cuppa? There's no harm in that.' Alan looked over Sheila's shoulder into the chalet.

'It's not allowed,' she said, looking up and down the row of huts. 'You can check with Bob in the morning. Goodnight.' She leaned forward and kissed his cheek.

'Is that it? Come here.' He put a hand around the back of her head and pulled her face towards his. Minutes later she pulled free and gasped for air. 'That's better.' He smiled. 'Plenty more where that came from.'

She stepped backwards into the chalet. 'Go and have your beer. I'll see you at breakfast.'

Alan leaned against the bar and looked around. Wooden masks and spears decorated the walls. Umbrellas, formed from bound reeds, sheltered bored-looking couples sitting holding hands. Light bulbs, concealed behind imitation rocks, splashed red, yellow and blue patches of illumination up the walls, adding a garish look to desiccated crabs and starfish entangled in dusty fishing nets. Stuffed fish in glass cases, rusty chains and anchors all failed to liven up the place.

Glancing at the saucy mermaid painted on the mirror behind the bar, Alan saw he had gained a white frothy moustache. He swiped his mouth with the back of his hand. The bartender mistook the gesture and came towards him. 'Same again?' he asked, breezily.

'I haven't finished this one yet.' Alan grimaced. 'Got any other beers? This one's not brilliant.'

The man behind the bar looked offended, but reeled off his complete stock of beers.

'Don't fancy any of them,' Alan said. 'Give me another of these, but chuck a bit more lime in, see if it helps.' He swallowed the last of his drink. 'On second thoughts, forget it. I think I'll call it a night. The excitement in here's getting a bit too much for me.'

Reaching his chalet, Alan pulled his sleeve back and peered at his watch. 'Is that all it is? I thought it must be midnight at least. I think I'll go and see how Sheila is. Wonder if she's got the kettle on?'

Green and cream enamelled lights, bolted high on the sides of the huts, cast pools of light onto the wet road. Alan sang, *Love me tender* as he strolled towards Sheila's accommodation.

He stopped at the end of the row of huts. A shadowy figure stepped out of a door about a third of the way down the line.

'Sheila? Where's she off to now? No, it's not. It's that bloody Bob again! Hang about! What are you up to?'

Bob turned and said something to Sheila. She closed the door.

'What's going on?' Alan demanded. 'What are you doing in her chalet?'

'Keep your hair on. She asked me to sort out the light. The bulb had blown. I stuck one in, and now I'm going back to my chalet. Goodnight, see you in the morning.' He grinned and walked off into the darkness.

Alan rapped on the door. 'Sheila. It's me. Open the door.'

The light inside the chalet went out.

'Right, that does it. I'm going to sort the bugger out.' He thrust his hands into his trouser pockets and walked off in the direction of Bob's chalet.

There was no light visible as Alan approached the Bob's accommodation. He pummelled the door with both fists. 'Open the door, you bastard. I'm going to knock your lying teeth down your throat.'

The door remained closed. Alan kicked the door again and again. The chalet opposite opened and a man in pyjamas stood in the doorway. 'Pack it in! People are trying to sleep.'

Alan turned and glared at the man. 'Shut your noise. I'm looking for Bob.'

'He's not in. Try the *Blue Lagoon,* that's where he usually goes.' The door slammed shut.

Does he? Okay, let's go and find him. Alan began to walk back towards the bar, but stopped when he saw Bob's car tucked away in the shadows between the huts. *I wonder what he's got in the boot. It must be worth something or he wouldn't go all the way to the docks in London. He might not have had time to unload, the bastard's been too busy chasing after Sheila,*

Taking a lock-knife from his pocket he approached the car. Checking there was nobody around he forced the blade into the crack of the door of the boot and levered. Paint flaked off as he applied more pressure. Suddenly the boot sprang open. Alan stood back and looked around to see if the noise had attracted any attention.

Satisfied he hadn't been heard, he reached in and removed the top box. Walking back to the road between the chalets he held the box in the glow of one of the lamps. '*Romeo y Julieta* cigars?' He sniffed the wooden box. 'Sound a bit poncy, but they smell great, bet they don't come cheap.'

Alan returned to the open boot of the car and counted. 'There's hundreds of the buggers. Now I can see why he goes to the docks.' He snapped his fingers together. 'Gotcha! And I saw a phone box by the entrance. This could be very interesting.'

'Hello…no, it's not an emergency. Sorry, but I need the police and I don't know the number. What? Hang on a minute.' Alan breathed over a glass panel in the door. As the man repeated the number, he traced it in the condensation. 'Thanks.' He put the phone down. Picking up the hand-set again he fed in some pennies and pushed button A when his call was answered.

*

'Hello, Alan,' Sheila said, sitting opposite him in the communal eating area.

He mumbled into his cornflakes and ignored her.

'Have you seen Bob?' she said, looking around the room.

'No. I haven't seen your precious bleedin' Bob.'

'There's no need to be rude. I only asked you a simple question.'

'Did you, well I don't care where he is, or you for that matter. I'm going back home.'

'What? I thought we'd come all this way to be married.'

'So did I. But there's something going on between you two. All that bollocks about fixing light bulbs, you two must think I was born yesterday. And he makes my skin crawl the way he calls you, Pet.'

Sheila blushed. 'Don't be silly. It's all in your imagination.'

'Is it? Then why are you asking where he is? You're supposed to be with me.'

'Because I want to know about the jobs he promised us. I need to make myself look presentable if we're going for an interview. We have to do as he says. Don't forget it's his sister we're going to stay with while we qualify for Gretna Green.'

'Please yourself. But I'm not going to marry you after all I've seen and heard. I've already written to my mum. I just need to post it. She'll send me my fare home and then it'll be goodbye to you, *Pet*, and that slimy northern git.'

'It's not fair. I haven't done anything. I left home to be with you. You said you loved me. Now what's going to happen?'

Alan looked up and grinned. 'How about visiting your new lover? In prison? How does that grab you?'

'What do you mean?'

'Just that the coppers came last night and took your Bob away for questioning. Seems he had a load of dodgy cigars in the back of the car when he stopped to pick us up. They want to know where he got them from.'

'How do you know all this?' She stood up and glared down at him. 'Did you shop him to the police?'

'Me? Why would I do that? Besides, I didn't know he had anything to hide, did you?'

'If you're telling the truth and Bob's been arrested then there's no future here for us.'

'He'll probably get off with a couple of years. You could wait for him to be released, then *he* can marry you and good riddance to you both.'

'I can't…he's already married. He told me she doesn't understand him, said I was the girl for him. He's going to ask her for a divorce then –'

'So he did fu–' Alan thumped his fists on the table. 'You bitch! You wouldn't let me have it, would you. Oh no. *We have to get married first,* you said. *I'm saving myself.* You're just a tart.'

'It wasn't like that,' Sheila protested. 'I didn't mean it to happen. It just sort of did.'

'Well now you can just *sort of* sling your hook. I told you, I'm finished with you.'

She gave a deep breath. 'I can't blame you. It was a daft thing to do. It won't happen again, I promise. I haven't got any excuse…but I *am* sorry if that helps.'

'It doesn't.'

'So…what do we do now? If Bob's gone like you say, where does it leave us.'

'As I said, I'm going home. You do as you please. As far as I can see nobody seems to know why we're here, so I reckon it'll be a while before anyone realizes we're not on holiday.' He rattled a spoon against the side of his cup. 'We've got a chalet each, the meals are free, so it'll give you time to sort things out with your parents. I've given my mum this address to send me some money. You'll have to do the same, or stay here until that prat, Bob, comes back. It's your choice.'

*

Opening the door Mrs Reardon stooped to pick up the postcard from the doormat. 'Look,' she said, 'The postman's been while we were at the ponds.'

'Who's sent that?' John grunted.

She held the card closer to her face. 'It's from Alan. It's hard to read. Looks like he scrubbed out the first lot, then wrote it all again.'

'Sounds about right. He never gets anything right first time. I remember –'

'Funny. The picture's Blackpool but it's postmarked Whitby. I wonder why?'

'Does it matter? What's he after?'

'He's not after anything. If you just shut up a minute, I'll read it to you.' She coughed. 'He says, ''Hello Mum. Going to marry Sheila. Got a job and a place to live. Will write again soon. Alan.'' See, he just wanted to let us know he's safe.'

'Shame. I thought we'd heard the last of him.'

'You wicked so-and-so. Leave him alone.'

John pushed her towards the kitchen. 'Go and get my dinner on, all that raking around looking for a missing kid's made me hungry.'

She pushed past him and out of the front door. 'There's cold meat in the larder, make yourself a sandwich. I've got to take this to the police, they can stop looking for Alan now.'

Chapter 42

The second day's hunt for Tommy proved fruitless despite the efforts of a large group of volunteers. The police advised Mr and Mrs Green they would widen the search area beyond the village, and, with their permission, would contact the newspapers as this had brought results in the case of Alan Reardon. They also confided that the magician, Mysto, had been released as they had no evidence he was in any way connected to their missing son, despite being heard to make a vague threat against him. His details had been recorded, they said, should anything come to light at a later date.

Tommy's parents were distraught. Their son was no angel, but he had never stayed away from home before. They both feared the worst.

Margaret Reardon sought to raise their spirits. She told them of her joy when she received a postcard from Alan after he had been missing for nearly two weeks. In return, after thanking her for her concern, they pointed out there was a big age difference between Tommy and Alan. Tommy would not be able to fend for himself as Alan had managed to do.

Carl Lyonaisse instructed Douglas and MacIntyre to ignore their normal duties and concentrate on searching every inch of his estate until the boy was found. Elizabeth took to her room despite her husband's assurances lightning doesn't strike the same place twice. She argued that the adage *there is always an exception to prove the rule* may be more appropriate.

Brian and Anna held hands as they walked the grounds discussing their future.

At the end of the day, as rain-clouds obscuring the sun hastened the end of daylight hours, Carl thanked everybody for their efforts and asked for a repeat effort in the morning.

He told them the marquee would be left in place and tomorrow he would organise hot and cold refreshments.

John opened the door and stepped inside. Margaret tugged at her head-scarf as she followed him. An envelope lay to one side of the doormat. She picked it up. 'It's from Whitby. It must be a letter from Alan. But it was posted six days ago, what's up with the mail these days?'

John banged a fist against the wall. 'Oh God, I knew it was too good to last.'

'What do you mean. He's our son.'

'You don't need to remind me. What's he want this time?'

'Oh, shut up. You're getting on my nerves.'

'And you get on mine. You always thought more of him than you ever did of me.'

'I wonder why,' she retorted. 'Perhaps it's because he's twice the man you are.'

'Huh! That's your opinion. Now, stop shouting and tell me what he's after.'

'What exactly does that mean?' Margaret's jaw jutted forward.

'It means,' John said slowly, 'I hoped we'd seen the last of him.'

'Well, you're out of luck.' She clutched the letter to her bosom. 'He says here he's coming home.'

'Over my dead body.'

'If only.' She sneered. 'Let me tell *you* there'll always be a home waiting for him here.'

'Why's he coming back anyway?'

She read the letter again. 'He's coming because the girl he was hoping to marry has changed her mind. And he's been let down over the job he thought he was going to get.'

'No job? Well there's a surprise. He wouldn't know a proper day's work if it bit him on the arse. And he's *not* moving back in here.'

'That's what you think. My sister got me this house. I'll have whoever I want living in it. If you don't like it, you know what you can do.'

'Yes, and that's exactly what I *will* do. I've been thinking of leaving you for years. I'll get from under your feet just as soon as I can sort something out. Are you satisfied now?'

'Yes, and the sooner the better as far as I'm concerned. Alan can have our room and I'll move into his. He needs the space.'

'He wouldn't do, if you hadn't hidden all his rubbish.'

'Just as well I did. He'll be able to play his records all day long when he gets back home. I can't wait.'

'And how's he going to do that, all the way from Blackpool or wherever he is?' John smirked. 'Walk?'

'Of course not. He's asked if we can send him a postal order for his train fare.'

'Then he's out of luck, he can go and whistle for it. I'm not sending him a penny.'

'But I will. I'm going to the house to ask Carl for an advance,' she yelled.

'Good for you. I'm sure *our* son will pay you back. If he ever gets a job.'

*

'That's a great pity, Mrs Reardon. But I must admit I've always had a feeling all was not well between the two of you.' Carl gave a deep sigh. 'But if your marriage has reached this state then perhaps you are better to go your separate ways.'

'Yes…I feel quite relieved in a strange sort of way. We've been at each other's throats for years.'

'What are your plans? Will you move away?'

'I had hoped you'd be kind enough to let me stay on. I know Patricia doesn't need me now Brian is so much better, but I enjoy working here. Alan would love his old job back too, I'm sure.'

'Hmmm…it *may* be possible…but on the other hand Douglas has asked me to help him find a home for Brian and Anna. The house you're living in would certainly fit the bill.'

'But I've nowhere else to go. I'm not even on any council list.'

'Calm yourself, my dear. I didn't mean to imply you *had* to leave, far from it. I'm sure the small cottage would serve you well. Elizabeth's health hasn't been improved by this unfortunate incident with Tommy, she will need close attention. Perhaps we could find you some more hours to help with your financial situation.'

Margaret swallowed. 'Yes, please. That would be very kind.'

'Nonsense. I would feel more at ease knowing someone is at hand to help Elizabeth. She's taking all this very much to heart.'

'If I could ask one more favour,' Margaret fidgeted. 'Alan has asked us to send him his train fare but my husband –'

'Consider it done. Let me know how much you need. We can come to some arrangement later. The most important thing is to get your son home. Where is he by the way?'

'According to the letter he's staying at a holiday camp just outside Whitby. It's called *Sunnyside,* but from what he says the weather is much the same as it is down here.'

'Is he on holiday? Seems a long way for a young chap to go?'

'No, evidently he and this girlfriend were hitchhiking to Scotland. They planned to get married at Gretna Green.' She dabbed at her eyes. 'He knew we wouldn't give our consent so he ran away.'

'Don't upset yourself, my dear. Here, have…' He withdrew the open box of cigars. 'Sorry, force of habit. Do go on.'

'As I said, it's our fault he went missing.' She paused. 'A man working at this *Sunnyside* place picked them up in his car and offered him a job but it didn't work out. He said the man was a crook and the police came to the camp to take him away.'

'The man I hope, not Alan.' Carl smiled.

'Yes, that's what I meant. Alan wouldn't get involved in any real trouble, I'm sure. I know we worried about him when he went about in a Teddy Boy gang, but it's different down here in the countryside.'

'It is…but we still have our problems. Take Mary for example, and Tommy of course. How *do* children go missing in an environment like this?'

Margaret sighed. 'I can't imagine. John and I were worried…no, that's *not* true. It was *me* who worried something terrible had happened to Alan.' She took a small step back from Carl.

He extinguished his cigar. 'I do apologise, Elizabeth insists I give these up, but…'

'I didn't mean to be rude, it's your house,' she said. 'You carry on.' She chewed her lip then took a deep breath. 'But I've been wondering, do you think the magician we had at the fete has got anything to do with Tommy?'

'It's possible, I suppose. But the police have released him from custody. They couldn't build a case against him. I'd be more inclined to think he may be implicated if he had been in the area when Mary disappeared.' Carl spread his hands open. 'But then again, thinking along those lines, Brian Miller *was*.'

'But surely you don't –'

'Of course not, my dear, perish the thought. It's just that it's easy to jump to conclusions. Anyway, let's get back to Alan, how much is his fare?'

'He said he needs five pounds. Is that too much to ask?'

'No, consider it done.' He glanced at his watch. 'I'll have the cash ready for you later, you can take it to the post office in the morning. Send the postal order by registered post. Meanwhile we will continue to search for Tommy. But for my money, he's not on my land. I'm certain even though *we* couldn't find him, MacIntyre would have done. I think the police are right to shift their attention elsewhere.'

'Thank you, I really am most grateful.' She looked down at the floor. 'I know this is going to sound trivial in the circumstances but I'd like your advice.'

'You flatter me. Have you another problem?'

'Yes…George at the police station has asked me to go to the cinema in town…I don't know if I should go with him.' She twisted the wedding ring on her finger.

'If you and your husband have reached the end of the line, so to speak, then why not?' Carl smiled. 'We all deserve a little happiness in our lives.'

*

Mr and Mrs Green, Carl, Douglas, Brian and Anna sat around the table discussing what to do next in the hunt for Tommy. Rex stretched out at Douglas's feet. A Thermos jug of coffee and plate of biscuits stood beside a large-scale map of the local area. Smoke spiralled up from a cigar stub balanced on the edge of the brass ashtray in front of Carl. Anna divided her attention between what was being said, and Brian.

'I think if we draw a blank today,' Carl said, 'then we'll have to face up to the fact the police are correct and Tommy is not on the estate.'

Mrs Green stifled a sob. 'Oh, dear…oh, dear.' Her husband put his arm around her.

'But let's look on the bright side,' Carl said. 'MacIntyre has been searching the woods since early light. Who knows, he may be on his way back with Tommy even as we speak. In the meantime, I suggest we do as agreed. Douglas is taking Rex. Brian and Anna are going together and Mr and Mrs Green, you will make up a third team. If you stick to the areas we've talked about, you should be able to cover all of the grounds. Good luck everybody!'

Mr Green stood up. 'Thanks for coming everyone. We won't forget your help and kindness.' He turned to Douglas. 'And I'd like to express our gratitude to your wife for stepping into the breach and keeping our shop open.'

Carl held up a hand. 'And please don't forget, there's a cold lunch laid on here for around one o'clock. As you know, I'd like to come with you, but I've had my doctor's orders.' He coughed apologetically. 'If necessary, you can all go back out again this afternoon. But let's hope for the best.'

Brian stood up and helped Anna from her chair. 'Are you ready? If it gets too much for you, just say so and I'll bring you back.'

She smiled up at him. 'I will be fine. Back home I walk the long ways.'

Douglas reached down and stroked his dog. 'Come on lad, let's get the day started.' Rex trotted at his heels as Douglas headed towards the woodland.

Mr and Mrs Green headed for the formal gardens. Carl shook his head. *I don't think you two are going to find anything. You look as if you're in a dream…or a nightmare. And I do know how you feel.* Settling into a chair he watched the searchers disappear from view.

Chapter 43

Douglas called to Rex, busy sniffing a discoloured area of grass. 'Leave it, boy. Come away.' The dog dutifully loped back to him. 'There's nothing there for you. That's just the latrines I filled in after the scouts got rained off this year.' A few hundred yards further, on the pair entered the woods. Rex put his nose to the ground to follow scents only a dog's nose can detect.

Ferns beneath the trees cloaked the ground. Large fungi added splashes of colour, red, cream and white. Fallen branches were slowly decaying and returning nutrients to the soil. 'This is nice,' he said to Rex, gazing around. 'I don't think we've been in this part of the woods.' The dog stopped and looked ahead, tilting his head from side to side.

'Keep going, boy, we've got a lot of ground to cover. No time for dawdling.' Douglas urged the dog forward.

Rex stayed where he was, ears erect and nose twitching.

'What is it? Can you hear something I can't?'

MacIntyre came crashing through the undergrowth. 'What are you doing here?' he demanded. 'This is my part of the woods to search.'

'Is it? That's strange, Carl asked us to check this area.'

MacIntyre waved his stick back the way he had come. 'You'll be wasting your time going any further. I've looked, he's not there.'

Rex lay on the path, head cocked to one side, a low growl coming from deep down.

'What is it, Rex?' He looked at MacIntyre. 'The dog's onto something. Come on, let's see if we can find what it is. When you appeared, I thought it must be you he'd heard, but look at him.'

'There's nothing. I told you, I've just searched these woods. Your dog's probably picked up the scent of a squirrel.' He brushed a hand across his forehead then wiped it down his trousers.

Douglas frowned. 'No, I don't think so. He'd be chasing it by now.' He bent down. 'Off you go, boy. Show me what you've found.' He turned to face MacIntyre. 'Are you coming?'

'No. Complete waste of my time. I've got work to do. You and your dog can chase shadows if you've a mind to.' Pushing the undergrowth aside with his stick, he walked back into the trees.

Rex ran ahead. Douglas chased after him and was lucky to see him turn off the main track. The dog stopped and cocked his head to one side before charging further into the ferns.

'Good *boy*. Go on, find it.' Douglas urged.

Rex was pawing the ground at the foot of a large tree when Douglas caught up with him. 'What have you found? Badgers?' He approached the dog. 'Don't go down that hole, I might not –' Douglas stopped and cupped a hand to one of his ears. 'Stop, Rex, I thought I heard something.' He listened intently. 'Yes, I thought I did. Come out of the way. Let me see.' Pushing Rex aside, Douglas got down on his knees and put his head between the tree's roots. 'This is no badger set,' he said. It's far too large. I can't see much, it's so –'

A low moan, deep within the earth, stopped him in mid-sentence. 'Jesus Christ! There's somebody down there. Tommy, is that you? Answer me.' Rex nuzzled his way in beside Douglas who pushed him back. 'Stay. Stay there. Good boy. I don't want you falling in.'

He leaned further into the darkness and yelled. 'Tommy, I'm going for help. Wait where you are!' As soon as the words left his lips, he shook his head.

Getting to his feet, he saw a rope tied around the trunk of the tree, hanging down into the darkness. He scratched his head. 'Strange? I wonder who did that. Tommy? No, he wouldn't have a thick rope like this.' Patting Rex on the head he said, 'Let's get back. We need help. And I'm going to flatten some of these ferns so we can find our way back. Come on, boy, let's go.'

*

'You think you've found him,' Mrs Green cried out, dropping a cucumber sandwich to the floor. 'Take me there, please, Douglas, take me to him.'

'Please, Mrs Green. Calm yourself.' Carl patted the air in a downward motion. 'Douglas can't be sure what he's discovered. It could be an injured animal.'

'With due respect, sir, it didn't sound like that. We need to get back with ropes and torches.'

Carl bobbed his head in agreement. 'Of course, we do. But I don't want Mrs Green to raise her hopes.' He looked around. 'Where's MacIntyre when he's needed?' Getting out of his chair he said, 'Come with me, I know where he keeps things.'

'Is this all you need, Douglas?' Carl pointed to the coil of rope. 'and the torches?' He paused. 'I agree with what you say, best to leave Mrs Green with me. It will be quicker if you and Mr Green go back together…do you think I should alert the police? Or the fire brigade?'

'Not until we know for sure there's something to report. If there is, then we *will* need their help. If Brian shows up, tell him where we've gone.'

*

Rex led the way back. Crushed ferns confirmed the dog was heading in the right direction. Douglas carried the rope over his shoulder while Mr Green, torch in each hand, struggled to keep up.

'Here we are.' Douglas pointed. 'See? There's a rope already tied to the tree as I said, but I'd rather use ours. At least I know it's up to the job.'

Mr Green crawled to the gap between the roots. Shining a torch down he gasped. 'Tommy! It is you! Hold on, son, we'll soon get you out. Are you hurt?'

At the bottom of the shaft Tommy turned his head and looked up. 'Dad? It's –' He groaned. 'It's my –' Silence returned as he lapsed back into unconsciousness.

Mr Green turned and caught hold of Douglas. 'He sounds in a bad way, we've got to get him up and quick.'

Douglas tore himself free and wound the rope around the tree twice before tying a knot. Taking the remainder of the coil he stuffed it between the roots and yelled, 'Look out, Tommy.'

Grasping the rope Douglas leaned back and gave it a jerk. 'That's fine,' he said. 'Now, shall I go, or will –'

'No, Dad, leave it to me. I'll do it. *Is* it Tommy?'

'Hello, Brian, I didn't hear you coming. Yes, it is…is Anna with you?'

'No, she back at the house with Carl. Give me the rope, you just shine a light down for me.'

Brian sat on the edge of the hole, grasped the rope and swung himself into the void. Douglas and Mr Green shone their torches and watched his progress.

Minutes later Brian's voice echoed back up the shaft. 'I'm down. Good job you brought another rope, the original one's far too short.'

'How's Tommy,' Mr Green yelled.

'Give me a minute. His leg's twisted under him…it looks broken I'm afraid.'

'Can we move him?' Douglas called down.

'No, Dad, we're going to need the experts. There's no way I could get him up by myself. Not in his condition.'

Getting to his feet, Douglas said to Mr Green, 'You stay with your son, I'll go for help.'

After cutting a section of tree root away, the fire-crew worked to bring Tommy to the surface. With a splint applied to his leg, he was carried out of the woods on a stretcher.

Douglas, Brian and Rex followed the procession. 'Well done. You were right not to let me go down,' Douglas said, breathlessly. 'If I had, I'm sure I'd have needed rescuing too.'

Brian smiled. 'Glad I got there before you tried, Dad. It's made *my* arms ache. How he got down there, Heaven only knows.'

'And Tommy…he does too,' Douglas answered. 'I bet he'll have a tale to tell.'

Chapter 44

Mr and Mrs Green stood outside the hospital ward, speaking to other anxious parents, waiting for visiting hours to commence. The door opened and a nurse stepped aside as the tide of visitors rushed in.

Tommy was visible only from the chest down, his face hidden by the comic he was reading.

Pale blue pyjama trousers he had outgrown, allowed the plaster cast on one leg to protrude.

'There he is,' Mrs Green said, grasping her husband's arm. 'Come on. And put that cigarette out, you've only just had one.'

Mrs Green shook Tommy gently. 'Hello, love, we've come to see you.'

Tommy reluctantly closed the latest issue of the *Eagle* and turned his head. 'Hello, Mum,' he mumbled.

'Your dad's here too.'

'Hello, Dad.'

'Here you are, I've brought you some more comics from the shop,' Mr Green said, holding them out. 'Now, tell us what happened.'

'Yes, we want to know. Did somebody push you?' She spat on her handkerchief and wiped jam from the side of his mouth before he could react.

'Urghh, Mum, do you have to?' He wiped his face with the bed sheet.

'Stop whinging,' she said. 'Just look at your poor leg. Tell us the truth about how you managed to get into this state.'

'It wasn't my fault.' Tommy managed to raise himself up onto his elbows. 'It was those stupid dolls. I bet I could have found them if they'd been put in *proper* hiding places. Next year *I'm* going to show Mrs Harrington where–'

Mrs Green put a hand to her forehead. 'Slow down, you're making my head spin.'

'Yes, forget about the treasure hunt, tell us how you fell down that hole.' Mr Green took out his cigarettes, saw the look on his wife's face and put them back in his pocket.

'I didn't fall, well not at first. And it wasn't my fault. If they hadn't hidden those rotten dolls in the woods –'

'There weren't any in there. Mrs Harrington gave MacIntyre strict instructions,' Mrs Green interrupted.

'Yes, but I didn't know, did I.'

'She gave you a map of the grounds. Surely you could see the woods weren't on it?'

'I thought it was a trick. Or perhaps she hadn't given me the same map as the other kids. Anyway, when I couldn't find the last three dolls I went in there.'

Mr Green shook his head, disapprovingly. 'And ended up breaking your leg. Very clever.'

'Take no notice, dear.' She placed a hand on Tommy's head and patted him gently. 'Just tell us what happened.'

'I got bored looking for stupid dolls so I started to track Julius Sneezer and his Roman soldiers.'

'Julius Caesar, dear. His name is Julius Caesar.'

'Is it? Not in my *Beano* it's not. Anyway, that's how I found the rope tied around a tree.'

'And couldn't leave it alone,' Mr Green grunted. 'Typical.'

'I bet you were the same when you were a boy,' Mrs Green countered. 'He must get it from someone, and it certainly isn't me.'

Tommy helped himself to a sherbet-lemon sweet from the bag on top of his bedside locker. 'These are jolly good. Can you bring me some more? And some dandelion and burdock? My throat's all dry. The nurse said it was probably the Annie's fetic they gave me when they put me to sleep.'

'You mean anaesthetic. And what happened to please? Where are your manners?'

'I probably lost them down the big hole.' Tommy grinned. 'But I did find these.' Opening the cabinet drawer he grovelled around, produced some small objects and proudly held them out. 'Lucky beads. Lots of them. Can you take them home for me and put them in my bedroom?'

'What on earth *are* they?' Mrs Green shuddered. 'They're dirty and horrible. Throw them away.'

'Not likely, they *must* be lucky. They saved me when I fell off the rope. Well, almost saved me, I still broke my leg.'

Mr Green frowned. 'You're lucky it wasn't your neck. All these scrapes you get into. What about the time –'

'You still haven't told us where you found these revolting things.' Mrs Green glared at Tommy. 'Did you pick them up in the woods?'

'No, Mum. They were in the hole I fell down. The rope ran out before I reached the bottom. I tried to climb back up but I couldn't. Then I lost my grip and fell. I heard my leg snap and then everything went black. When I woke up, I almost started to cry because I thought I'd never get home again.'

Mrs Green reached out and held his hand. 'Don't upset yourself, dear. You're safe now, thanks to Douglas and Rex finding you.'

'Can we hear about these?' Mr Green held out the small objects. 'Your *lucky* beads?'

'Yes, Dad. I tried to stand but I couldn't. I tried crawling around to find a comfortable place. I couldn't see much, it was really dark. It felt like there was a cave and that's where I found them.' Tommy moved the sherbet-lemon from one side of his mouth to the other. 'They're really good beads, aren't they. I'm going to drill holes in them when I get home and make a necklace. Not a soppy girl's one, mine will be like the one Geronimo wears in my comics.'

Mr Green pointed at Tommy. 'Don't you go touching my tools again. The saw you *borrowed* wouldn't cut butter now. If you want holes in these, *I'll* do it.'

'Thanks, Dad.'

Chapter 45

Patricia Miller took her hands out of the sink and shook them. She reached for a teacloth. 'Stay there, I'll go, dear. I'm the nearest.'

Opening the door, she was surprised to see Mr Green. He held out a box of chocolates, a jar of sweets and a tin of pipe tobacco. 'It's not much,' he said, 'just a small thank you.'

'Oh, you shouldn't have, really. Come in, the kettle's on. Douglas is putting his feet up. Carl gave him a day off.'

'Oh, okay, thank you. But I won't stop. We're off to the hospital again soon.'

'Douglas. Brian. It's Mr Green. He's brought us all something.'

Douglas entered the kitchen. 'Good morning. I wasn't expecting to see you, I thought you'd be at the hospital. How's Tommy? Doing all right I hope.'

'As well as can be expected, as they say. Apart from the broken leg he's been a very lucky boy.'

Patricia passed him a cup of tea. 'Do you take sugar? It's under the muslin cover, keeps the flies off.'

Mr Green reached for the bowl. 'Thank you.' He added a spoonful to his tea and stirred it.

'So...what happened? Has he told you yet?' Douglas opened the tin of tobacco and sniffed the contents. 'Hmmm. Lovely. Thanks for this, very nice of you.'

'Not as much as you deserve. From now on anything we have in the shop is yours, free of charge.' His expression changed from gratitude to puzzlement. 'I don't know what got into him that day. He says he went on some sort of treasure hunt. He had a map –'

'That's right,' Patricia said. 'I helped –'

'Don't interrupt, dear. I want to hear Tommy's story.'

'As I was saying, he told me he had a map and said he was determined to win first prize. Ten shillings it was. He found seven of the dolls but couldn't find the others. So…Tommy being Tommy, he decided they may be hidden in the woods.'

'No, MacIntyre had clear instructions about –'

'Please, dear, let Mr Green finish.' Douglas turned back to their visitor. 'Sorry, do carry on.'

'After a while he started playing one of his games, tracking Romans or some such thing. Then he found a tree with a rope tied around it.'

'And couldn't resist it.' Douglas grinned.

'I expect you're right. According to Tommy, he lowered himself down, lost his grip and fell. The firemen said even if he hadn't broken his leg, he still wouldn't have got out by himself. The rope was too short for a start.'

'Lucky Rex heard him, I didn't. Not until I stuck my head down the hole. Poor kid, although he's certainly got the luck of the devil.'

'Talking of luck,' Mr Green fumbled in his pocket. 'Look. He found these down there, he says they're lucky beads.' He held out his hand. Small, grey-white pieces sat in his palm.

Douglas picked one up, walked to the window and held it up to the light. 'If I'm not mistaken this is a bone. Perhaps a rabbit fell down the hole.'

'Is it? I didn't pay them a lot of attention. He asked me to take them home and put them in his bedroom. I've got to drill some holes in them, *when* I can find my drill.'

Douglas frowned. 'No…this isn't from a rabbit. I've seen lots of rabbit bones.'

'Oh, so what *are* they from? A squirrel perhaps?'

'Let me see the others,' Douglas said. Mr Green tipped them into his open hand.

Douglas took them to the kitchen table. 'There's a bit of a mixture, but these large ones look as if they belong together.

I think we need to show these to the police. I'm getting a bad feeling about this.'

Mr Green pushed the tiny bones around. 'I see what you mean. You don't think –'

'It could be. Leave it to me. I'll take them down the station, see what George thinks.'

'Okay.' Mr Green swallowed hard. 'Let me know when you're going and I'll try to come with you.'

*

George rested both arms on the counter inside the police station and leaned towards the visitors. 'I have shown the bones to my sergeant and we are both of the opinion they are human remains.' He cleared his throat. 'Finger bones of a young child to be precise. Did Tommy tell you anything more?'

'Human?' Mr Green gasped. 'Yes, he did. It seems when he came to after his fall, he tried to move around, tried to get comfortable. He said it was very dark, but he could feel an opening leading from the main shaft. He tried, but couldn't drag himself into it. But it's where he found the lucky beads as he calls them.'

'And,' the sergeant said, 'it's where I think we're going to find the answer to Mary's disappearance.'

Douglas put a hand out to steady himself against the counter. 'Surely not. How could she possibly have got down there?'

Chapter 46

Carl Lyonaisse paced back and forth. 'I can't believe you didn't know about this Dene hole on my land. You walk those woods every day,' he said, glaring at MacIntyre.

'It is a very large wood, sir.'

'Yes, and you must have covered every inch of them over the years. I find the whole thing most incredible. Are you sure you didn't know it existed?'

'I can assure you, sir, I have never seen it before.' MacIntyre shifted his weight from one foot to the other. 'Is that all, sir?'

'Yes, MacIntyre, it is for now. The police have rung to say they will be back this afternoon to inspect the place where Tommy was found. It seems the boy found something down there, but they won't tell me what it is.'

MacIntyre stepped towards the door. 'With your permission, sir, I'd like to go back to my place. I have something to attend to.'

*

The skeleton lay on a tarpaulin. It was tiny compared to the men gathered around. Discoloured clothing disclosed the sex of the deceased. Mrs Fluffy, Mary's teddy bear, confirmed Douglas's worst fears. The sudden glare of a flash bulb lit up the trees, momentarily casting grotesque shadows. 'That should do it,' a fresh-faced youth in civilian clothes said. 'Easier up here. Trying to get a picture of the remains down there was no joke.'

Douglas stared down at the pitiful sight. 'How am I going to tell Carl? He and Elizabeth have kept their hopes alive all this time. Now this.' He gripped the sergeant's arm. 'Would you do it? I don't think I'm up to it.'

'It's my duty to do just that. Don't you concern yourself. I'll break it to him as gently as I can.' He pointed towards the hole at the base of the tree. 'I don't want it left like that. Now the root's been cut back, it's very dangerous. Can you organise a safety barrier of some kind?'

'Leave it to me,' Douglas assured him. 'I'll find MacIntyre and get him to help me. We can use the rope from the fete.'

'Good man. I'll leave it in your capable hands. We need to get back to the station so I can organise a visit from forensic experts.'

Douglas took one last look at the human remains and some much smaller bones put to one side. 'Those look like they're from rats,' he said, pointing.

George nodded in agreement.

*

Rex padded beside Douglas as he walked up to the path leading to the gamekeeper's cottage. He knocked on the door and waited for MacIntyre to answer. 'Come on, man, open up.'

As he knocked again, the door moved. Douglas pushed it. He tapped his pipe out on the door frame and frowned as he stepped into the dwelling. 'MacIntyre. It's me, Douglas. We've got a fence to put up.'

The flies appeared to be more of a nuisance indoors than in the garden. Rex lay on the floor, head resting on his paws. A low growl warned his master something was wrong.

Douglas stopped and bent down. 'What is it, Rex?' he said, stroking the dog. Straightening up, he moved towards a strange buzzing sound coming from the rear of the cottage. Flapping his hands at clouds of flies, he entered the room. Iridescent blue and green blowflies were feasting on blood and tissue. Douglas retched. Putting a hand over his mouth, he ran through the cottage into the garden. Bending over the lavender he emptied the contents of his stomach. Rex nestled against his legs and waited.

Wiping his mouth with the back of his hand Douglas glanced back at the open door. 'Come on, Rex. Let's get away from here.' He started towards the tree line. 'Hurry boy, we've got to reach the police before they leave.'

*

Douglas, George and the sergeant watched as the body was removed from the cottage. 'What a terrible way to kill yourself,' Douglas said, looking down at his feet. 'Why did he do it?'

The sergeant looked at the sheet of paper he was holding. 'Guilt,' he said.

'Is that a suicide note?' Douglas asked.

'You could say that. But it's more of a letter. He must have spent his last moments on earth unburdening his conscience.'

George held out a hand. 'Can we see it?'

The sergeant held it out. 'Why not. It'll be read out at the inquest anyway.'

Douglas moved closer to George so he could read.

You will have found her by the time you read this. I want to tell you it was an accident. I never intended to harm Mary. I was walking my rounds when she came running towards me. She had her teddy and wanted to go into the woods to see if she could find where the bears have their picnic. We searched for a while then sat down and I started telling her a story.

Something came over me. I swear I have never done anything like it before. I came to my senses before anything serious happened. I told her she must not tell her parents but she said she was going to ask her daddy to show her his teddy's friend.

She got upset when I shouted. I put my hand over her mouth. She went to sleep in my arms. I was going to bring her to the house and say there had been an accident. But I panicked when I realized they probably wouldn't believe me. As I walked with her in my arms, I saw a large hole between some tree roots. I thought I could hide her there until I could think what to do.

As I pushed her into the hole, she fell away from me. As you have found out by now, it isn't just a hole. But I didn't know that. I swear I didn't. She dropped into the dark and I reasoned she would never be found. But now you have found Tommy my guess is you have found her too. I can only imagine what this will do to people. You may or may not have suspected me, it but it doesn't matter. I have lived with this for too long and I cannot do so any longer.

I would like to say how sorry I am.

'So that's why he shot himself,' Douglas gasped.

'It's plain enough,' the sergeant agreed. 'I always thought he was a little different…bit of a loner I'd say.'

'But who would have thought he could be capable of murder?' Douglas said. 'I know he had a thing about guns, but…'

'If you'd been in the service as long as I have, you'd know people are capable of just about anything. For the family's sake I just hope she didn't suffer, but I'm afraid we'll never know.'

George swallowed. 'Poor little Mary. All the time we hoped she may turn up. Now we have to face the fact she never will.'

Chapter 47

Margaret ran her tongue across the flap of an envelope and grimaced. 'Urghh. Alan always said they make this glue from dead donkeys.' She licked the back of a stamp and stuck it in place. As she rose from the table, John entered the kitchen.

'What's that?' he grunted.

'Alan's postal order. Carl lent me the money. I'm to pay it back out of my wages each week.'

'More fool you. The little sod won't thank you for it.'

'He must take after you then.'

John raised his hand as if to strike her.

She took a step back. 'Don't you dare. When Alan gets back, I'll tell –'

'Tell him what you like. I've found a flat and paid a month in advance. The taxi will pick me up at one o'clock. Then I'll be free of both of you.'

Margaret took a deep breath and exhaled loudly. 'Good. Now perhaps me and Alan can –'

'See what I've been on about? Me and Alan. Me and Alan. It was me you married, remember?'

'How could I ever *forget*. If I hadn't been expecting…' She paused. 'Do you know they found poor little Mary?'

John looked away. 'Yes. And I heard about MacIntyre. This place is a nightmare, I can't wait to see the back of it.'

*

Margaret put her lipstick back into her handbag, smiled at her reflection in the mirror and opened the front door.

As she approached the gates, Brian and Anna approached from the house. 'Good morning,' Brian smiled. 'Are you going to the village?'

Margaret held out her envelope. 'Yes. I've got to post this letter. You wouldn't believe how silly I've been. I walked all the way into the village yesterday to buy a postal order and if I'd written the letter I could have sent it while I was there. Now I've got to go all the way back again.'

Anna looked puzzled. 'I do not understand,' she said.

Brian gently squeezed her hand. 'We could take it for you, we're going to the High Street.' He pulled Anna towards him and grinned. 'We are going to look at engagement rings.'

'*Congratulations!* Oh, I'm so pleased for you both.' Her smile deserted her as she continued. 'My Alan was going to get married but his girl let him down. Mind you, I'm not surprised. Why he had to pick up with a gypsy girl, I don't know.'

'Sorry to hear it didn't work out for him.' Brian looked at Anna then back at Margaret. 'But it's better than making a mistake and having to live with it for the rest of your lives.'

'I wish somebody had told me that,' Margaret said, regretfully. She handed Brian the letter. 'You will be sure to post it, won't you? It's very important.'

'Don't worry. You can rely on us. Oh, and if you see Mum or Dad, please don't say anything. We haven't told them yet.'

*

'Come in,' Carl said. The door of his study opened and Margaret entered. 'Do sit down, please.' He waved a hand towards a chair. 'I have some more bad news I'm afraid.'

Margaret tucked the folds of her dress beneath her as she sank into the plush upholstery. Her knuckles whitened as she clutched her handbag. 'Oh, dear,' she said in a low voice, 'now what's happened?'

'I had Elizabeth admitted to hospital. Finding Mary –'

Margaret put a hand over her mouth. 'Oh. Oh, dear. How bad is she? Will she be away long?'

'It's hard to say. Elizabeth couldn't deny Susan's death, but she's always clung to her belief Mary would be found alive.'

'Poor Elizabeth.' She looked across at Carl. 'And you, of course. Sorry. It's been such a shock. I can't begin to know how you feel.'

'Numb. It's as if this is all happening to somebody else and I'm watching. And to think I was employing the man who murdered…'

'Yes, I understand. But you can't really blame yourself.'

Carl leaned back and gazed up at the ceiling. 'I don't know what to do. I feel like all the troubles in the world have fallen on me.'

'We're all here for you. Me, Douglas, Patricia, Brian and Anna, oh, and my Alan too, when he comes home.'

'When do you expect him?'

'Anytime next week. I can hardly wait. Brian and Anna posted the letter for me.' She smiled. 'They told me they're planning to get married.'

'Married?' He chewed his bottom lip. 'I didn't know. But that's splendid, at least there's some good news on the horizon.'

'Oh…I really shouldn't have said anything. I'm sure Douglas and Patricia don't know yet.'

'Don't worry, I'll act surprised when I'm told.'

'Douglas said Patricia is worried Brian and Anna will move away.'

'Surely not.'

'Yes, he's quite concerned. But I've been thinking. Now Elizabeth doesn't need me for a while, perhaps I should be the one to go. John's left me, so they could have our house.'

'I won't hear of it. No, you must stay. Elizabeth will recover soon, I'm sure. Then I will be relying on you to make sure she is well cared for. You and Alan must stay on.' He lowered his voice. 'Douglas isn't getting any younger. Your son could become head gardener in the years to come.'

'Thank you.' She hesitated. 'I don't know if I should say this…'

'Please, do carry on.'

'What…what are your plans for the gamekeeper's cottage?'

'Do you think anyone would want to move in there? After all that's happened? No, I don't think it's an option.'

'Sorry, of course you're right, I shouldn't have suggested it.'

Carl put a hand beneath his chin and squeezed the flesh. 'Yes, you should…I think you've solved the problem. I'll have it demolished and a new cottage built in its place. Perhaps Brian can be my gamekeeper.'

Margaret stared at her hands, folded on her lap. 'Or he may be better suited to helping Douglas now John won't be around. Not that my husband was ever much help to anyone.'

Chapter 48

Douglas put a hand on Brian's arm. 'Brian, I have a message from Mr Lyonaisse. He asked for you to see him up at the Big House. I said you'd go after lunch. Is that all right?'

'Yes, of course. But why does he want to see me? Do you know?'

'Not really. Probably something to do with the funeral arrangements I expect.'

'Will Anna be there?'

'Possibly, but it may be something private he wants to talk about.'

'Oh. I'm not sure I can go on my own. Will you come with me? I'm sure Mr Lyonaisse won't mind.'

*

Carl sat back in his chair and gave a deep sigh. 'So, that's it in a nutshell. I've let it be known Mary's remains are to be sent out to her parents in Australia to prevent any awkward questions in the village. I want the funeral to be a strictly private affair.'

Brian nodded. 'I fully understand. I'll be proud to help.'

'And you appreciate *if* Anna is to attend, she must be told our secret?'

'Yes.'

Douglas patted his shoulder. 'I'm proud of you too, son. Anna seems to have found the imaginary switch you spoke about once.'

'That's a good way of putting it, Dad. I don't have so many nightmares now and I'm beginning to feel there is a light at the end of the tunnel.'

Carl smiled. 'That's good to hear. I'm sure when Stanton is sent to prison, you'll be able to put the whole episode behind you.'

Brian stood up and held out his hand to Carl. 'Thanks again for asking me. If you'll excuse me, I'll change these clothes and get started.'

'Now Brian has gone there's something I wanted to ask you.' Carl reached for his cigar box. 'A little bird told me he's planning to marry. Is it true?'

'Yes, sir. I was going to tell you but it didn't seem right somehow after hearing about your poor wife. How is she? Will she be home for the funeral service?'

'I'm afraid not. I spoke to the convalescent hospital this morning. No *real* progress yet, but they say she will improve. I've just got to be patient.' Striking a match, he lit his cigar. 'Changing the subject, there's another matter I have to resolve. MacIntyre. I'm going to need another gamekeeper. Do you think Brian would be interested?'

Douglas sat bolt upright. 'Brian loves the open air, but he doesn't know anything about the job.'

'Point taken. I suggest I offer Brian a choice. He can choose between becoming my gamekeeper, or taking that John fellow's place. If he prefers to try his hand at keeping, I will bring in somebody to train him. How does that sound?'

'Very generous, sir, but there's a small problem. When they marry they'll need to find somewhere to live. I've been asking around the village but there's nothing available to rent at present.'

'Hasn't Mrs Reardon told you of her suggestion? About demolishing and re-building MacIntyre's cottage? It will take time of course, but it can be my wedding present to Brian and Anna.'

Douglas gripped the arms of his chair. 'She never said a word. I'm sure they'll both be delighted. I can't wait to tell them, and Patricia.' He stood up. 'Unless you would rather tell them yourself, sir.'

'Nonsense, go ahead. But perhaps it may be better to wait until after the service.'

'Of course. I fully understand. If there's nothing else you'd like to discuss, I'd like to see how Brian's getting on.'

'That's fine. But don't do any heavy work.' Carl tapped his chest. 'We don't want you to end up in hospital.'

*

'Good morning, son,' Douglas said, looking up from his breakfast. 'I didn't expect to see you up this early. Did the hot bath help last night?'

Brian put both hands in the small of his back and winced as he stretched back and forth. 'Yes, Mum was right, the Radox certainly did the trick.' He bent one arm and felt the raised bicep. 'And after all that digging, who needs a Charles Atlas course?'

'Carl did appreciate your offer to dig Mary's grave. It must have been difficult for him to let you and Alan into his confidence about her parents.'

'It was the least I could do. Anna was shocked when I told her.'

Douglas coughed to clear his throat. 'Are you up to coming to the service this afternoon?'

'Don't worry, Dad, Anna and I will be there. We want to pay our respects.'

*

Douglas stood with his arm around Patricia, Brian held hands with Anna. Carl, Margaret and Alan completed the group of mourners lining the graveside. Patricia eased a handkerchief up under her black veil, dabbed her eyes and shuddered. 'Try not to cry, dear,' Douglas said softly. 'I know it's hard. It is for all of us.'

'Poor Elizabeth,' she snuffled. 'She waited all this time, and now she can't be here.'

'Carl says he'll arrange another service when she's recovered. The headstone should be in place by then.'

The vicar led the prayers and paid tribute to the joy Mary's short life had brought into people's lives.

Tears trickled down Carl's face as he tossed a bunch of wild flowers from the meadow onto the tiny casket. 'Give Mrs Fluffy a hug from Grandma and Granddad.' He turned to Patricia. 'I had her bear put in with her. They were never apart.'

'And she loved the flowers in the meadow.' Patricia sniffed.

'It was Elizabeth's suggestion,' he replied, huskily.

Brian used a shovel to send a shower of earth into the grave. As it struck the coffin the sound released the floodgates of emotion. Sobs and sniffles accompanied the mourners as they left Brian to finish the burial.

Carl glanced back. A light breeze rustled through the copse of trees surrounding the last resting place of Mary and her parents. Their child had returned to them at last.

End

Printed in Great Britain
by Amazon